MURDER IN MASON

Janet Slater

Pinetree Books

ISBN: 9798712784424

First Printing, 2021

Pinetree Books
Kings Mills, Ohio, USA

www.facebook.com/janetslaterbooks

Contents

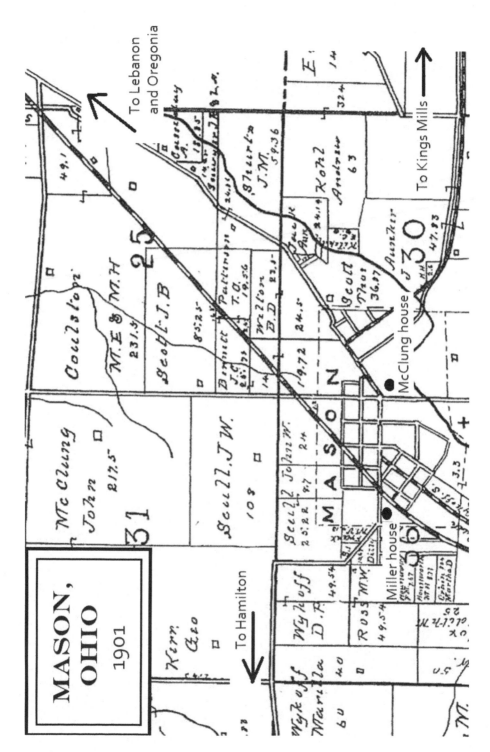

MASON,
OHIO
1901

To Lebanon
and Oregonia

To Kings Mills

To Hamilton

McClung house

Miller house

3

A HORRIBLE BLOODY MURDER
COMMITTED FRIDAY AT MASON.

The Victim an Aged and Helpless Woman.

On Friday morning of last week Mason was aroused to a realization of the fact that one of the bloodiest and most brutal murders imaginable had been committed in its midst. As the awfulness of the crime became known the harder it seemed to comprehend that it had occurred within the limits of the peaceful village and at

night to inherit his fortune. This thought may have so preyed on his mind that he was wrought up to a condition that fired his brain and nerved his arm for the bloody deed. A alike that any sane could that sane could that his life compan

mitted was the center of attraction Friday, Saturday and Sunday, people coming in from far and near. In spite of many theories as to the

OLD MAN M'CLUNG
SITS IN SILENCE

He Only Holds His Head and Has Nothing To Say.

GUARDED BY TWO OFFICERS

And Under Arrest on the Serious Charge of Murder — Coroner In His Finding Says The Old Man is of Unsound Mind—Dr. Van Dyke and Others Minds As to The Guilty Party

MRS. M'CLUNG
KILLED WITH
A HEAVY CLUB

Little Town Of Mason Thrown Into State Of Great Excitement.

WOMAN'S SKULL WAS CRUSHED

No Evidence Of Robbery Because Nothing In The House Was Disturbed—Blood On The Husband's Clothes And How He Explains It—The Coroner Has Closely Questioned The Aged Husband—No Arrests Have As Yet Been Made.

TRANSCRIPT
FROM
CRIMINAL DOCKET.

Mayor's Court
OF THE
MUNICIPAL CORPORATION OF

Village of Mason

THE STATE OF OHIO

John McClung

CERTIFICATE.

STATE OF OHIO,
arren _____ COUNTY, ss.
age of Mason

the undersigned, Mayor of the said ipal Corporation, hereby certify that thin and preceding is a full and true cript of the proceedings had by and be-

Clippings from Lebanon's *Western Star* (top), *Hamilton Evening Democrat* (middle and bottom left); cover of Mayor's Court Transcript from preliminary hearing in Mason's Opera House (right)

4

Note to the Reader

This book is fiction, but much of it is true. Like all historical fiction, this book is built on a foundation of research— months of asking questions that lead to other questions, shuffling through a dizzying maze of census records, newspaper articles, court records, legal documents, maps, photographs, atlases, and genealogical records to find bits of information that lead to answers or partial answers or just more questions. If I were writing a strictly informational account of the events in this book, you would read an organized account of those discoveries.

But in historical fiction, these facts are only the bones; the writer wants to go beyond the facts to tell a compelling story with characters that think and talk and feel, drawing the reader into their world with all its smells and sounds, hardships and joys. A census record reveals a name, family members, a birth date and location, and sometimes an occupation, but sheds no light on character. Fiction puts flesh on the facts.

The details of the McClung murder case and the other crimes described in this book are all taken from legal documents and contemporary newspaper articles, with real names used. Most of the other characters named in the book were real people, too, although I have invented their actions, thoughts, and conversations. In the back of the book you will find a list of the real people and a bit of information about each of them. The town of Mason is a real place, and I am grateful to the Mason Historical Society, the Warren County Museum, and the residents of Mason who have written books and articles about the town's history and people, for their invaluable help in my research. Any historical errors in this book are my own.

The narrator of our story, Isabel Miller, is invented, but her family is real; her father was the undertaker for Rebecca McClung and the Miller house still stands proudly on the west side of town. Hans Schmitt, too, is invented, but his experiences are based on those of people of the time.

Finally, the house where the McClung murder took place still stands on a prominent corner in the middle of the city of Mason, Ohio; it is now a Thai restaurant. Many say the ghost of Rebecca McClung haunts the house, but the owners set a place for her every evening at a table in her upstairs room, and she seems to be at peace.

PROLOGUE

Mason, Ohio, 1951

I only saw her face a few times, through a window; but even then, only in shadow. I never spoke with her. She was fifty years older than me, and to my knowledge she had never emerged from her big, gloomy house during my lifetime. I touched her hand once; but that was only after it was cold and lifeless.

So you might wonder why I should take such an interest in Rebecca McClung. I suppose there were several reasons; the first being that I passed her house countless times, for it was just down the street from where I lived. It was surrounded by a picket fence and the shutters were closed up tight every day of the year, which led some strangers in town to think it might be an asylum of some kind. The place had an air of mystery about it that instilled a mixture of fear and leaps of imagination in the minds of the town's children.

As a girl of eleven when Rebecca McClung was murdered, I was at an age when I had an idealistic sense of justice in the world around me. Adults were good and upright citizens, like my parents, or they were evil, such as murderers and people who kicked dogs. So when Rebecca McClung was murdered, I expected the wicked person who had done the deed to be brought swiftly to justice and then perish in hell. When things did not go as I thought they should, I couldn't stop trying to make sense of it in my mind. Of course, as I matured, I understood that few people are purely good or purely evil; but my compulsion to know the truth about Mrs. McClung's murderer continued throughout my life.

But probably the biggest reason I care about Rebecca McClung and her murder is represented by a piece of paper fifty years old. On it is a drawing made by Mrs. McClung. No one would admire it for its artistic merit. But the drawing, signed with her full name, was made for me, and it cemented a relationship between the two of us, however short and unusual it may have been.

I'm staying in her room now, the one she died in fifty years ago. It's only temporary, until the room my brother Frank is adding to his house is ready for me; he convinced me to return to the town where I grew up and be with family now that my eyesight is almost gone. And now that I'm boarding here, with time for my thoughts to travel back and my typewriter with me to put them into words, it seems right to finally tell the whole story.

CHAPTER ONE

The first time I saw Mrs. McClung was on the second day of fifth grade, in the fall of 1900. I remember the occasion because it was the same day Hans Schmitt received his special welcome to Mason School from a few of his more mischievous classmates. The event coming on the second day of school rather than the first was perhaps an act of mercy; more likely, it was from lack of opportunity.

I was on my way home from school in the roundabout route I took four days a week, walking with Ethel Rebold up Main Street in the opposite direction from my house so I could pick up our family's mail at the post office. The post office was in Seward's drug store, just east of the town's main crossroads, and Ethel and her family lived in a little house just a little further on. I didn't mind the extra walk because I could chat with my friend all the way there. I stopped for the mail every school day except Friday, when my father picked it up because he had to go to the druggist anyway to pick up his weekly "supplies," which were probably cigars.

Ethel was a year ahead of me in school, but we were in the same classroom with the same teacher because Mason was just a very small town back then. Our school was the biggest one in the district; scattered about the surrounding countryside were one-room schools for the farm kids.

Ethel was filling me in on what to expect from our teacher, Miss Dill, because this was her second year with her but my first. You might think Miss Dill would be one of those old maid schoolteachers with a face as sour and wrinkled as her name, but that was not the case. Miss Dill was young and one of the prettiest women in town, with full, rosy cheeks and kind blue eyes. Many years later she would be elected as Mason's first female council member.

Ethel's little sister Alice ran ahead of us, pigtails flying, excited to tell her mother about her second day of school. I reminded myself that next year, when my own little sister Mildred would start school, I'd have to encourage her to do the same rather than be a party to our big-girl conversations.

Alice was far down the street when we reached the drug store, so Ethel had to quickly say goodbye and keep on toward home even though her father's store was just next door—in the same building, actually, but with a different door—as Seward's drug store and post office. Mr. Rebold's establishment was a dry-goods store, with all manner of mundane things people needed, plus a few more interesting things just in case they wanted to buy something they didn't really need but would enjoy having, like a comic book or a bit of costume jewelry to dress up a hat or scarf.

Just as Ethel hurried off after Alice, Seward's door sprung open and Mrs. Tucker burst through, clutching her baby and a small paper bag in her arm.

"Good afternoon, Isabel," she said. "Is school out already? Dear me, I need to hurry home. Robert and the girls will be there ahead of me. It's Mabel's first year, and she was a bit nervous this morning."

I said hello and she hurried off behind Ethel. Mr. Seward was alone in the store then, stepping out from behind the long line of glass cases to shift to his postmaster role on the other side of the room because he saw me coming.

I don't think there was any mail that day; about half the time there wasn't. The other half it was usually something for my father's business, because he was an undertaker and someone was always trying to sell him something or thanking him for his care of someone who died. So after telling Mr. Seward that the school day was fine, because he asked, I told him goodbye and left. I had just started walking back down Main Street, carrying only my history book because I had a chapter to read that night, when I saw the commotion in front of the McClung house next door.

For someone just entering town, the first evidence of approaching the big square house on the corner of the two main streets in town was the smell. Not from the house, mind you, but from the town dump that was on the other side of Section Line Road, behind Drake's stable. It reeked of rotting garbage, and you could smell it blocks away, but the stench of rotting garbage heightened alarmingly as you approached that corner. Of course, there were lots of unpleasant smells in those days, more than we have now—smoke from the blacksmith's fire, horse and cow and pig dung in the street, manure on farm fields, and, of course, all those outhouses—and we were used to it.

We had concrete sidewalks on all the main streets in town by that fall of 1900, much appreciated by anyone who wanted to keep their shoes and stockings clean. The roads were a different story, however. Every day, rain or shine, horses' hooves and cart wheels, wheelbarrows and boot heels, pigs and sleighs and cows and drays pounded, rolled, trampled and ground their way through the mud and dirt, leaving ruts and bumps that threatened to shake out your insides. On this day in September, we had been more than a week without rain, so the rugged topography of Main Street was as hard as the cement sidewalks.

Dust was swirling in the air as four of my male classmates slowly tumbled toward me in a boisterous knot of arms and legs across the road, heading toward the big brick house beside me on the corner of Section Line Road. In the center of the clump was Hans Schmitt, the new boy, and he was fighting the other three every step and stumble of the way. A dark cloth tied tightly across his mouth restricted him to emit only grunts and squeals in protest.

When the boys reached my side of the road Pearlee Spuhler broke off from the pack and posted himself on the sidewalk in front of the McClung house, looking this way and that, but ignoring me. He knew I was just a girl, no older than they, with no authority to stop their shenanigans (and probably no desire to do so, either, for to be known as a tattletale was to be shunned as a traitor to children everywhere). The other two boys, Leavitte

11

Pease and Robert Tucker, continued to drag Hans all the way up to the McClungs' front door. I wondered if Robert knew his mother was at that moment hurrying back to their house with the baby, expecting to see him shepherding his younger sisters. There was no sign of the girls; probably they had cut through the yards behind the school to get home more quickly.

Leavitte, the biggest of the boys, held Hans in a bear hug while Robert tied one end of a rope to the doorknob. The other end was already tied around Hans's wrists. Leaving Hans secured to the front door of the McClung house, Leavitte and Robert, closely followed by their lookout Pearlee, flew down the street ahead of me to Spuhler's Lunchroom, where they paused outside the door just long enough to smooth their hair, paste on smiles, and look relaxed before they followed Pearlee in to help his father clean up from the afternoon meal and get the restaurant ready for the next day.

Meanwhile, Hans was raising just about as much of a ruckus at the McClungs' front door as anyone can make with a gag in his mouth and his hands tied. He pulled against the rope, kicked the door, and squealed like a pig stuck in a fence. I could just see Robert Tucker's head of dark curls poking out Spuhler's door down the street, no doubt intent on what would become of the sacrificial lamb the boys had left on old man McClung's stoop.

It wasn't long before I saw the curtain slither open on the only second-floor window with an open shutter, and I got my first look at Rebecca McClung. I couldn't see her well, of course, as it was dark inside the house; at first there was just a pale hand on the curtain and a silhouette of half a head. But as she nudged the curtain aside and leaned into the window to try to see what was happening below at her front door, I saw her face. It was soft and delicate, maybe even pretty. And she looked no more startled than she would have been to see a cat prancing up the sidewalk with its tail in the air.

That is, until Mr. McClung yanked open the front door, pulling Hans to the ground, and stood over the boy with a large knife in his hand.

I had seen Mr. McClung many times before, of course, because he didn't sit inside the house all day like his wife. He was an ancient man with a white beard who owned a big farm just north of the village, but had moved into town several years earlier when he got too old for farm work. I don't remember who farmed his land after he moved to town; tenants, most likely, or one of his brother's children, as the McClungs had no offspring of their own. It's a good thing, I suppose, because Mr. McClung clearly did not like children. We knew he was the one who got a law passed years earlier that prohibited children from playing ball or even marbles in the village streets. If you were caught, you could get a fine or even twenty-four hours in the calaboose. Thank heavens that law had quietly crept into the dusty corners of town hall and the only ones who stopped our games when they got too rowdy in later days were our parents.

There were two things every kid in Mason knew about Mr. McClung: he was mean, and he was rich. His brick house stood like a fortress on a corner in the center of town, filled with tall windows that were seldom open, the closed shutters downstairs and the heavy drapes upstairs hiding untold secrets within. He had his own stable out back, even though he lived almost next door to Drake's Stable where most people kept their horses, and where my father kept his hearse. But I don't think Mr. McClung boarded his own horse so he could treat it to apples and carrots every day, because Mr. McClung no doubt believed that horses, like children, should dine only on hay and water. I believe he wanted to pay no one else to keep his horse primarily because he was stingy.

I knew he was miserly because he and his wife still had a privy out back. Of course, lots of people did then, but we had a real flush toilet in our house and the McClungs were richer than we were. I had heard from the best sources at school that Mr. McClung kept a big barrel of money in his house, and every time he went out the door he made his wife sit on it until he returned. We had not one but two banks in our town even then, the largest on the ground floor of Sprinkle's Opera House, but apparently

Mr. McClung didn't trust anyone else with his fortune except his wife. The fact that he kept her shut up in the house all the time probably meant he didn't trust *her* much, either. I used to picture her sitting there atop the barrel, a wrinkled hook-nosed crone with a tight gray braid, swinging her feet that wouldn't touch the floor while leafing through a year-old *Ladies' Home Journal*, waiting for her husband to come home.

I also knew Mr. McClung was stingy because of the hullabaloo going on around that time over the sidewalks. My father, who knew everything that was happening in Mason, said the old man wouldn't allow the cement company onto his property to install the new walk. He sued the village and its officers, complaining they were taking a strip of his land without his permission. Maybe he was afraid some of us would play marbles on it. So until the court ruled on the case, sidewalks lined the streets of Mason everywhere except in front of the McClung house.

But poor Hans Schmitt didn't know any of this about the McClungs that day, because his family had just moved to Mason that summer of 1900. All he knew as he sprawled on the stoop, still tied to the now-open door, was that a very old, angry man dressed in grubby overalls was swearing at him and waving a knife over his head.

That's when Mr. Albert Dill happened to walk out the front door of the Mason House Hotel across the street. Mr. Dill was undoubtedly related to our teacher, Miss Dill, but I never knew just what the connection was. Mr. Dill not only lived there in the long red brick building; he owned the hotel. My father always thought it strange that someone with as much money as Albert Dill lived in only one room like all the other boarders in the hotel, eating some of his meals with them in the dining room. But Mr. Dill was one of those rare adults who made you feel like you were just as important as anyone else, even if you were a kid, and he always seemed to have time for anyone who wanted to talk. I never saw him angry, or blowing cigar smoke in anyone's face, or strutting around like he was some important person in town, even if he was.

So when I saw him, I didn't hesitate, but dropped my history book and stormed across the road, yelling in panic. "Mr. Dill! Mr. Dill! You've got to stop him! Mr. McClung is going to kill Hans!"

Mr. Dill caught my arm before I crashed into him. "What's wrong, Isabel? Who's Hans?"

All I could do was thrust my free arm toward the McClung house, waving it frantically. "Hans—the new boy—they tied him to the door—and he's going to kill him!"

Just as we turned to look, a horse and buggy hurtled around the corner from Section Line Road, right in front of a stake wagon that had been rumbling closer all this time from the west end of Main Street, piled high with crates picked up from the train depot for delivery in town. The wagon driver yanked on the reins and the horse reared back with a snort while two wooden crates slid off the top of the heap and crashed into the road.

"Hey!" Mr. Dill yelled at the buggy driver. "Slow down! This is a town, for God's sake!"

Ours was not the sleepy little out-of-the-way village you might imagine. The main route from Cincinnati to Lebanon and on to Columbus came up from the south on Pike Street, turning the corner east onto Main and running right through the town's center. Section Line Road, too, was busy, the major north-south route through the county. People and horses, carts and wagons and buggies were always driving too fast through our streets, kicking up dust and mud and digging ruts in the road. The town being on the main route was good for local businesses, surely, but the traffic was often a subject of complaint.

Mr. Dill ran over and calmed the wagon horse as the driver salvaged his damaged freight from the road, and I looked over to the McClungs' doorstep catty-corner across the road. By this time Mr. McClung had stopped yelling, and he was holding Hans's hands in one of his while he slipped the knife under the rope to cut him free.

"I don't think it's a murder scene," Mr. Dill said to me, and smiled. Then, still holding the horse's bridle, he turned to Mr. McClung. "John! You need any help over there?"

Mr. McClung looked up and let go of Hans, who took off running.

"Hans!" I called out. "You forgot your book!" Hans stopped and looked up in surprise as I ran to pluck his school book, a twin of my own, from the road where it had fallen and brushed off the dirt from the cover. *Epochs in American History*, the cover declared in jaunty pointed letters with a fresh gouge cutting across the capital E. Hans would have to do a bit of repair work or he'd be in trouble for the damage. We met on the side of the road and as I delivered the book to him, he turned away to wipe his eyes so I wouldn't see he had been crying.

I was panting a bit from all the excitement, and Hans was rubbing his wrists. They were red and scraped from pulling against the rough rope, but he quickly dropped them to his sides and set his mouth in a tight line, attempting to guard his pride. I smoothed some strands of hair that had come loose from my ponytail and tucked them behind my ears, a bit self-conscious myself. My hair was so fine and thin it always seemed to slither out of any order I might impose upon it.

We were headed the same way, as Hans lived in a rented house just west of town, and we began to walk. I felt sorry for him, but I hardly knew him. What if he thought I was somehow aligned with the boys who were out to humiliate him? I had to say something.

"I'm sorry that happened, Hans," I mumbled awkwardly.

He kicked a pebble fiercely. "Vat kind of boys do you have in zis town?"

"They're really not so bad. They do this to every new kid at school."

"*Every* kid?"

"Well, the boys, anyway. The girls usually get some surprise in the classroom—like a toad in their lunch pail, or something like that. It's a kind of initiation, I guess you would call it."

"In-issi . . ."

"You know, to make you officially part of the group." The irony was not lost on me, and I could certainly not condone their behavior. "But this was especially bad, picking the McClung house like they did."

"Zat old man . . ." He trailed off, and pushed a flop of blond bangs out of his eyes before looking over to Spuhler's restaurant where the boys had disappeared inside.

I followed his glance. "Pearlee's family owns that lunchroom," I said. "He's really nice, when you get to know him." I pretended not to see Hans's scowl. "He's got five sisters, all younger than him, that follow him around like baby ducks. He's good to them, too; I've seen him. But I imagine he's glad to get away from them and hang with the boys when he can."

Hans looked at me directly for the first time. "They do zis because I am German?"

I paused a moment, startled by the beauty of his eyes. Red-rimmed, yes, but sky blue with gold specks, sparkling in the sunlight like my grandmother's sapphire ring. I watched him scowl as he looked down again and kicked a rock.

I considered. He did have a strong accent, sounding a lot like the Katzenjammer Kids in the comics if you read them out loud. In fact, one of *them* was named Hans. But this escapade went the other way. It was Pearlee, Leavitte, and Robert who were acting like the naughty Katzenjammers, and they spoke perfect English.

"Hans, nobody cares if you're German; lots of people here came from Germany." Just then we passed the bakery on our left, where Mother sometimes bought our bread. "Mr. Zacharias, for instance. You've got to try his doughnuts; they're like gooey clouds. He's from Germany. The Spuhlers, even—I'm sure Pearlee has relatives back there somewhere. And the Kohls—you must have met them; he's the carriage maker. Pearlee Spuhler practically worships Otto Kohl. You'll meet him; he's in high school. And you know Elmer Lambe, in our class? His parents both came from Germany. I think they even go to the church in Fosters where the service is in German."

17

Hans nodded. "Ja, ve go dere too. I'm friends vith Elmer." As he turned his head, the sun caught his hair and it burst into a hundred shades of gold. I could see all of it, even the top, because I was a head taller than Hans. I was awkward and gangly, always the tallest girl my age at school. How I would have loved to have hair the color of his—I always felt mine to be nothing but plain, halfway between my mother's light hair and my father's dark, and I wished it to be one or the other, anything but the same plain brown as my shoes (which, I might add, were already as big as Mother's).

We had to wait for a wagon piled high with hay and pulled by two horses before crossing Pike Street. Down that road to our left four or five other kids with their backs to us headed home from school. We continued toward the west end of Main Street in silence for a bit, and I remember looking at Hans's hands. His left clutched the history book, and his right, closest to me, was rough and tan below the red marks on his wrist. I imagined him pitching hay, slopping pigs, dragging a plow.

"Listen, Hans," I said as we neared my house. "This—thing—today was mean, I know, but it's over now. Try to forget about it. Robert and Pearlee and Leavitte might snicker a bit tomorrow in school, but that's the last you'll hear about it. They're really not bad boys. You'll get along fine."

That day marked the beginning of my friendship with Hans. I thought more than once about his blond hair in the sun, his sapphire eyes, and the shy smile he gave me when I turned in at my gate, and looking back now I wonder what he thought of me.

I also wonder what Rebecca McClung thought when she peeked through her curtain and saw her husband with that knife.

Treasure

Spring, 1831

John tugged at Mary's hand. "Come *on*. We're falling behind."

"I'm tired."

"You're just too *little*, that's all. Too little to go to Ohio."

"I am not. I'm this many, and I'm not a baby." Mary held up three fingers with her free hand. Two fewer than the full hand John could show if he weren't too old now for that kind of counting.

"Then walk faster." He tugged again.

Mary stumbled and fell onto the stony road.

"You're *mean*," she wailed, pushing herself up with her hands.

Charity, several yards ahead, heard her sister's cry and turned. She ran back and scooped up Mary in both arms. "How would you like to ride on Malachi?" she asked the little girl.

Mary glared at John from over Charity's shoulder as they jogged up past the family wagon. Bits of gravel and hardened mud crunched under Charity's high-button boots, already scuffed and dusty from two weeks of travel. Charity handed the little girl to her older brother Joseph, who lifted her up on one of the two horses that pulled their wagon along the National Road.

John pulled the sides of his broad-brimmed hat to fix it more firmly on his head, and then ran to catch up to the wagon's rear left wheel. It was just the same height he was, and it ground along beside him tirelessly. It pulled in front of him again as he slowed, and he could see his mother sitting in the shadows inside the wagon, nursing the baby. Rebecca's lacy bonnet lay in the straw beside them, not needed in the shady wagon, and John could just see a bit of her downy black hair against Mother's breast. Next to them little Elizabeth leaned forward and pointed. "Don, Mama. Don, Don."

Elizabeth was two, and she loved to say his name, even if she couldn't get it quite right yet. John smiled at her before running into the tall grass beside the road. He ran ahead, the dry brown

19

stalks from last year crackling against his shins below his rolled-up overalls. When he was far ahead of the horses, just before the wagon ahead of them, he plopped into a patch of new spring grass and lay on his back, looking up into the blue sky and afternoon sun. Not a single cloud broke the blue, and the sun warmed his face.

He slipped his hand into his overalls pocket and pulled out his special stone. The sun glinted off the tiny facets, bits of glitter stuck in the chunk of gray.

It must be gold, he thought; it was a treasure, a real treasure, and it was his. A boy named Nate had given it to him; Nathaniel, his mother called him. But he had said to John, "Hi, I'm Nate. Are you going west?"

And together the boys had explored the field beside the road while they waited for the caravan of wagons to begin. John had never seen so many people gathered together, not even in church. They had come from many different places, and the only ones John knew were those in his family who had traveled with their new wagon since early morning. The men shook hands and inspected horses while the women carried last-minute supplies from the town stores and tucked them into baskets and bins under the canvas that stretched in curves over the wagons. Children ran and kicked stones and shouted in excitement, or eyed each other shyly. John and Nate hunted for treasure.

Nate had found the first piece, and held it out for John to see as he turned it in his hand, watching the facets flash in the sunlight. Nate tucked it into his pocket, but he kept looking. The second stone he had given to John.

That had been weeks ago. Since then, the wagons had spread out like a line of ants on the National Road that led west, and people traveled mostly with their own families until the sun set and they gathered in groups for safety and to cook and socialize. Now, John sat up and searched the line of wagons, looking for Nate, but didn't see him or his wagon.

"John!" His mother, walking beside the wagon now with baby Rebecca on her hip, waved to him from the road. "Stop your lollygagging and get over here!"

He saw the river before Frank did. The brothers had been munching hardtack and kicking stones as they walked, kicking them farther and farther in an unspoken contest to outdo the other. The sun had just started its afternoon journey toward the horizon in front of them when John spotted the stripe of gray-brown lined with trees in the distance, beyond the first of the wagons that snaked along the road.

"The Ohio!" cried out his father from up ahead. He laid one hand on Sophie's mane and shielded his eyes with the other. "Susanna, children, we've come to the river!"

Mary, up in front beside her mother, pumped her short legs to reach their father before the boys. "Are we there now?" she asked excitedly, pulling on her father's trouser leg. "Da, are we there? Are we in Ohio?"

"No, we're not there yet," said Frank, showing off his eight-year-old knowledge. "The *river* is called the Ohio. The *land* Ohio where we're going is a state and it's on the other side of the river. But even when we get across, we have to keep going for a long time."

"Why a long time?" wailed Mary, crestfallen.

"Uncle Joseph and Aunt Chloe live on the other side of Ohio."

John had never met his aunt and uncle, because they had left Maryland before he was born. He knew they were his aunt and uncle twice over, though, because Uncle Joseph was his father's brother and Aunt Chloe was his mother's sister. They had cousins he had never seen—James and another John, his mother told him, both bigger than he was, and Cousin John was even bigger than his own brother Joseph. They had farmland in Ohio, a lot of it, Mother had said, and they were saving some of it for them. When Frank said they lived on the other side of Ohio, John didn't know if he meant the other side of the *river* Ohio or the

21

land Ohio, but right now it didn't matter. He ran after Frank toward the water.

By the time they reached the river, the first of the wagons was being loaded onto the ferry. The two horses walked down the grassy riverbank and then up the wooden ramp all the way to the front of the boat, the wagon settling on one side of the ferry. John and Frank watched as another wagon was loaded beside it, and then two more behind, with the various animals and people that accompanied them. The ferryman untied the ropes that held the boat to the shore and then called out to the four horses, a pair on either side of the boat, the ones that had been on board before the wagons were loaded. They stood in two small open stalls, one pair facing forward and the other pair back, and when they began walking the boat began to move.

It was not until their family's turn came to board the ferry that John learned the mystery of these four horses that walked all the way across the river and back without ever moving from their stalls. Under the deck, Joseph explained to Frank and John, was a great wooden wheel. Two rectangles had been cut in the deck under where the horses were enclosed, so they stood on the wheel, and when they walked they made it go around. The wheel was connected under the deck to shafts that turned the paddle wheels, one on each side. So as the horses walked a circular wooden road that moved under them, their power moved the boat across the river, and all the ferryman had to do was steer the rudder against the current.

John made his way through the people and the horses and the wagons to the fence that guarded the side of the boat. The top rail was just at his eye level, so he sat on the deck holding the bottom rail and let his legs dangle over the river. He had never seen so much water in one place. The wagon horses shifted nervously, their sudden movements punctuating the jostling from the waves and currents of the river. John felt in his overalls for the treasure stone as he clutched the rail tighter with his other hand. It felt good in his hand, solid and familiar. His finger touched the pointy end. The glittery part was right below the point, he remembered, and he pulled it from his pocket just to see that he was right.

"Don! Don!" Elizabeth stumbled across the deck toward her brother. "Wada, Don! Look! Bi-i-i-g wada!" John turned his head toward her just as a horse on the far side of the boat neighed in fright and reared up. The boat shifted and Elizabeth tumbled to the deck face-first, sliding under the deck rail. "Don!" she wailed.

John pulled himself to his feet and lunged for her just as her head slid over the edge a few feet away. He reached under the rail to grab her leg, and he held on with all his might.

"Elizabeth!" Charity's startled cry rang out over the rushing water and the snorts of the jostled horses. She pushed her way through the packed deck, losing her bonnet on the way, and reached for the little girl. In a moment John gladly released his grip and Elizabeth was in Charity's arms, crying and bleeding from a scrape on her forehead.

After much hugging and scolding and smoothing of dresses, Charity carried the little girl back to the family's wagon, and John was again alone. Panic suddenly rose from his stomach and enveloped him: where was his treasure stone? Frantically he searched his pockets, and then the deck around him. He had been dangerously close to the water when he took the stone from his pocket. Why hadn't he kept it where it was safe? Maybe it had bounced the other way and was still on the boat. Bent over the soiled wood, he backed into the legs of a man around him, who grunted his displeasure. But John stayed focused on the floor, peering around legs of horses and men, reaching to examine each piece of gravel or lift a trampled leaf.

The boat reached the big island in the middle of the river, and one by one the wagons were unloaded. Their owners would hitch them up and pull them to the other side of the island, where another horse-powered ferry would take them the rest of the way across the river. But John hung back as long as he could, looking back across the channel they had just crossed, picturing the gold glitter of his treasure stone fading to nothing as it sank through the deep, dark water and settled into the mud at the bottom to be lost forever.

CHAPTER TWO

I asked for this room when I needed a place to stay, the one she died in fifty years ago. They say you can still see the bloodstain on the wooden floor; they've scrubbed and scrubbed but it won't go away. It has become a part of this room, this house, this town. I can't see it, of course, as my sight is all but gone now. But I can still see the light that comes through her window, the one Rebecca McClung was peering out of the day Hans was tied to the doorknob.

It's a room in a boarding house now, and I don't mind the bloodstain on the floor. Even if I could see it I wouldn't mind. I grew up with blood and death in my house, and they are no more alarming to me than the cut flowers in the vases that sat on either side of the caskets in the parlor where the funeral services were held. Death is a part of life, something every one of us will experience one day or another, and blood is just the stuff that flows through us to keep our minds sharp, our toes warm, and our cheeks pink while we live on this earth.

After the McClungs were gone, and before the Scofields bought this house in 1920 for boarding, it was a hotel called The Modern. If ever there was a misnomer, that was it. Even today it has no indoor bathroom facilities. Boarders here, just like the McClungs themselves over fifty years ago, must use the privy out back. At least we've got running water; there's a pump in the kitchen that sends it up to a tank in the attic so it can flow to the sink.

Of course, bathrooms were a rarity in the McClungs' day. But I had enjoyed the privilege ever since I was seven, when my parents built our house on the west end of Main Street. It was home both to our family and to my father's business, the C. C. Miller Funeral Home.

It was a grand house, and it still is. The day we moved in from our humbler house outside of town, I took little Milly's hand and pulled her along with me toward the front door as Mother handed baby Everett to Father so she could climb down from the coach. I opened the front door and stepped into the parlor. The room was big and open, its walls framed with generous polished wood molding adorned in carved medallions at each high corner of the room. The front window curved out toward the front yard, and above it the sun shone through a colorful stained-glass window featuring a lyre like King David's.

I gazed at the big fireplace in the parlor surrounded by beautifully carved wood molding. But it was the tiled artwork on the sides of the fireplace that especially caught my attention. A handsome, but somewhat girlish-looking, young man lolled on one side while a beautiful young maiden adorned the opposite side—and both were *naked*. I was aghast—and laughed nervously. Did my mother know there were naked people in her living room, right there where any visitor and her own children could see them when they first walked in the front door? She must have known, because she only smiled as my father enlightened me.

"See the letters here?" He traced a phrase inscribed on the tile just below the top wood molding, its curved letters framed by floating cherubs. "*Amor et Psyche*," my father read. "Amor, the boy, is Love. And Psyche, the girl, is the Soul. They are from an ancient Greek story, and eventually, they marry."

Classical myth and architecture were in vogue more at the turn of the century than they are now, and the beautiful tilework apparently identified us as more refined than most of our neighbors as well as providing elegance in a parlor that doubled as a place for funerals and visitations for my father's business. But for me, the classical art in my living room served to impress my playmates not with my social class or my father's occupation but as an interesting oddity to identify me: Pearlee's got a cat with six toes on one foot; Izzy's got naked people on her parlor fireplace.

But what I knew would be the best part of the house was what I wanted to explore that first day after I tore myself away from the parlor artwork. I ran up the center staircase to the second-floor hall, barely glancing into the spacious bedrooms as I searched for the door that led to the magical flight of stairs hidden behind a hallway door. I scrambled up the narrow, steep wooden steps until I reached the very top, the grand turret that crowned our castle, and entered what became my royal domain.

No attic or garret, this. With ceilings as lofty as those on the lower levels, the spacious turret was divided into three rooms, all with tall windows to look out over the town. I naturally headed for the largest room, the semi-circular one. You had to take a step up to go inside it, like entering a throne room. It was more windows than walls. And each looked a different direction, so you could twirl around and get a sweeping view from the farmed fields on the west of town to the houses across the way and then down Main Street to the east.

Mason at the turn of the twentieth century was a small town with fewer than seven hundred people, but it was no isolated hick town sprinkled with local yokels. Because it was about halfway between the big cities of Cincinnati and Dayton, we saw lots of people passing through, stopping in Mason to get a drink at one of our two saloons or to stay overnight in one of the hotels. People from the surrounding farms came into town on a regular basis, too, visiting family or friends or to pick up supplies.

The Cincinnati-Lebanon road led right past the McClungs' house through the center of town, bringing carriages and wagons that kicked up dust and rutted our roads, but along with them interesting people with money to spend in our little town. The rail line, too, passed through Mason with passengers and freight traveling to and from Cincinnati and Dayton and even places beyond. Everyone in Mason knew Mr. Collins, who was the train conductor from before I could remember until I was in my thirties, who always answered a "How d'you do" with "Still pokin' along," a tip of his hat, and a smile half hidden by his big, bushy mustache.

Most all we needed was right here in town, and we were hardly backward. By 1900 we had cement sidewalks and kerosene street lamps on all the corners, cleaned and lit each night by our lamplighter and extinguished every morning. Electricity was the latest improvement, installed first in the town hall, my school, and a few businesses. There were telephones in the mayor's office and the larger businesses, including our funeral home. You were allowed to call anyone in town for free and talk three minutes on each call. You could even call other cities and states, but those calls you paid for.

Right on Main Street you could buy groceries, meat, clothing and shoes; there were two drug stores, a harness shop, a blacksmith, a tin shop, and a crockery store that sold practical items like oil lamps and milk jugs. There was even a carpet weaver just outside town. Townspeople and visitors could keep their horses at one of the two stables. Drake's, the largest, was two stories plus a basement, and had an elevator so buggies could be lifted from the ground floor to the upper level for storage.

Sports enthusiasts could enjoy horse races at the track in Lebanon; several of the race horses were boarded at a barn in Mason. Baseball was popular, too, and a couple of our local ball players even made it to the big leagues. A day at the ball park to watch the Cincinnati Reds, America's first professional baseball team, was a short train or trolley ride away. Closer to home, the Mason Croquet Players competed on a grassy field next to Town Hall.

From the turret I looked down on all this, my new realm, and I was the queen. As Milly and baby Everett grew and as my brothers Frank and Robert joined the family, the turret was the children's playroom, home to blocks and marbles, dolls and board games, and pillows to lie against while reading a book or just gazing outside at the clouds. The only claim our parents had on the room was a row of hooks along one wall where they hung winter coats and other bulky clothing they wore only occasionally.

This was the room I ran to after leaving Hans that second day of school in the fall of 1900. I dropped my history book on the parlor table and flew up the front stairs, down the bedroom hallway, and up the spiral stairs to the turret. From the western window I watched Hans plod along the road until it became little more than path leading to the Wikoff fields where he and his family worked as tenant farmers. As he disappeared behind a row of tall brown cornstalks, I found myself thinking of Fridays, when I didn't have to go to the post office after school.

Not many of my classmates lived west of the school, like we did; the few who did go my way were boys. But this year, Hans was one of them, and the rest of that first week I was secretly looking forward to Friday when we'd both be walking the same direction.

So, I felt a flutter of excitement when Miss Dill dismissed class at the end of the week. But I hadn't even gathered my books before Hans shot out the door right on the heels of Leavitte Pease. With determined calm, I said goodbye to Ethel Rebold and made myself walk, not run, out the school door. My hopes fell, however, when I didn't see Hans out front. In fact, I realized none of the boys in our class were out front, and a sinister dread clouded my happy anticipation. Boys were bound to settle scores, I knew, and usually by very physical means. I circled around the back of the school, fully expecting to see my new friend intent on revenge, flailing at his enemy while a fiendish grin spread on the broad face of Leavitte Pease. As the bigger, stronger boy, Leavitte would first play it cool, allowing recognition of his dominance to sink in—and then smash Hans to the ground with a single blow.

What I found instead was Hans standing by calmly while Leavitte bent over and drew a large circle in the dirt with his finger. Robert Tucker was sitting on the ground nearby, sorting a pile of marbles, and Farlane Dwire approached just as Leavitte stood up. Farly was a year or two younger than the others, and longed to fit in with the older boys. Mostly, they tolerated him.

"C'mon, Farly, you always lose," Leavitte said, pulling a marble bag out of his pocket. "You got enough marbles left to play?"

Farly plopped down on the dirt and emptied his marble bag in front of him. "You really think you're something, Leavitte. This bag will be full by the time we're done today."

Hans watched as Leavitte dropped five colorfully glazed marbles in the center of the ring, followed by Robert who did the same. Farly added his five, all but one of them plain brown clay. He was down to his dregs.

Hans pulled a bag from his pocket and stepped closer to the ring.

"I figgered you could just watch today, Hans," Leavitte said quickly. "You'll want to know what you're up against before you play with us." After dismissing the new boy, he suddenly realized I was standing there. "You can watch too, Izzy, if you want." Leavitte was always glad for an admiring audience.

Rather than retreating a respectable distance to watch, Hans took another step toward the ring. "I vill play," he announced.

Leavitte looked at him in surprise. "Well, if you want. Okay with you guys?" Robert and Farly nodded.

"We'll just play friendsies then. You shouldn't play keepsies when it's your first game."

Leavitte probably wished he hadn't spoken so soon when Hans stepped into the ring and opened his bag. One by one he dropped five of the most beautiful marbles any of us had ever seen.

The sunlight shone *through* them, not just *on* them. They were perfect clear orbs of glass with bright ribbons of yellow, red, orange, green and blue swirling around a maypole of white lattice strung through the center of each. Beside them even Leavitte's best blue glaze was nothing but a painted ball of clay.

Leavitte hesitated a moment, trying hard to hide his amazement. But then he stepped up to the line on one side of the circle. "I'll lag first. Then you can go, Farly, then Robert and then Hans."

Leavitte crouched and made a fist on the ground with a yellow-green marble propped against his thumb. He closed one eye to take his aim, then squinted at one of Hans's marbles as he popped the shooter off his thumb. Narrowly missing Hans's marble to the left, the shooter rolled across the circle and tapped one of Farly's brown clay spheres.

Then Farly knuckled down, blew on his shooter for luck, and aimed for the same swirled blue marble of Hans's. He, too, missed, but his dull shooter smacked one of Leavitte's green-glazed clays and knocked it out of the ring. After a smug look at the bigger boy, he aimed his second shot at another of Hans's marbles, and missed.

Robert was the first to knock one of Hans's beauties out of the ring, a yellow swirlie bright as the sun. Then he hit one of Farly's brown clays. He missed on his third shot, and it was Hans's turn to step up to the ring.

Hans crouched at the line and rolled his shooter in his palm, its ribbons of red twirling through his fingers. He took a deep breath, let it out, and knuckled down.

Plunk! One of Farly's brown marbles rolled out of the ring. Hans retrieved his shooter, then plunk! Farly's only colored clay was gone. Hans glanced at Robert before knuckling down the third time, and took aim at one of his dull yellow glazed marbles. That, too, flew from the ring, followed by two more of Robert's marbles and one of Farly's.

As he retrieved his shooter the next time, he looked at Leavitte, who immediately studied the ground. Hans knuckled down and eyed Leavitte's best rich blue marble. Leavitte barely moved as it shot out of the ring and landed near his foot.

"Gosh darn!" breathed Farly. "Do you *ever* miss?"

Hans smiled at him after picking up his shooter. This time he aimed at another of Farly's dull clays. The shooter slipped past it on the right and rolled out of the ring.

Leavitte didn't say anything as he crouched for his next turn. He then managed a smile as one of Robert's marbles left the ring. He followed this by smacking Hans's red-ribboned beauty, and missing his next shot at the green one.

By the time Hans's turn came around again, only three marbles remained in the ring—one of Leavitte's and two of his own. He quickly dismissed his own two shining beauties from the ring. Then as he stooped to pick up his shooter the second time, he casually bumped his elbow into Leavitte, who glared at him but said nothing.

Hans rolled his shooter in his palm and aimed. Zing! Leavitte's marble left the ring, leaving it empty.

Hans stood and gathered his marbles, and the other boys reluctantly did the same.

"Zank you for zee game, fellas," said Hans. "Next time vee play keepzies, *yah*?"

Tears

Winter, 1835

Ohio is not good for females. So why do Father and Mother keep bringing forth girls? There must be a sickness here, John thought, one that seeks out the women, even before they are born, perhaps; a sickness that can peer even into a mother's belly and hover about the house, plotting when it will strike its final blow. It was a sign, probably, that the McClungs should have recognized, when Sophie, the horse who, alongside Malachi, had pulled their wagon all the way from Maryland to Warren County, Ohio—never complaining even when the sun beat on her neck and back in the afternoon, so hot that even the field daisies wilted—just lay down and died in Uncle Joseph's stable a week after they arrived, not living long enough to get a stall of her own.

John was nine now, and used to girls, of course, and some of his sisters were thriving in Ohio. Charity was fourteen, almost a woman, and she loved the open spaces of farmland and prairie that stretched so far they seemed to have no end. She liked the outdoor chores the best, laundry and tending the chickens and the vegetable garden, but she also could cook whole meals by herself and they weren't bad at all. Mary and Elizabeth liked to be indoors with their mother. At seven and six, they were best-friend sisters, sharing a bed and clothes and just about everything else. And Rebecca, four, was bouncy and mischievous and loved trees and creeks and animals. John couldn't count the times Mother had sent him to roust her out of the stable or the cornfield, a difficult task when she'd disappear between rows of corn higher than her head.

But these four sisters had all been born in Maryland, not Ohio. They were of hardier stock. The problems began early in Ohio, even before the family left Uncle Joseph and Aunt Chloe's big farmhouse to move into their own.

The first Ohio baby, born only weeks after Father had planted his first crop on their new land—a little late, but it grew fine just the same—was a little girl who was so small and weak from the start that Father and Mother didn't give her name, calling her "wee one," holding her like a baby bird with a broken wing, sad, pitying looks on their faces rather than smiles. She didn't even last the summer.

Next was Susanna, who came while Father and Joseph were harvesting the corn the following year. She was born with a shock of light brown hair that leaped from her head at all angles, and a strong cry so insistent you'd think the house was on fire. Rebecca, who turned three shortly after she was born, patted and tugged and babbled to her new sister like she was her own baby doll, making her crude toys out of cornhusks and pebbles that Mother had to keep taking away so she wouldn't choke on them. When Susanna could pull herself up on Mother's skirt or a table leg, Rebecca would take her by both hands and walk backwards, encouraging her to toddle across the wooden floor, a pair of giggling, drunken dancers that always landed in a pile of arms and legs and tangled skirts. By summer, Rebecca and Charity were taking their little sister outside every day, letting her wiggle her toes in the mud by the creek and throw corn to the chickens. She'd always come back in need of a bath. One day, she shivered when Charity lowered her into the tub, even though the water was warm. She had been less exuberant that day, sitting in her eldest sister's lap by the creek instead of venturing near the water.

"Susie's caught a fever," the girls told their mother.

Mother tucked the baby into her cot, smoothed back her wild hair, and lay cool, wet cloths on her forehead. For several nights Mother was by her cot when John went to bed, and tipping medicine off a spoon into her mouth when he rose to do his chores in the morning.

On the fourth day, John was awakened by his mother's keening wail as Susanna died in her arms, just two weeks shy of her first birthday. All the family went to the funeral service at the church that hot, windless day, and even Uncle Joseph, Aunt Chloe, and all the cousins traveled in their wagon to Springhill Cemetery, just the other side of Bethany. Aunt Chloe wrapped her arms around Mother as the men tossed the first shovelfuls of earth over the white-painted coffin next to the small stone marking the grave of the wee unnamed sister who had gone before.

Mother was teary for weeks after, talking little. And Rebecca was heartbroken. Why did God take away her little doll-baby sister? She checked the cot in her parents' room so many times— just in case—that Father put it away on a high shelf in the barn. All that dirt and mud and water—it was too much for someone as young as Susanna, especially a girl, John thought. Maybe if you had kept her inside where it was safe, John told his mother, she would not have gotten sick.

And now it was happening again. This last baby was born just a couple of days ago, in the dead of winter, another girl. John never saw her, because she didn't even live to draw her first breath. But he watched as Father and Frank eased the tiny wooden box into the ground while gentle snowflakes fluttered down like tears. There was no church service this time, and no one else there to say goodbye.

CHAPTER THREE

Walking home from school on Fridays became a regular thing for Hans and me. We didn't talk with each other much at school; we both seemed to understand the teasing we would get from the other kids, accompanied by fake "smoochy" sounds behind our backs, if we seemed to have more than the usual relationship among classmates of the opposite sex. But after school on Fridays, Hans became my next-best friend after Ethel Rebold. He told me of his long sea voyage from Germany when he was six, and the train trip that brought him to Ohio with his family. He taught me some German words, too, and we'd always part with a "*bis bald.*" I had never been out of Ohio, so I craved to know more about the faraway places Hans had seen. He, in turn, asked me about words he didn't understand, or why we had fireworks on the Fourth of July or why children put their baby teeth under their pillow when they fell out.

A few times Hans joined both Ethel and I on days other than Fridays when we walked toward the other end of town, if one of his parents had asked him to bring back something from a store. And if he was with us when we passed the McClung house, he and I would glance at each other, wrinkle our brows, and then smile.

One Friday in October Hans wasn't at school. I didn't think much about it; kids got sick or were needed at home sometimes. He had seemed perfectly fine the day before at school, however; I saw him run off into the schoolyard to play marbles with the other boys as I left with Ethel.

When Hans returned to school on Monday, his face was badly bruised on one side and his arm was in a sling. Outside at lunchtime, I pulled him around the corner of the building.

"Hans, what happened?"

He looked down and shook his head. "Nutting. It vas nutting."

"Obviously it was something! Look at you!" He pressed his lips together in a tight line.

Suddenly it struck me. That marble game after school the previous Thursday. "It was Robert and Leavitte, wasn't it?"

"No!" he said quickly.

I didn't believe him. "You won their marbles from them, and they got mad, right? They're not going to get away with it. I'm telling Miss Dill." I started to run off.

Hans grabbed my sleeve. "No! Don't say anysing. It vasn't zem!"

I stared at him, and saw the anguish there. "Then what—"

He dropped my sleeve and stomped off. I didn't find out what happened—not until much later. But I better understood his silence when a couple of weeks later he had to pick up some elixir for his mother at the pharmacy after school and walked with me. We were on our way home, he with the elixir and I with a letter for Mother, when we passed the McClung house.

"Did I ever tell you," I asked Hans, "that the day—the day you were at their house—I saw Mrs. McClung's face in the window?"

"*Nein*. Vat did she look like?"

"I couldn't really tell; it was more like a silhouette. But I wonder if she's up there now."

Hans followed my glance and saw the small gap in the shutter. "She might be vatching us now." He smiled.

We kept walking, and I kept thinking. "I wonder why she never comes out. No one has ever seen her, not for a long time, anyway."

Hans just shrugged and said nothing.

"Don't you wonder what she does up there? Why she stays in that dark house all the time?"

Hans sighed deeply. "*Nein*, I do not."

"Really?"

"Izzy," he said, stopping for a moment and looking at me. "Vat happens in zee families is sier own business, and is better for everyone if vee don't ask questions."

I had always pictured Mrs. McClung as an old crone with a long, pointed noise marked with a wart or two, a pointed chin, and eyes that looked in two different directions. She had a permanent crook in her back, with her hair hanging over her shoulders in tangled strings, or maybe tied up in a knotted scarf like the witch in Hansel and Gretel. I think most of the children in town thought of her that way, if they thought of her at all. If Old Mr. McClung—who was dirty and mean and wore clothes older than we were—showed his face in town occasionally, how much worse his wife must be if she stayed locked up inside. She was probably afraid people would faint or scream and run the other way if they saw her.

This image I held of her was challenged that fall before the murder due to an odd experience I had one morning before school. I had left earlier than usual because Father had an important letter that needed to go out in the mail that day. I figured I could drop off the letter and then meet up with Ethel as she passed the post office, so we could walk to school together. I was on the sidewalk, just approaching the livery stable, when I saw a man standing by the McClung house inside the fence, right up close to the corner that faces Section Line Road. You never saw people standing on the McClungs' property, except perhaps if the old man was with them, and as I got closer I saw it was Mr. Dawson, the shoemaker. His cobbler shop was nearby; I had passed it on the other side of the road just a few minutes earlier. I had been in it several times, most recently to drop off a pair of Father's funeral shoes to be resoled. Today Mr. Dawson was standing beside one of the tall shuttered windows and talking—to the house. I couldn't hear him well enough to know what he was saying. There was no one else around. He must be crazy, I thought.

I told my mother about it that night as I peeled the potatoes for dinner, and she laughed. "He was talking to Mrs. McClung," she said. "He does that every once in a while. You know, he's her brother."

"She has a brother?" It was hard to believe a witch had family members like other people.

"She has three. The other Dawson brothers used to live in town when their mother was alive, making wagons and ploughs and such. Mrs. McClung was a Dawson before she married."

"Have you ever seen her?"

Mother bent to put the roasting pan in the oven. "Oh, yes, but it's been a long time."

"What was wrong with her? Was she really ugly?"

She laughed again, shut the oven door and faced me, her hands on her hips. "Now where did you get the idea something is wrong with her?"

"If there's nothing wrong, then why does she stay in that house all the time with the shutters closed?"

Mother's face turned serious as she moved to the sink. "Well, that I can't tell you. But I do know she is a beautiful woman, or at least was at one time. My mother knew her; Rebecca Dawson was younger than her, but they did run into each other on occasion. She said Rebecca was the most beautiful girl she had ever seen."

I puzzled on that while Mother scrubbed a mixing bowl. Mrs. McClung was not an old crone at all, and she had family members and maybe even friends.

"Doesn't she miss seeing people? Why doesn't her brother at least go inside if he wants to talk to her?"

"Well, I don't think Mr. McClung thinks too kindly of his wife's brothers. But that's none of our business. I do know that Mrs. McClung not only talks to her brother through the window, but she also watches what goes on outside, through the louvers in the shutters or the curtains on her window upstairs. People say she knows everyone in town, from a distance."

What a way to see the world, I thought. Like looking through a knothole in a fence all the time. And she knew everyone in town?

I wondered if she knew me.

Goodbye

Spring 1839

"You've got to come now, John," Mary said when she caught her breath from her sprint across the field. "Father says it's time to say goodbye." She had run from the house to the back of the hemp field where John was guiding the plow horse in straight rows. He had just turned thirteen two days earlier, and was big and strong enough now to do almost all the tasks his father and brother Frank could do. He felt proud to have the family rely on him for serious work, especially since Mother had become sick with dropsy.

Mary, at only eleven, had taken over many of Mother's simpler tasks by then, laundering and mending and cleaning, while Charity handled most of the cooking. These last few weeks Mother could not even get out of bed, and the older girls helped her with the chamber pot when she needed it. Elizabeth and Rebecca had charge of Sarah, the baby, and Rachel, three, bringing them to play on Mother's bed for a half hour every morning, and to Charity when their mothering skills fell short.

Frank should be with him, John thought as he hung the reins over Jack's harness, but Frank had taken the wagon into town for supplies and probably wouldn't be back for more than an hour. So while Mary ran back to the house, John trailed behind, walking alone. He hung his hat by the door and pulled off his muddy boots, moving slowly, delaying the visit to his mother's room as though circumstances might change in that extra moment or two.

As he climbed the stairs and approached Mother's sickroom he heard gentle crying. The door was open, and he stood there a moment, not wanting to go in. Father was sitting in a straight chair pulled close to the head of the bed, holding Mother's hand.

43

Rachel was next to him, holding on to Father's leg as though it were a rock in a rushing river that was trying to pull her into its fury. Charity stood on the other side of Mother, holding Rebecca's head against her chest and stroking her hair. Mary had already joined Elizabeth to sit at the bottom of the bed, her legs hanging over the side, her head against her sister's shoulder.

Mother's head was propped against the headboard with pillows; her eyes, ringed with dark circles, were closed. Her face was pale and sunken, but her distended belly pushed out the sheet that covered it. John knew that beneath her belly her legs were grossly swollen, the skin pulled tight until it was white, and she could no longer stand on feet blown up like balloons. Every day she had swallowed a dose of the foxglove tonic the doctor had prescribed, but she kept getting worse. Dropsy was a brutal way to die, swelling the body with fluids while robbing all its strength.

Seeing his sisters surrounding the bed, John couldn't help but think that each of them, and himself, too, was partly responsible for Mother's imminent passing. At age 40, she had given birth twelve times, and John pictured each birth biting off a piece of her strength. Those she loved most were taking her life, yet they loved her dearly. He thought of baby Sarah, napping in the next room, who would never remember her mother. Mother's legs were horribly swollen in the time she carried her, and the birth had been difficult. Yet Mother's smiles and the light in her eyes were no less bright than when Rachel had come two years earlier, and probably the same as when John himself had been born.

Charity looked up at John and motioned with her hand, urging him into the room. As he reluctantly approached, she stepped back so he could stand at the head of the bed. He gently placed his hand on Mother's shoulder, feeling through her thin gown the one place not swelled grotesquely. Mother turned her head on the pillow toward him. She strained to open her eyes, but the lids only flickered.

"Mother," John said, his voice gravelly, hesitating. "It's John." She nodded slightly. "I—I want to say—" What *did* he want to say? "You're a good mother."

44

He frowned. That did not sound right at all. But no other words entered his head. He bent to kiss her on the cheek, stepped back with one last look, and then quickly walked out of the room.

CHAPTER FOUR

The Christmas of 1900 stands out in my memory—mostly because of a gift I didn't get.

The younger children (and perhaps me, too, if I would admit it) felt the wait was interminable before my Miller grandparents finally arrived about nine o'clock that morning. The tracks from the carriage and the horse had made a trail through the light snow down Main Street as far as we could see, and the horse snorted as Grandpa tied him to the hitching post, his breath making a little cloud in the cold morning air. Aunt Inez, eleven years older than me, had come too, of course, because she still lived with my grandparents, and she and I helped unload the packages they had brought for all of us children from the carriage and carry them into the house. Aunt Inez was the fun aunt, the one who paid attention to me and the younger kids. She worked as a stenographer in the county courthouse in Lebanon, taking the train every day to work, the next stop up the tracks from Mason. She was a grown-up with an important job, but she still knew how to laugh and play, and I wanted to be just like her when I was older.

We all were drinking hot spiced cider, about to open presents, when there was a knock at the door. I ran to open it, and there stood Ethel Rebold. She bid me "Merry Christmas" with a big grin, and stepped to one side so I could see past her where a shiny red bicycle stood propped up against a pillar at the bottom of our porch steps.

You first must understand that before 1900, bicycles were for adults. Some of the men in Mason, for example, rode a bicycle to their jobs at the gunpowder and cartridge companies in King's

Mills, the next town over. Others might ride to Lebanon, where there were more businesses than in our village.

My father never had a bicycle, but he often told the story of the time he tried out one of the old high wheelers that belonged to a friend. The front wheel stood as tall as he was, and the pedals were attached in the center of it. Just climbing up on it took some skill, and once you got it rolling, it was all about balance—not just side to side, but front to back, too. The little wheel in the back was hardly enough to keep the contraption on the ground if you got stopped suddenly by a stick or a rock. My father was enjoying coasting at top speed down a hill on his friend's high wheeler when he hit a rock in the road that sent him flying over the front wheel, head first onto the dirt road. He wrapped his shirt around his bleeding head to walk home, and said he was still pulling gravel out of his forehead a year later.

Around that same time the new "safety bicycles" came out, with two wheels the same size. The name reflected the obvious advantage of being lower to the ground and less front-loaded. The bikes also had a gear and chain to send pedal power to the rear wheel, so they were much more efficient as real transportation. This was the kind of bicycle we saw around Mason when I was a child, and they didn't look too much different than the ones people ride today.

"Do you like the new bicycle, Izzy?" Ethel's excitement fairly burst out of her, tumbling across our front yard as dazzling as the sun glinting off the shiny red frame.

"Is it *yours*, Ethel?" She was at least half a foot shorter than me, and the bicycle looked awfully big for her.

Her smile faded a bit. "Well, not really. My mother got it as a Christmas gift from Pa."

I pulled on my boots that stood at the door and ran down the porch steps, oblivious to the cold. "What's she going to do with it?" I ran my hand over the smooth metal, and slipped my fingers around one of the handlebars.

"Pa thinks she's going to learn to ride it and they'll go on trips through the countryside together."

"Will she? Learn, I mean?"

Ethel laughed. "Well, maybe. But today she didn't want to, and said I could be the first to ride it."

She patted the seat. "Do you want to try?"

I hesitated. Of course I did. But when Mother learned I had once tried Ethel's father's bicycle, the one he used sometimes for small deliveries from his store, it got me into trouble. It was not *ladylike*, Mother said, because I had to pull up my skirt and kick my leg high over the bar to get on. I hadn't gotten far with it, either, losing my balance and catching a boot heel in my hem as I tried to keep from falling. I ended up with a skinned knee and a tear in my skirt.

But this bicycle had one big difference! Instead of the horizontal bar crossing straight from the handlebars to the seat, there was a graceful S-shaped tube that swept down from the handlebars all the way to where the pedals connected, leaving plenty of room to mount the bike with barely lifting a leg. And there was even a special guard around the chain area that would keep a skirt from getting caught. I had heard of bicycles made for ladies, but this was the first one I had seen. How could Mother object?

I glanced up at the house, and then down the almost-empty street. No one was watching. So Ethel held the bicycle for me while I got on—no skirt-hitching needed. I was able to sit on the seat, too, because I was about the same height as Mrs. Rebold. I lost my balance with the first couple of pedal pumps and hopped to the ground, but then I got back on by myself and wobbled down the street with Ethel running after me. Steering got easier as I picked up speed, and by the time I reached Dawson's cobbler shop I had the hang of it and Ethel was left far behind.

When I turned around to come back, Aunt Inez was standing on the porch calling to me. "Izzy, get in here! The other kids are about to launch a riot if we don't start opening presents."

I coasted back to the side of the road in front of our house as Ethel ran to meet me. I reluctantly passed the handlebars to her and she climbed on. Then I watched her march up and down on

49

the pedals in front of the seat of the too-big bike, wishing it could be mine.

When I joined the rest of the family in the parlor, my siblings didn't care about hearing about the new bicycle; they just wanted to open presents. But I couldn't get it out of my mind. That bicycle rode off with a bit of the excitement I had felt earlier as I had carried in the packages from my grandparents' carriage. None of them were anywhere near big enough to hold a bicycle, and I couldn't think of anything else that would be nearly as wonderful.

My present from Grandma and Grandpa Miller was a rich blue dress with white collar and cuffs and fancy shell buttons on the front. I liked it all right, and it was special because Aunt Inez had had it made for me at a shop near where she worked in Lebanon. Inez brought candy for all the children, a popular but short-lived treat.

My parents' gift to me was a book that Father had bought on one of his trips to Cincinnati. It was called *Beautiful Joe*, and the picture on the front showed the dark silhouette of a dog sitting under a tree, looking out on a hilly landscape under a blue sky. It is a sweet, sad, joyful story "written" by a dog who was cruelly mistreated as a pup and goes on to have many adventures. It's based on the life of a real dog, who of course could not write, but the fanciful twist was effective in making me imagine what it's like to be helpless when others don't care who they hurt. Beautiful Joe became as real to me as our dog Cerbie, and instilled in me a great empathy for animals. But it also opened my eyes to the cruelty of some human beings and the evil that exists in the world, right along with the good. That insight was to help me in the months and years to come.

It turned out Mrs. Rebold never took to riding a bicycle. A disappointed Mr. Rebold talked about selling it, but he never set it up in his store with a For Sale sign on it; I think they decided to keep it just in case Mrs. Rebold ever changed her mind, or one of the girls eventually grew into it. Whatever the reason, I am grateful to the Rebolds for letting me borrow it almost whenever

I liked. Mr. Rebold kept it in the storage area in the rear of his store, so I would walk the half mile or so to get his permission and then wheel the bicycle out the back door. I'd just have to be sure to return it before his store closed, and I never could have it on Sundays, of course. Before spring arrived, Mr. Rebold took Ethel to the Wright brothers' bicycle shop in Dayton and got her a sky-blue girl's bicycle in a size that fit her, and then we could ride together. But I still enjoyed days of riding by myself, relishing the feel of the wind in my face and the freedom of venturing beyond where my feet alone could take me. It was on one of those solo rides that I first connected with Mrs. McClung.

One especially warm afternoon in early March I had picked up the red bicycle at the Rebolds' house and pedaled down Main Street to the eastern end of town where I turned right onto the road to Kings Mills. There was a lovely little bridge over the creek just down that road, and I crossed over the rushing water and continued past fields in varying stages of plowing and planting, smelling of damp earth and pungent manure. The road was bumpy and eroded from early spring freezing and thawing, and it was a rough ride. I had to dodge potholes and puddles so the wheels wouldn't throw water up the back of my skirt.

A cow grazing near the road looked up at me in surprise, a clump of grass hanging from her mouth. I pumped the pedals hard to pass a young couple in a buggy, and the horse shook his head at me as though to say, what's the world coming to? I rode all the way to the village of Kings Mills, stopping in front of Mr. Ahimaaz King's mansion with its fancy carriage house and its fountain in the front yard. I hopped off the bicycle, holding it up as I looked around me. Hello, world, I thought; here I am, in another town, and I got here all by myself.

I pedaled a bit slower on the way home, my legs tiring and my behind a little sore from being jostled on the rough road. When I reached the creek bridge just outside town, the gurgling water looked so refreshing that I steered off the road, lay the bicycle in the fresh green grass, and pulled off my high-button shoes and stockings.

The creek was full and moving quickly, as it often was in the spring, but the day was warm enough to make it inviting. So I held up my skirt and picked my way down the grassy bank and stepped into the edge of the water. I drew in my breath at the sudden cold, but held my stance on the rocky bottom until I gradually got used to the temperature and enjoyed the feel of the water surging against my ankles. The sun sparkled on the water where it found its way through the overhanging sycamore trees. A female cardinal flew across the creek and perched on a nearby branch. Small fish I couldn't see in the turbulent, muddy water nibbled at my toes, darting away when I jumped back in surprise. Spring was peeking around the corner and it was glorious.

Refreshed, I scrambled back up the bank and dried my feet with the bottom of my skirt (Mother would not like this) before pulling on my stockings and boots. After walking the bicycle back to the road, I stood on the pedals to build up speed until my hair blew out behind me. The road was smoother on this side of the bridge because there had just been a street repair day a few days before. All the men in town were required to donate two days of labor per year working on the roads to keep them passable. Mr. Reed, the marshal and the lamplighter, was also the street commissioner, and he kept careful records of who worked when. Men who shirked their duty had their names published in the Mason newspaper. Every spring Mr. Reed hired a team of horses to pull a big scraper down the road, smoothing it and clearing it of debris and mud. The men would follow behind and shovel the scrapings onto a flatbed wagon that would haul and dump it.

So I appreciated the smoother surface as I banked around the corner onto Main Street and coasted into town. Exhilarated by speed, I wasn't ready to return the bicycle yet, so I continued on past the Rebolds'. As soon as I neared the McClung's big brick block of a house on my left, I looked up to the second-floor windows. Framed between the curtains in the one window not shuttered closed, I could just make out the silhouette of a head.

I don't know what made me do it. Maybe it was the newness of the first warm spring day; maybe it was my feet still tingling from the cold water, or maybe just the freedom of speeding past the people shuffling along the sidewalk. But I didn't think twice.

I waved.

And she waved back.

Each time after that when I rode the bicycle past the McClung house, I looked up at that window. Sometimes the light wasn't right and I couldn't tell if she was there or not, but I always waved, just in case.

Land

Fall 1855

John's sister Rebecca pressed a tear-moistened cheek next to that of her six-year-old niece Sarah, whispering final endearments John couldn't hear as he waited for her to climb up next to him on the wagon seat. Sarah's brothers Granville, age five, and Taylor, age nine, had already said their goodbyes with little emotion and hurried off to the barn to play with the week-old kittens. Little Sarah clung to Rebecca, the only female around now that her mother had passed away.

John grasped the reins impatiently, and looked out again over the cornfield he and Jesse had harvested just weeks earlier. Jesse LeSourd was their sister Charity's husband, and John and Rebecca had spent the last six years on their farm in Fairfield Township, Rebecca helping with the children and house chores and John with the farming. Those were long days, those final weeks of harvest, when the weather was fair. Jesse and John strapped husking hooks over their gloves early in the morning and spent most of the daylight hours cutting, husking, and stowing the crop until their shoulders were sore and their necks were red and leathery from the sun. Jesse's oldest son Taylor was good help, too, but Jesse wouldn't let the boy miss school or homework to work in the field. If I had my say, thought John, things would be different. A boy learned more and got stronger working hard on a farm than he did sitting at a school desk. Especially when teachers wasted hours on ancient history and useless stories they called literature. School should teach a boy to cipher and read, and that's all he would need.

But none of that mattered now that Charity had died. In a few days, when the sale of this farm was completed, Jesse would load up what he could carry in his wagon along with his three children and head to his parents' farm in Liberty Township, less than ten miles away. He would leave Sarah there to live with his parents, and he would take his sons Taylor and Granville with him to Indiana where Jesse would study to become a preacher. He was done with farming, ready to consider what he called the important questions, ready for a new life.

Six years of John's life, wasted. Sure, Charity and her family were his kin, but as John saw it now, he had been even less than a hired hand, with nothing to show for all his work. He was leaving with nothing more than he came with: a secondhand wagon, a horse, and a sister who was already past prime marrying age.

Rebecca reluctantly handed Sarah back to her father and climbed up next to John, brushing away a tear with the edge of her sleeve as Jesse carried the little girl around the back of the wagon to the driver's side. John clutched the reins in his right hand and didn't reach for the child, but Sarah grabbed his neck and slipped into his lap. She held his face in her little hands to get his attention.

"Uncle John, I don't want to go live with Gran and Gramps LeSourd," she whispered. "Can I go with you and Rebecca?"

John considered her earnest face and sighed. Sarah didn't belong on the McClung farm, its long history of females notwithstanding. She was Jesse's responsibility and none of his. If her father chose to leave the girl with her grandparents, that was his business.

John shook his head. "No. There's no place for a child at our house."

"I'll be really good, just like a grownup," she said quickly. "I'll do all the chores you tell me to."

John pulled her hands from his face and looked at her sternly. "You can't come with us, Sarah. That's just the way of it."

Sarah looked down at her lap, then raised her lips again to John's ear. "Then I want to go to heaven so I can see Mama and Sammy."

John looked away, out to the dry cornfield. Children were always saying foolish things, things you couldn't even answer to. People died; it just happened. There was no reasoning with it, no answers to it, nothing to be done about it. Sarah would learn to forget her little brother, gone half a year now, and her mother Charity, gone barely two weeks. It's what you have to do.

He lifted the girl from his lap and handed her back to her father and wished Jesse success in his new life. The children and their father watched as John clicked his tongue to the horse and the wagon clattered away from the house.

It was only about an hour back to their father's farm, where a houseful of family was expecting them. There was Father, in his sixties now, and Mary, the woman he had married just a few years after their mother died. John didn't think much one or the other about her, but she could cook and did her share of the chores. All the younger girls were still at home, too—Mary, Sarah, Rachel, and Elizabeth. His brothers Joseph and Francis had both married and moved out, both working a farm in Turtle Creek that belonged to Joseph's elderly father-in-law.

John, almost twenty, was now the only son in the family who would still be working his father's farm. Kin or no kin, he would still be working for someone else. But there was a difference—his father was getting up in years, and John would be the only son left on the farm when his father died, meaning it would one day be his. Then he'd bring in his own crops and his own money, and he'd buy up other land, too. And if there ever were any children to tend, they'd be his own and not someone else's.

With a slap of the reins, John turned the wagon away from a life working for others and pointed the horses toward land that one day would be his own.

CHAPTER FIVE

If Christmas was a bit like vanilla ice cream, good but not very exciting, my birthday on March 23 was like an ice cream sundae with all the toppings. First of all, it was on a Saturday—no school, no homework. Right after breakfast, before Father started work in the embalming room, he asked me to come out to the ice house with him. I knew something was up, because I had never had to haul ice before, and Mother had a strange smile on her face as we passed her in the kitchen. I was no less puzzled when we walked out the back door and there was the Rebolds' red bicycle leaning against the ice house. I just looked at Father.

"Well, don't you want to ride it?" Father asked. Oh—he had picked it up at the Rebolds for me so I could go for a birthday ride.

"Sure, I guess so."

"When you get back, bring it in the carriage house. It's yours now."

I was just as excited as if I had gotten the bicycle brand new on Christmas morning. I loved that bike; it was an old friend by now, and I wouldn't want any other. Now I could ride it whenever I liked, even when Mr. Rebold's store was closed, and I wouldn't have to walk across town to pick it up.

I did take it for a ride that birthday morning, stopping at the Rebolds to thank them for selling it to my father; Ethel joined her mother at the door to give me a birthday hug. Then I rode a mile or so out the road to Lebanon before turning around at the Pattersons' farm. The freedom I had first felt coasting across town and out the other side a couple of weeks earlier was now doubled—the bicycle was now my own. In my joy, I waved at people on the street and at a passing carriage. And, of course, I waved at the tall curtained rectangle of Rebecca McClung's second-story window.

As I neared our house, there was Hans on the walk approaching our front door. I called out to him, and he stopped and waited for me to ride up and prop the bicycle against the side of the porch.

"What are you doing here on a Saturday?" I was a little out of breath from the ride, but smiled broadly.

"I brought you somezink." He smiled. "But vere did you get zee bicycle?"

I stroked the frame lovingly. "It used to be the Rebolds', but Father bought it from them for my birthday. I'm eleven today."

Hans beamed. "I know! Zat's vye I came today." He reached in his pocket and pulled out something small. "Hold out your hand."

I did, and Hans placed his gift on my palm. "Happy Birzday!"

It was a shiny glass marble, a large shooter, clear with white inside. I lifted it into the late morning sunshine and examined it. The glass was pure and transparent, and inside—how did it get inside?—stood a delicate white angel, her graceful wings stretched open behind her, her skirt intricately draped in tiny folds.

"It's not so good as a bicycle," Hans said. "But I hope you like it. It's from my uncle's shop in Germany."

I could not take my eyes off it, turning it in my hand. The angel was perfect from every angle, the tiniest statue I had ever seen, encased forever in a glass sanctuary. "It's beautiful, so beautiful." I finally lifted my eyes to Hans, who relaxed and grinned. "Thank you."

That evening after supper my family sang "Happy Birthday" and I blew out eleven candles on a chocolate cake with white seven-minute icing. Even baby Frank, not yet a year old, got a small piece. He swirled his finger through the airy white topping before stuffing the treat in his mouth—although more of it ended up on his cheeks and hands.

Before it was dark, I ran out to the carriage house to look at my bicycle one more time. It stood proudly against the wall, next to our family carriage, and looked like it belonged there. I thought of my ride that day, different because the bicycle was now mine. And I wondered if Mrs. McClung had seen me pedal past her house. Even if she had, she wouldn't know I was riding my birthday gift. I could not have explained the desire, but somehow, I wanted to share this special day with her.

Suddenly I had an idea. I latched the carriage house door, ran in the house, and found Mildred in the kitchen, helping Mother put away the last of the washed dishes. "As soon as you're done, come up to our room and get out some paper and your crayons," I told her, "and I'll draw pictures with you."

Since I was usually trying to get Milly away from me, she was excited at the offer to do something together and joined me in our bedroom moments later. She pulled out a stack of clean white paper from a drawer of her chest and the box of Franklin Rainbow Crayons she had received the Christmas before. Mildred was a girl of order, and she liked to keep all her seven crayons the same length by using them equally. So she lay them all on the wood floor in front of the throw rug, side by side, and chose the two longest for me to use.

"You can have orange and violet," she said. "But you have to give them to me if I need them for my picture." She started making a big blue arch in the middle of her paper—the start of another rainbow, her favorite subject because her crayons were all the right colors.

There was no point in arguing with Mildred, so I picked up a pencil instead and started to draw.

By the time I had finished my sketch, Milly had skipped off to show Mother her finished picture. So I was free to use the red crayon to color in the frame of the bicycle I had drawn, and adorn the rather poorly drawn figure of myself astride it in a yellow dress that was much brighter than the one I had actually worn that day, but my choices were limited to the Rainbow colors in the box. Then, with the pencil, I carefully printed my name at the bottom: Isabel June Miller. Mother said Mrs. McClung knew everyone in town, but I wanted to be sure.

I folded the paper in quarters and printed her name on the outside. Then, the next morning, I left for school early so I could track down Farly Dwire before class started. He lived at the Mason House hotel, right across the street from the McClungs' house, and his father was the innkeeper.

"Farly, I am hiring you to do something important for me," I instructed him sternly. "Here is a nickel. You are to give this paper to Mr. Dill at your hotel, and ask him to deliver it to the McClungs. You also must tell NO ONE. If you blab, you have to give back the nickel, and I will tell EVERYONE about the day you wet your pants when that cow mooed in your ear at the fair."

Farly's eyes widened, and he nodded his head solemnly.

I knew I was taking a chance. But Farly usually liked to please the older kids so they'd let him hang around, and with the trust I was showing him and the threat I had given him, I felt chances were good the paper would at least reach Mr. Dill. Then Mr. Dill, one of the few people who seemed to have regular contact with his reclusive neighbors across the street, would need to give it to the McClungs. Delivery to Mrs. McClung was far from certain, but I didn't see I had anything to lose. No one could be upset with a child's drawing of a girl on a bicycle.

When I was twenty-two, I prepared to move out of our house at the western end of Main Street. As part of that process, some of the things I had accumulated through the years were thrown away or passed along to my younger siblings. But there were a few things that, although they served no practical purpose and would not be used in my new home, I saved in a box I labeled "Keepsakes." Among these were my high school final paper on the influence of Shakespeare on modern literature, which earned a ten out of ten; funeral cards from the passing of loved ones; and sentimental small gifts from family and friends.

One of those special items is sitting here beside me now, nestled in a little box that I lined with a scrap of blue velvet—the marble from Hans. The lid is open, because I was just enjoying the beautiful marble again. I haven't been able to see it with my eyes for more than year now, since I lost most of my sight to glaucoma, but this morning I held it below the warm sunlight coming through Rebecca's window and in my mind I again admired the perfect, tiny white angel twirling in glass as I rolled it in my palm. It is the best gift I ever received, and I love it still.

Another gift, almost as dear to me, is in my box of special items that is still in a closet at Frank's house, awaiting my return. A few days after I had given my drawing to Farly following my eleventh birthday, an envelope had been waiting for me at the post office, and I couldn't wait to get home and open it—the first letter just for me that I ever received, addressed to Miss Isabel J. Miller.

Inside the envelope was a drawing—done in pencil on a plain piece of writing paper; nothing fancy or especially artistic, but it delighted me more than if I had opened a painting by Rembrandt. It showed a ladies' bicycle with two seats, one behind the other. In the front was a girl in a dress, leaning forward to pick up speed, with her hair flying out loose in the breeze. Behind her, on the rear seat, sat a prim woman with a bun on her head, with one hand on the girl's shoulder and a smile on her face. Underneath was penciled in a spidery script: "Isabel June Miller and Rebecca Dawson McClung."

CHAPTER SIX

Nothing good happens in the dark. That's what Mother usually said if on a beautiful summer evening I complained about the curfew, rung out every night at 8:30 from the bell atop the town hall. Once, when I was being smart, I snapped back something like wasn't that what the streetlights were for, lit every night by Mr. Reed, the town marshal? Since that comment was punished with a soapy mouth-washing, I limited my protests to quiet grumbles.

But that April, the nothing-good thing that happened in the dark occurred in the morning hours, before daybreak.

April 12 started out cool and calm. It was a Friday, and I was practicing spelling words in my head in last-minute preparation for the end-of-the-week spelling test as I started my walk to school (*Apprehension: two Ps, "shun" with an s, not a T*). Cerbie walked with me as far as the railroad tracks, as he always did, anxious to test the smells of the day. He moved in for a pat on the head before turning and trotting back home, finding nothing out of the ordinary.

But he hadn't gone far enough, for the excitement was farther down the road. More people than usual were in the street and along the sidewalks ahead of me on Main Street—many more. They clustered in small groups, fanning out from a nucleus that seemed to be centered at the corner of Section Line Road in front of the McClung house. I picked up my pace until I got to the school, and then stopped, torn. I should be heading to my classroom, but I still couldn't see what people were interested in up ahead. Besides, I could just make out some of my schoolmates in the crowd, some with a parent, some with their friends. If they could be late for class, then so could I.

Farly Dwire was standing near the back of the crowd, next to his father, who was talking with Mr. Rebold, Ethel's father. I didn't see Ethel anywhere. Since the Dwires lived in the hotel right across the street from the McClungs, and Farly's father was the innkeeper, the Dwires would know what was happening, if anyone did.

"Farly, what's going on?" I was almost breathless from sprinting up the road.

Farly glanced at his father, who was deep in hushed conversation with Mr. Rebold, then back to me. "It's Mrs. McClung," he whispered, his eyes wide. "She's dead."

Something dropped in my chest. Dead? How could she be dead? It had only been a few weeks since she drew the picture of us on the bicycle built for two. This couldn't be. I had thought we might be friends, but I hadn't ever really met her. Now I never would.

Something else was wrong. What were all these people doing here? Their unease and sheer numbers seemed exaggerated for the death of an old woman no one ever saw.

"Why is everyone hanging around?" I asked Farly.

"Izzy," he hissed in my ear, grabbing my arm and demanding my full attention, "somebody *killed* her. It's a *murder*."

He voiced the word with a reverence and awe generally reserved only for God himself, a word seldom heard in our small town and certainly never from the lips of a young boy like Farlane Dwire.

My mind raced. Who in the world would want to kill Mrs. McClung? She never went out anywhere, so how could she cause offense to anyone? Maybe Farly was wrong. He wasn't even ten yet, after all.

I looked around for Mr. Dill. He lived here at the Mason Hotel, too, and knew the McClungs probably better than anyone. But he was nowhere to be seen.

"Farly, have you seen Mr. Dill?"

"No, but I know where he is. In *there*"—he pointed to the house with an accusing finger—"with the sheriff and Deputy Smart. In there with *her*—her that's *dead*."

Mr. Dill? In the house of the murdered woman, with the sheriff? What did that mean?

"Farlane," said Mr. Dwire, "you go off to school now. You're already late, if I'm not mistaken. And Isabel, you'd best be on your way as well."

I walked away, but not to school. How could I? The morning bristled with excitement and horror. Most everyone in town was outside the eerie big house on the corner, most of its shutters open now. They were on the new sidewalk in front, in the road, and spilling around the corner into the side yard and even around back. And they were all talking in hushed tones, questions and gossip spilling out in a fury I'd never seen before.

"It happened while Mr. McClung was doing his chores, out in the stable. You know how he goes out there early every day, always the same time; feeds the animals, milks the cow."

"They were after his money, had to be."

"He sure had enough of it. Hidden in the house, I hear. Never did see him use a bank."

"But why kill her if they were after money?"

"She must have been in the kitchen, and they had to get her out of the way."

"No, no. She was in bed. I heard it from the doctor himself. Killed right in her bed, she was."

"William says he saw a man on horseback, riding off from the house, about that hour."

"That could have been anybody."

"I bet you double to nothing it was that group of Negroes been down the pike there putting that fill dirt in the cemetery."

"It could have been the old man himself, you know. He's an ornery one."

"Old McClung? He's an odd one, all right, but he can barely get himself around let alone kill his own wife. I heard her whole head is smashed, bared to the brain."

"It had to be someone after his money. It's no secret he's got a houseful of it."

"Listen to this. Mr. Springer just told me, and he saw it himself. There was a man running from the house, right at the time it happened, just before the marshal got here. And mark my words. He was wearing a *dress*—a woman's dress."

Wife

Spring 1870

At age 44, John was finally to be married. There would be another Rebecca McClung, when she took his name. It sounded good to him, since his sister with that name had died three years earlier, less than a year after she finally married. And she had been a good woman.

The ceremony would be small—family members, mostly—at the Universalist Church the beginning of May. Just in time to start planting season with a wife. And what a treasure she was. The first time John saw her, Rebecca Dawson was still a girl. John had come to pick up a new wagon wheel from her father Ezra, the wagon and plough maker. He had hardly noticed her then. But she grew into a beautiful woman, the most beautiful in the county, John thought. At least of the ones he had seen. But not foolish like the others.

Since she grew up with brothers, and had a sensible mother, she hadn't been as exposed to all the frivolities of other females. She dressed simply, but that made her beauty shine all the more because it didn't have to compete with all the lace and geegaws that spendthrift women wore. She was quiet, staying at home, not running off to all those female club and society meetings that had become popular in town.

As the oldest child in the family, Becca (as John had come to call her) had grown up helping her father—and, later, her brothers—manage the business side of their profession, and when John bought the first new plough of his own, a few years after his father died, it was young Rebecca who had taken his money and carefully printed a receipt and recorded the sale in the account book where she kept all the records of sales and supply purchases.

John would bring Becca home to the farmhouse he grew up in, just north of Mason, on land that was now his. She wouldn't be burdened with the farm work, as John hired laborers for that, but she would help his stepmother Mary with the household chores. Rebecca came unencumbered from other family members, her father having died several years earlier, and her mother well provided for by Becca's three younger brothers—the older two, Vete and Nicholas, who had taken over their father's wagon-making business, and the youngest, Pen, a journeyman shoemaker. John figured her brothers would be happy to no longer take the responsibility of caring for their sister.

Of course, they were careful about who she would marry. She was desirably buxom and beautiful, but she was thirty now. Certainly there were others who had taken a fancy to her that her family did not see as worthy. John, on the other hand, was prime marrying material. His age brought with it experience and stability; his head for business and hard work had made him one of the wealthiest men in the township. Yes, the Dawson family was fortunate to have such a match for their sister.

And John, too, was more than fortunate—a beautiful, sensible woman was hard to come by. Rebecca was to him a fine treasure—and he would be careful all the rest of his life to keep her safe.

CHAPTER SEVEN

We had to stay inside the school building all that day, eating lunch at our desks and "reading quietly" at recess. I don't know if that was because of official order of the marshal, the teachers fearing that there may still be robbers or murderers in the streets, or just that children would be in the way of the investigation. But every chance we got we were peering out the windows, trying to see the people on the street, imagining the manhunt that must be going on to find Mrs. McClung's murderer.

Besides our town marshal and his deputies, our law enforcement team included the Mason Horse Rangers, formed in the early years of the town to combat a group of horse thieves that had been victimizing the area. Each proud member of the group wore a shield-shaped badge and had a blue sign posted on his house with white letters reading "Member of Mason Horse Ranger Company." Unencumbered by the more formal legal system, these men were probably already searching on both horse and foot for the man in women's clothing seen running from the scene of the murder. Most of us would have given anything to join them rather than sit inside identifying subjunctive verb forms and reciting in order the kings of England.

There were more than the usual number of hands raised for permission to sharpen a pencil or get a drink of water or use the outhouse, and we'd walk slowly past the tall, narrow windows, our view of town like watching a ball game through a slatted fence. The biggest news came when Leavitte Pease returned from the outhouse with the whispered report that a man in a fancy suit was out in the McClungs' front yard looking over a suit of clothes spread out on the grass; he said the coat looked like the one the

71

old man wore when he went out. Lots of the townspeople were watching from the side of the road, he said. I hoped my father might be one of them, so I could get the full report after school.

After Miss Dill finally dismissed us, I was about to race home to find out if Father had been there, when Robert Tucker grabbed my arm.

"Izzy," he said earnestly, looking around the schoolyard to be sure no one could hear him. "Your father is the undertaker. He's going to get old Mrs. McClung's body."

You'd think the possibility would have occurred to me earlier, but it hadn't. Like most of the town, I was still trying to understand who might have killed the poor woman and why. I wondered what Robert was getting at.

"Maybe, but . . .well, you know my father isn't the only undertaker in town."

"No. But Leavitte saw the marshal walking down to your house about an hour ago, along with some papers."

I thought about that. It made sense, actually, because our funeral home was the only one in town that could hold services and viewings. Mrs. Bursk, the other undertaker, followed the tradition of holding a viewing in the home of the deceased or of a relative. The McClung house was the scene of a murder, hardly a place for a respectful viewing.

Robert glanced around again and brought his face so close to mine that I could smell the liverwurst he had had for lunch. "You want to earn some money?"

I drew my head back; this was getting strange. "Robert, what are you talking about?"

"Her body," he whispered, mysteriously. "We want to see it, me and Leavitte."

I yanked my arm out of his grasp and pulled away.

"Robert Tucker, you are *sick*." I whirled away from him, but he grabbed me again before I could get away.

"There's fifty cents in it for you," he said. "Me and Leavitte will each put in a quarter. All you have to do is get us in to see her."

I stared at him. "There's no way my father would let you in."

"That's why I'm asking *you*. We could come at night, while everyone's asleep. We won't touch her or anything. What's the harm in just looking? And think of what you could do with that fifty cents," he added slyly.

I confess, selfish desire elbowed its way into my good sense. I had been wanting the board game *Around the World with Nellie Bly* ever since Ethel Rebold told me her father had gotten some to sell in his store. So, although I knew everything about Robert's idea was wrong, I stood there a moment too long.

Robert, mischievous but astute, caught my indecision. "Listen. They'll probably bring her body over later today, right?"

"I guess."

"Well, we'll watch for when they move her. But assuming it's tonight, Leavitte and I will be outside your back door at midnight. All you have to do is open the door, let us in to where the body is, we'll take a quick look, you let us out again, and you've got fifty cents."

I knew no good could ever come from stooping to Robert's level. So I squared my shoulders to stand taller than he was. "I don't think so, Robert," I said in my best holier-than-thou voice.

"You think about it some more," he hissed. "Midnight. Leavitte and I will be waiting."

It turned out Robert was right about the marshal going to our house. When I got home Father was already hauling blocks from the ice house out back into his embalming room, preparing for the body he would soon pick up in his hearse. He was always tight-lipped about the details of his business with the deceased, saying they had a right to privacy and respect even in death, so it was Mother I went to. As busy as she was with household duties and several small children, somehow she always knew what was going on in town.

But not today.

"Frank is teething again, slobbering and crying most of the day," she said, bobbling him on her hip with one arm while stirring something on the stove with the other. "Cerbie threw up

73

on the parlor floor while the marshal was here, and Everett's coming down with something. All the excitement that's going on in town, and I can't learn a thing about it because I can't get out of the house."

"I can find out for you," I said, in a less-than-selfless attempt to turn the situation from my benefit to hers.

"Peel these potatoes for dinner and put them in some water, get Everett to take two spoonfuls of that tonic, and then you can go. But take Marshall with you. He's been driving me to distraction and he needs to get out and run off some energy. Mind you keep a careful eye on him, though—there's no telling what could happen in that hubbub down the street."

I whirled through the chores, probably being a bit too strong-handed with Everett and the tonic, and called to Marshall. He was delighted to be going somewhere, and burst out the door with his chubby legs churning.

"Marshall, you stay on the sidewalk," I called to him sternly, "or you'll have to go back home. Do you hear me?"

He nodded solemnly and jogged ahead on his short legs, flapping his arms like a bird.

There was still a crowd outside the fence around the McClung house, spilling into the street, and I found Ethel there with her father. I scooped up Marshall and set him down firmly next to me near the side of the road and took his hand.

"What's going on?" I asked Ethel in a hushed voice.

"The marshal and a couple of the deputies have got old man McClung in there. The coroner's been talking with Mr. Dill and Mrs. Baysore, she's been living in there with them, you know, the past few weeks, they say she and Mr. Dill bought the place but let the McClungs stay upstairs, can you imagine why anyone would want to live in there—with *them*?, and they've finished searching all over the house and the yard and the barn, my dad says, and they haven't found anything—"

Ethel's father grasped her arm and shushed her. "Listen. The coroner's going to say something."

The coroner was a tall, robust man with a salt-and-pepper beard and thick droopy mustache that pulled down bags under his eyes. He was dressed in a black derby hat and clothes fancier than most of the folk around, so he would have stood out even if he hadn't been standing on the step in front of the house. He was patting the air with his arms to get people to quiet down.

"Thank you, Mason citizens," he boomed authoritatively. "My name is Carey, George Carey, and I'm the county coroner. I'll give you a brief update before we continue with our business here."

Mr. Carey pulled a sheaf of papers from his coat pocket and held it in the air. "I have completed an inquest in the matter of the death of Mrs. Rebecca McClung, and am prepared to present my findings." He pivoted, taking in the large assembly of people. "The marshal and myself will be escorting Mr. McClung to the mayor's office in the firehouse where we will conduct a hearing. The hearing is open to the public—" his voice trailed off a bit— "if the public can fit." The problem was obvious. The firehouse was a simple, small building that doubled as a town hall back then.

"Will you tell us your findings, Coroner?" someone shouted from the back of the crowd. "I think we've got a right to know." A few others chimed in, agreeing with the demand.

Mr. Carey looked around at the crowd, then licked a finger and shuffled through the papers. "After viewing the body and hearing the evidence," he read, "I find that the deceased came to her death from blows upon the head by some blunt instrument in the hands of her husband, while under mental aberration."

A moment of shock and silence—followed by gasps and murmurs. Many shook their heads, some out of disbelief, some out of disagreement. Mr. Carey turned from the crowd and went back in the house. I didn't know what mental aberration was, but figured it meant something was wrong with Mr. McClung's head.

Mr. Tetrick, the carpenter who had done work in our house as well as many houses in town, threw his hat on the ground.

"They're railroading him!" he shouted. "This was the work of robbers."

"He could have done it," said the man next to him. "McClung is one peculiar man."

"You can't accuse a man of murder for being peculiar!" Mr. Tetrick retorted.

"I think you're right, Tetrick," said Farly Dwire's father. "Everyone knows he keeps money hidden in that house. It was bound to happen one of these days that he'd be robbed. And the poor woman surprised them."

"They say he beat her to death with a stick of wood," said a servant girl from the Bennett farm. "How's that old man strong enough to do that? He can hardly walk."

Suddenly I realized Marshall was no longer holding my hand. I looked frantically about, but it was hard to see a two-year-old in the sea of arms and legs in the gathered crowd.

"Marshall!" I called, just as the door to the big house opened again and the people quieted down. I looked up just as the other marshal—the one who policed the town—appeared on the stoop, followed by Mr. McClung, who was led and supported by Deputy Williamson. The old man looked up, squinting at the sun, and scowling when he saw the crowd. Behind them was Mr. Thompson, the village attorney, and the coroner. Mr. McClung hung his head again as the group of men moved across the lawn. The people parted to make way, but weren't ashamed to stare.

And then I saw Marshall. He emerged from a maze of legs to run across the lawn, right in front of Mr. McClung. The old man almost tripped over him. I dashed out to grab my brother, and had to get closer to the accused murderer than I had ever been before. I don't know if the man even noticed me; he seemed dazed and confused.

Everyone followed the little procession a block down Main Street to the firehouse and town hall building. We waited outside while they went in to the Mayor's office to prepare for the hearing. But a few minutes later Mayor Lowe appeared outside the door, with Mr. Thompson, the town's attorney, at his side.

"Folks," he said, taking off his hat. "We've had a change of plans. Mr. McClung's lawyer, in Lebanon, could not be reached today, so the hearing will take place Monday at ten a.m. And I see we can't accommodate this crowd in my office, so the hearing will be held in the Opera House. This has been quite a day, and now it's time for everyone to go home."

The Opera House was the perfect place for the murder hearing. If that sounds odd, it's because folks today are not familiar with what opera houses were back then. Despite the name, they seldom hosted operas, but they did host most every other form of entertainment in town. Opera houses were event and community centers, used for band concerts and high school graduations, Farmers' Institute meetings and vaudeville shows.

Our Opera House was owned by Mr. Sprinkle, who ran several businesses in town and whose very name radiated joy. Behind that joy, however, was personal tragedy: Mr. Sprinkle had lost all his family—two children in infancy and a teenage son to suicide, and his wife at age forty-eight. The Opera House was a tribute to his resiliency, showing he still believed that life should be enjoyed and shared. The Opera House brought countless good times to the people of Mason, and although a murder hearing was far from a happy event, holding it there was not only practical, but symbolic: the murder of Mrs. McClung had become a town event.

CHAPTER EIGHT

I'm not proud of this, but to be honest, I did consider Robert's "offer" of fifty cents in exchange for a look at Mrs. McClung's battered body. The opportunity to be the first of my classmates with a brand-new *Around the World with Nellie Bly* board game was a lot more attractive to me as an eleven-year-old than it sounds now. What could be the harm in a couple of boys just *looking* at the body? I had seen many of the bodies Father handled in his business. Less than a week earlier, Father had wheeled the body of Robert Hines into his embalming room as Mildred and I watched. He had died of consumption, at only age eighteen.

No one would know if I took a peek at Mrs. McClung. And yet, I knew underneath it was wrong. Not only was I forbidden from entering the embalming room; my parents had also instilled in me the importance of showing respect for those who had passed on to the next life. Their bodies may be useless and lifeless now, but they represented the precious life that had once filled them. In the same way that our flag represented our country, the body a person left behind represented that person, and should be treated with the same respect it deserved while living.

So I was torn. My brief contact with Mrs. McClung edged out the temptation, and I went to bed Friday night at my usual eight o'clock, not planning to rise until morning.

But that's not what happened.

I awoke with a start. I don't know if what startled me was something in the house or something in my dream, but my eyes popped open. The house was silent and dark. Pale light from the streetlamp near our house filtered through the sheer curtains, casting a slanted rectangle on the floor near Milly's bed. She lay still beneath her blanket, her doll next to the pillow with a thin stuffed arm hanging over the edge of the bed. I knew the night was far from spent, for outside the crickets still sang with gusto and I felt far from rested.

Wide awake, I lay in bed thinking about the day to come. It was a Saturday, so there would be no school, but there would be a lot happening. The body of Mrs. McClung, delivered under cover the evening before to our back door and now lying in the embalming room, would keep my father busy most of the day as he prepared it for the viewing and funeral on Sunday. Various McClung and Dawson family members and lawyers and officials might come and go during the day as well, and Mother must be dressed and available to greet them and help Father handle business arrangements. That meant I would be responsible for the younger children, keeping them upstairs and quiet and out of the way. My father's undertaking business directed all of our lives.

But if our family had to make some sacrifices for the undertaking business, we also reaped the benefits of Father and Mother, for a short time, becoming almost part of the families they served, who by necessity shared the thoughts, feelings, and raw emotions bared as the bereaved experienced one of the most significant and stressful times of life. When I was younger, I had little interest in learning details like who had an estranged child or brother or parent and if that person should be invited to the funeral; or that someone's grandmother's favorite color was lilac, and she ought to be buried wearing the fancy hat with lilac flowers on it, so could Father make it sit right on her head while she's lying in a casket? Now that I was eleven, however—almost an adult—I began to appreciate the advantage of occasionally being privy to inside information.

Of course, Father took very seriously the trust given him, and he was very careful to respect the one who had died and to guard the privacy of his or her family. So when I burst out with my question at the supper table that evening, Father had hesitated.

"You were in the McClungs' house, Father!" I had exclaimed. "What was it like?"

Father was quiet for a moment as he spread butter on a piece of bread. "Well," he finally said. "It's a nice house, has lots of rooms inside on both floors."

Mother's fork dropped loudly on her plate. "Oh, please, Charles. We know that. What is it *like*? How do they *live*?"

Father slowly chewed the bite of bread in his mouth, but he looked at Mother and his face lit up.

"All those rooms, and they don't use half of them," he said with feeling. "While I was there to get the body, Mrs. Shurts was cleaning the house, and made some interesting discoveries." Mrs. Shurts was a neighbor; her daughter Erma had just started first grade in September, so with both her children in school now she was available to help out when needed.

"Well, what did she find?" asked Mother impatiently.

"Like I said, at least half the rooms in the house weren't used. They were closed up, and when Mrs. Shurts came in and opened them to see what needed straightening, she found they were rather bare, with few furnishings and those nothing special. But the closets were filled with clothes. She said a lot of them looked like they had never been worn and were fine and well-made, but were old styles and the wool ones full of moth holes. There were shoes, too, that looked like they had never been worn."

Father took another bite of bread, and I could see Mother's mind working. "Rebecca McClung must have dressed well if she had so many clothes she didn't need," she said.

"Oh, no. Sallie Baysore said she only wore only ragged housedresses. When I viewed the body, she was wearing just a plain white shift she had slept in."

"Remarkable," said Mother. I found myself wondering what Mrs. McClung would have worn if she really had ridden a bicycle-built-for-two with me. In the drawing, she had just sketched the outline of a simple dress.

"And that wasn't all Mrs. Shurts found," continued Father. "One room was stocked with canned fruit and jellies and all manner of provisions. I can't imagine they could eat them all before old John passes away. In another, the closet held tall stacks of good fabric—muslin, linen, wool; ginghams and calicoes—that had never been made up into anything. Just sitting there for who knows how long. But in that same room there was a heap of rags in the corner that looked like maybe someone had slept on it at some time."

Father looked over at me and undoubtedly saw my deep interest in all he had described. "Isabel June," he said, using my full name to signal I'd better heed him or I'd be in deep trouble, "you do not speak of this with anyone else, do you hear me?"

"Oh, Charles," sighed Mother, before I could answer. "If Mrs. Shurts and Mrs. Baysore and Marshal Reed and three deputies and a doctor or two were all in that house, you know the whole town will know all about what you said and more, right down to John's collar size."

I put my hand over my mouth to keep from laughing, and never got to answer Father.

Father's description of what was in the house planted a picture in my head of Cinderella in her rags while her stepsisters got to wear lots of beautiful clothes. But Rebecca McClung didn't have any stepsisters. She could have worn all those clothes if she wanted to. Maybe she had at one time. But didn't she want new ones, made up of some of the fabric already in the house? All woman liked to wear nice things, didn't they?

I pictured her now as I lay in bed, thinking of her stretched out on the embalming table downstairs, dressed in her simple white shift. She would be cold and pale, maybe even bluish. Had they cleaned up the blood? I thought about the transformation Father would have to perform on her murdered body; he had assured the family the casket would be open for the viewing on Sunday morning. I knew he had a variety of cosmetics to help make her look alive, but how do you fix a face when almost all the bones are broken? What would she look like at the viewing? I would not be allowed downstairs to find out, and the casket would be closed after that.

Robert and Leavitte would not see her, either. That was a very good thing; they'd only gawk and brag about it later. But me?

The situation was entirely different. I cared about her and had reached out to her. I had barely been able to say hello, but I wanted to say goodbye. The idea might be foolhardy, but this was my only chance.

I sat up, quietly pulling away the covers. I eased out of bed slowly, tiptoed to the door to avoid waking Milly and noiselessly opened it. Gentle snores came from my parents' bedroom down the hall, so I knew that at last my father was asleep, resting for the busy day he would have tomorrow. Stopping at the head of the narrow back stairs, I strained to hear any sound from below, but only the ticking of the grandfather clock in the parlor and the distant rhythm of crickets played in the night. I eased down each step, keeping to the outside edge to avoid the creaky spots.

Gentle moonlight drifted through a window and shone off the freshly-waxed kitchen floor below. Startled by a sudden sound, I froze on the final step. But then I recognized the clicking of Cerbie's toenails on the wood as he crossed the room from his favorite sleeping spot near the stove to investigate. He stopped at the foot of the stairs, his head high and tail extended, on alert. When he saw it was only me, he relaxed and nuzzled his head against my leg as I stepped closer.

"Ssh!" I whispered near his ear as I sunk my fingers in his neck fur. "We have to be very quiet!" He seemed to understand, and followed me past the kitchen table and through the small family sitting room at the back of the house.

I stopped at the closed door on the far side of the room. It stood like a brick wall, seemingly of more substance than any other door in the house, although they were physically all the same. This door was always closed. Behind it was the forbidden room, the one we could never enter unless Father led us. The embalming room.

I had been in it only once, about a year earlier, when I had helped Father carry in a new piece of white-enameled metal furniture from the front porch where the delivery driver had left it. The strange piece had one central leg with a quartet of feet branching off the bottom like an X. The leg supported a shallow bowl in the center with two much larger wash basins connected to it on either side. After we had placed it near the large sink in Father's room, I had asked him what it was for.

"It helps me in preparing the bodies," Father had said. This vague information was not satisfying, but I knew not to press for more.

I gently wrapped my left hand around the doorknob, and hesitated, knowing that what I would do next would guarantee severe punishment if my parents found out. I looked at Cerbie, who raised an eyebrow at me.

"I'm only going to look," I defended myself in a whisper. "You'd better wait out here."

As I turned the knob it seemed to turn something in my stomach, too. I was deliberately disobeying Father's sternest rule, and I knew it.

I opened the door just enough to squeeze through, partly to keep Cerbie outside, but partly because it seemed a less flagrant violation than swinging it wide open. Slipping inside, I immediately eased it shut. I stood there for more than a moment, listening to Cerbie click slowly back to the kitchen.

The first thing I noticed was the smell. Metallic and pungent, it pinched in my nostrils. I had smelled it before on Father's clothing before he changed out of his working clothes, but never this strongly. I could see nothing in the blackness, for the only window in this room faced the backyard and was draped in thick navy fabric. I groped the wall beside me and found the switch.

The sudden light startled me, and I didn't move, feeling that it might startle the rest of the family, too. But that was silly; no one could see this light from upstairs. The room was twice the size of the sitting room I had just come from. The floor was a pale gray linoleum, different from the wood that lined the floors in the rest of the house. At the far side from the door was the large white enameled sink, and next to it the strange basins-on-a-stand that I had helped Father move. Cupboards lined the wall on either side of the sink. One of them had a glass front, and behind it stood bottles of various sizes and shapes. In front of the other cabinet and suspended on a metal frame was a large metal tank with a hose running from it that looped over a hook like an elephant curling its trunk. But it looked scarier than an elephant.

The brightest and most imposing shape in the room was the long table covered in a white sheet, its surface slightly inclined from the lower end positioned over the edge of the sink upward to extend into the room. The embalming table. I had seen it before, of course, the first time when Father explained it held the body while he worked, washing and embalming (I still wasn't sure what that was), and applying cosmetics to make the deceased look like a living person who had merely fallen asleep. It was his job to make a dead person look peaceful and pleasant, for the sake of those who grieved and out of respect for the deceased.

What a lot of work he would need to do for Mrs. McClung. They said her face was horribly smashed. Would there still be blood, or had the coroner or my father carefully washed it all away? I had seen broken bones before, and even the mutilated leg of a man who died of gangrene after a tree he was cutting jumped off the stump and pinned him to the ground. But a face with all but one of its bones broken? When I heard Father the night before telling Mother he would have a long day ahead of him, his voice lacked its usual confidence.

I tried to picture what was under the sheet. Mrs. McClung's toes lifted the fabric in two small peaks at the end by the sink. I wondered a few moments about the strange squarish bulge under the middle of the sheet before remembering Father passing through the kitchen the evening before carrying a small block of ice from the shed out back in his gloved hands, headed for the embalming room. I knew that dead bodies, just like food, stayed fresh longer when they were iced. Father didn't often do this when we had a body in the house; it was only when it had to sit overnight before the embalming. Mrs. McClung didn't seem to mind the wait.

I stepped closer to the sink, toward her feet, and then fingered the sheet at its edge. The sheet was wet in the middle from the melting ice, but the edge was still dry. I lifted it

85

cautiously, just enough to expose a foot—a wrinkled bare foot with crooked toes pointing toward the ceiling.

As I studied it, drops of water from the ice melting atop her belly hit the embalming table and I froze, startled. Each plop seemed to echo through that cool room like a pebble in a pool. I watched the drops run slowly into the gutter of the inclined table, each catching the ones ahead until a rivulet slid down past her foot, around the bottom corner, and through the hole at the end of the table, making a tiny waterfall into the sink.

With my left hand still holding the sheet, I ventured my right toward her foot. I knew it would be cold, but when my fingers touched her ankle it felt like a piece of slate in winter, and I pulled them back again.

The cold shock shifted something inside me. I had been thinking this stealthy trip would be a chance to finally meet Mrs. McClung in person, to touch her and say goodbye. But this cold body no longer held the person I wanted to know better. She couldn't see me; she couldn't return the squeeze of a hand. My contact with her would never be handshakes or hugs or passing cups of tea back and forth, or even talking face to face. We had a different kind of relationship—and, yes, it was a relationship, I told myself—and it had ended. Only thoughts and feelings would live on.

I dropped the sheet and left the room, turning off the light and easing the door shut behind me before returning to bed.

CHAPTER NINE

Hamilton Daily Republican News

Mason, April 13, 1901 – The old man passed a fairly good night on Friday, but at the mention of his wife's name he breaks down and cries piteously. In the past 24 hours he has aged very much, and looks as though he would not survive long. During the past twelve years Mr. McClung has not spoken to any of his brothers or sisters. The trouble originated over a lawsuit in settling their stepmother's estate. In his trouble, however, his people have come to him, and are trying to console him as best they can.

While I had been in the embalming room with Mrs. McClung, her accused murderer was sleeping in the house they had shared for twenty-two years. Because he was old and frail, he hadn't been put in jail but had been guarded at home by Marshal Reed's deputies.

On Saturday morning, the deputies threw open all the shutters on the house; ironically, it must have been brighter inside than it ever had been when Mrs. McClung lived there. Someone had draped black crepe on the front door, tied up with a black satin ribbon.

Father left shortly after breakfast to meet Mr. McClung at the cemetery, where he would choose the burial place for his wife. I was upstairs when he returned, and didn't see him before he shut himself up the embalming room for the rest of the morning. Meanwhile, Mother handled funeral arrangements with the Universalist Church and conducted other business, some by telephone and some in person. As it happened most days when there was a body in the house, I had charge of the younger

children. That primarily consisted of entertaining Marshall and
Everett, who seemed to be feeling better, while keeping baby
Frank out of trouble. At nine months, he could crawl all over,
usually toward his brothers' toys, and liked to pull himself up on
chair and table legs. He delighted in holding both my hands to
practice his walking—pulling to go faster on his chubby legs as I
kept him from falling. We were in the turret most of the morning,
for that's where the toys were, but by ten-thirty Frankie was ready
for a nap. I made Mildred, who was old enough to entertain
herself, temporarily responsible for the two other boys while I
took Frank down to the bedroom and laid him in his crib. I had
shut the door and was listening outside to be sure he was going to
sleep when I heard a man talking with Mother downstairs.

"He'll be coming to the viewing," the man was saying. "He
will be accompanied by my sister and I, as well as the marshal and
a deputy or two, I expect. Then we will go immediately from here
to the church."

Mother said something I couldn't quite hear. Then she said,
"Is the investigation progressing well?"

The man cleared his throat with something like a
"harrumph," and then spoke up loudly. "My brother is innocent.
That will be proved before long, I hope. He never trusted banks,
and perhaps that led to this tragedy. Many people assumed he
kept large amounts of money in the house, so this foul deed must
have started as a robbery. There have been a number of them
lately in this area, as you undoubtedly know."

After a moment of silence, Mother spoke in a soothing tone.
"I'm so sorry your family is experiencing this tragedy, Mr.
McClung."

"Thank you. I'll see that John remits payment to you
promptly."

The front door thudded shut as I started back upstairs to my
brothers and sister.

"What a strange day, Etta." My father paused fork and knife
over his pork chop a couple of hours later. He had sighed when

he sat down at the dinner table, glad to have a break from his work in the embalming room. "I don't think I've ever had to help an accused murderer pick out a cemetery plot for the murdered woman."

"I'm surprised they let him go to the cemetery," said Mother, spooning mashed potatoes onto Everett's plate.

"Well, Marshal Reed was with him, of course. He kept ahold of John's elbow most of the time; I think it was more to keep him from falling over than from running away. The poor man could only shuffle along, and his eyes were red and his face swollen from grief. But when I handed him my estimate, McClung just looked at it like it was a bill for a wagon wheel and said, 'Forty dollars for a casket? Can't I get a good one for thirty?'"

"I can't believe it, Charles. The man is one of the wealthiest in town, and he quibbles over the price of a casket for his own wife." Mother shakes her head.

"Reed couldn't believe it either," said Father. "He rolled his eyes at me. But it was a fair question. I've heard of undertakers who take advantage of the vulnerability of the grieving by overcharging. John should know I'm not one of them, but I don't think he ever bought anything without haggling over it. It's just the way he is. So I told John that was our basic model, nothing but padding and black silk lining added to it, economical but well-built and dignified."

"Well, his brother Frank said he'd be sure the bill was paid promptly," said Mother, firmly planting a fork in Marshall's hand after he picked up a bean with his fingers.

"I don't have any idea how many will come to this viewing," Father said after a few bites of his dinner. "Who does she have, anyway, besides her husband and her brother Pen? He's the only family that ever visited her, and she didn't even let him in the house!"

Mother set down her fork and sighed. "She may have, Charles, if John had allowed it. And she's got other family here. Even if they haven't seen her for years, they'll come. Believe me,

89

they won't give up a chance to take a look." She raised her eyebrows.

"Etta." Father scowled at her. "Your tone—"

"I'm sorry. But it's the truth. There are her other two brothers. The three men live together, you know, in Servetus's house, ever since his wife died."

"Yes. I guess Nicholas will be there, since he's a member of town council."

"Servetus will come, too. And Vete has a son, you know—he may come with his wife."

"I thought they had left Mason."

"They're just down the road in Pisgah, where they've got a farm."

"Children?"

"I don't think so; not yet. I hope they figure out how it's done."

"Etta!"

"Well, there haven't been any Dawson children since old Ezra passed; some of the McClungs are childless too, for that matter. But Albert Dawson seems a more normal sort than the rest of them. There may be hope yet for the family line."

"Etta."

Mother took a bite of potato. "Then there's Matilda Dawson."

"The maiden woman who lives alone here in town. She's a close relation?"

"Of course. She's Rebecca's aunt."

"Her *aunt*? But she can hardly be much older, living on her own as she is."

"I imagine not. But it was barely twenty years ago Rebecca's grandmother died. It would seem these Dawson women are long-lived. Except if they're *murdered*, of course. Long-lived, and poorly married, if at all, those Dawsons, both the men and the women. Two of Rebecca's brothers never married, Rebecca married a murderer, and Matilda's an old maid."

"Etta! That's enough." Father's eyes flitted to each of us children, our eyes sparkling and our ears attuned to this far-from-normal discourse at our dinner table. "You sound like a gossipy old woman. I won't have it."

Mother picked up her fork and knife and carefully cut a bite from her pork chop. "Charles," she said, her face composed, her baited fork poised in the air, "at least half the people in this town are going to pass through my house when they're dead, and you're going to see them all naked as the day they were born when they do, so—"

"Etta!" Father dropped his fork and it clattered to the floor.

"Well," said Mother primly, "I figure if they're going to bring all their privacy and secrets into my house when they're dead, I have a right to know some of them when they're alive."

Father picked up his fork and slammed it down on the table. "Children, you are excused."

Sidewalk

Spring 1900

Bert Reed, acting in his role of street commissioner rather than marshal, slapped the offensive paper in John McClung's hand and turned on his heel as John slammed the front door after him.

What right did those stuck-up councilmen have to take his property? Twenty-two years he'd lived in this house he built, on land he bought and owned. Now they wanted to take a whole piece of it, just take it, without his permission and without paying a cent.

It all started last August. That's when Council announced they were putting in cement sidewalks along all the main town streets, starting with Main Street. He'd have to take down part of the fence and move it back, they said. What do they think he's got the fence up here for? To keep people off his property, that's what. People like those kids a few years back. They were playing stickball right out front in the street, and one of clumsy kids went after a ball and crashed into his fence, knocking out one of the pickets. He heard the racket, and by the time he got to the door they were taking off down the street. But he'd seen them all; he knew who they were. The next time he saw them out playing ball again he sent for the marshal and had them all arrested. It was illegal to play ball in the streets; he had seen to that some years ago, getting Council to pass a law against it. They passed the law, but what good did it do if they never enforced it? John would make sure it was enforced this time! Preventing damage like that done to his fence proved exactly why they needed the law.

The marshal did his job, John would give him that. Made them pay the two-dollar fine. He should have made each boy pay the fine; but he let the lot of them get off on two dollars total.

93

You'd think that would've been the end of it. But not with boys like that.

Next thing John knew they had snuck into his barn at night and taken his cow. Walked her right out of there in the dark and hid her who knows where. When John discovered her gone, he knew who was responsible. He laid watch for them coming out of school and grabbed the ringleader. Shook him by the shoulders, and demanded the cow's return or they'd be forever sorry.

But what did that uppity rascal do? He weaseled out of John's grip, faced him and said John McClung wouldn't see that cow again until he paid two dollars to get her back. Then he ran off, saying he'd return with the cow, but the boys would take her right back to where she'd been hid if they didn't get their two dollars.

Well, he'd be damned if he was going to take the time to march over and report the whole thing to the marshal, who would probably just laugh in his face anyway, so he saw he had no choice. When the boys returned leading the cow, John threw two silver dollars at them and they took off leaving him to put the cow back in the barn.

So when Council wanted to put in the sidewalk on his property, John took the matter directly to court, and his lawyer was successful in getting an injunction against the councilmen and the town preventing them from trespassing on his property.

That worked for a while. People walked on the sidewalk up to the corner of Section Road, then after they crossed the street they'd walk around his fence until the sidewalk started up again in front of Rebold's store next door.

The arrangement didn't seem to cause people too much trouble, but Council wouldn't leave well enough alone. They officially condemned the strip of John's land they wanted for the sidewalk so people would be able to walk right across his property like it wasn't even his to start with.

He knew what he would do: he'd sue them all—both the town and the councilmen. And then he'd move—back out to the countryside where taxes were less and people could lay sidewalks where and when and whether they pleased, council and courts be damned.

CHAPTER TEN

Rebecca McClung had more people come visit her after she was dead than all those added together who saw her while she was alive. They came from miles around, many strangers to me, and certainly they could not all have known Mrs. McClung or actually be grieving her death. Mother called them "oglers," and figured they were all hoping to see the murdered woman lying in her casket. If so, they were sorely disappointed, because Father had firmly sealed the lid after the viewing at our house, and it was not opened again.

It had only been two months since the last big funeral in Mason, even larger than this one. Mr. Peter Wikoff was known throughout the countryside, married to a descendant of our town's founder, and he owned hundreds of acres of property in the area. Father had handled that funeral as well, and the service was also at the Universalist church where Mr. Wikoff had been a trustee. The building had been much too small to hold all the people who came to show their respects. Only close kin and the older folks could sit inside in the pews; the rest of us stood in the churchyard and the street, listening to the hymns and catching glimpses through the windows. When the service was over and the pall bearers had loaded the casket on the hearse, it was like Father was leading a somber parade. Dressed in his finest suit and top hat, he sat high up on the wagon seat with his back firm and straight, guiding our princely horses Ajax and Apollo along Church Street, turning right on Section Line Road, and continuing straight to Rose Hill Cemetery. The mourners—including almost everyone in Mason plus family and friends from as far away as Indiana and Tennessee—walked behind three and four abreast, mothers keeping a tight rein on their children.

There weren't many children at Rebecca McClung's funeral, however, although the pews were filled with adults. I had walked to the church alone, as my father had left early with the hearse to set up the casket in the church, and Mother was staying at home to tend to my sister and little brothers. She was good like that, making sure she didn't expect me to take over as mother more than necessary. It was a short walk, along Main Street past my school, then up a block and over one. In front of the wood-frame church with the little bell tower on top stood my father, smoothing the black mesh shawl on Ajax's back so the long fringe hung evenly on either side of the horse. He would stay outside with the hearse and horses, ready to assist the pallbearers with the casket after the service.

After entering the church, I looked around for room to sit. When I saw Mr. Dill on the end of a pew near the middle of the church, I slid in next to him. He smiled at me and squeezed my hand. Then I sat up very straight, stretching to get a good look at the casket in the front of the church. It was very plain. I knew all of the caskets Father carried, lined up in the showroom beside the parlor in our house. Each time someone died, Father would take the grieving family member there and gently explain the features of each sample. Mr. McClung hadn't been able to choose the casket in person, but he apparently had agreed to the price of the cheapest we carried.

It was good I had arrived early, for carriages continued to clatter into the street loaded with people who hoped to attend the event. A couple of the church deacons served as ushers, assisted by one of the sheriff's deputies, sorting out those closest to the family who would be given a seat and those who would be asked to listen from outside the windows and doors.

As the pianist played slow, soft music, I scanned the backs of the close kin in the front row, whispering with Mr. Dill about those I wasn't sure I knew. On one side sat Rebecca McClung's family: her brothers Nicholas, Pen, and Servetus, with Vete's son Albert next to him; and then Rebecca's aunt Matilda next to Albert on the outside end of the pew, the only woman remaining

98

in the Dawson family since Vete's wife had passed on years earlier and Rebecca was now gone.

In the front pew on the other side of the church sat the McClung family: John's brother Frank and his wife Ruth on the outside end, then John's sister Elizabeth and her husband Robert McClung (she had married some kind of cousin, I think), who now lived in Dayton. Most of John's siblings, Mr. Dill told me, were long dead. There was a large space between Robert and the inside end of the pew, as though to create as much space as possible between the McClung and Dawson families.

Soon, however, I learned that was not the reason for the open space. Just as the piano finished the final chords of "Nearer, My God, to Thee," three people entered the door behind us, setting off whispers in the pews, and all heads turned.

Sarah McClung Jordan, John's younger and trim widowed sister, supported her brother on her arm and the two walked slowly down the aisle, followed at a respectful distance by Marshal Bert Reed. Mr. McClung wore a rumpled black suit in a style long past, along with dress shoes someone must have polished for him, for their shine contrasted sharply with the old suit. His back was bent, and his head remained bowed as he shuffled along, clutching his hat in one hand. His sister looked over the pews, seemingly amazed at all the people gathered, but her mouth remained in a firm straight line.

The three sat in the front pew, with Sarah Jordan next to her brother-in-law Robert, Marshal Reed on the end, and John McClung between them. Mr. McClung sat quietly throughout the service, barely moving, looking straight ahead or down at his lap. I believe he drew more attention than his dead wife.

The officiating minister, Frank Blackford, stepped to the podium and led a prayer. I learned later that he was not really a Reverend, although his father was a Universalist clergyman; this Mr. Blackford was known by farmers throughout the state as the silver-tongued speaker at Ohio Grange meetings, where farmers would learn how to address problems like grasshopper swarms, droughts, and unfair pricing.

99

The choice of minister was fitting, in a way. John McClung was certainly one of Ohio's most successful farmers, owning almost a thousand acres of land and accumulating a net worth few others could match. Mr. Blackford would have respected his hard work and expertise. But I'm certain he had never met Rebecca McClung. Although women were included in the Ohio Grange, the reclusive Mrs. McClung would never participate in meetings. But Mr. Blackford eulogized her just the same—or his perception of her, at any rate.

"A man rarely achieves his success alone," intoned Mr. Blackford. "His wife, his God-appointed helpmate, supports him in a multitude of ways. For over thirty years Rebecca McClung was such a helpmate, the quiet partner in his success, enjoying the fruits of his labors in the fields while in turn meeting his needs at home. How blessed Mr. McClung has been to know his wife's tenderness and provision far into his elder years. Certainly he will miss her the rest of the days of his life."

In the pews around me, some of the women dabbed at their eyes with a handkerchief, but more than one mourner had a look that said they were believing none of the rosy picture of marital bliss Mr. Blackford was painting. How happy and loving can a woman be when she is confined behind locked doors and shuttered windows?

"Rebecca McClung's life on this earth has ended in a tragic way, but how comforting it is to know that she has now passed to her great heavenly home where there is no violence and no tears. And one day John will be reunited with her there, to live in eternity together."

Mr. McClung looked up then for the first time, but of course I couldn't see his face since he was in the front pew, so I don't know if the words comforted him or frightened him.

I couldn't help but wonder if Rebecca would really want to live in eternity with John. Wouldn't she be glad to be free of him in that beautiful place? I knew I was too young to really understand the feelings between a husband and a wife, but I had to think Rebecca would be glad to get out of that gloomy house, even if he hadn't murdered her, and surely she would enjoy heaven more if he wasn't there to boss her around. No doubt some others sitting there also hoped Rebecca might enjoy many peaceful days in heaven before John arrived to spoil them; others, I'm sure, expected that if God was indeed just, John McClung would never even see those pearly gates.

After Mr. Blackford's eulogy, there were two more hymns and a benediction. The six pallbearers came forward, including Rebecca's three brothers, John's brother and brother-in-law, and another McClung relative whose name I didn't know. Everyone stood as the men lifted the casket and carried it out the front door to Father's hearse that was waiting outside. Then the silence broke into murmurings that swelled in volume as the people made their way out of the church.

While the procession of clergy, pallbearers, and family formed for the short trip to the cemetery, most of the other people stood about and talked—and most of the talk was of the murder and the Mayor's hearing that would take place the next morning.

"I wouldn't miss it," said the father of one of my classmates. "I hear there will be some stunning revelations."

"Do tell!" said a woman near him. "What do you think they have found?"

"Maybe they've tracked down that man in woman's clothing someone saw fleeing down Main Street right after the murder."

The woman laughed. "Oh, Levi, didn't you hear? That was only Mrs. Brady, running with medicine for her sick mother. She talked with the Marshal yesterday."

"She *is* a right sturdy woman," said one listener, while others tried to hide a laugh.

"Well, perhaps they have found the murder weapon, wherever old McClung hid it."

"So you believe he is guilty?" said the woman.

"Well, if it wasn't him, then who was it?"

"It had to be robbers," said another man. "Probably the same rascals involved in those thefts outside town a few months back.

With all that money McClung had locked up in his house, it was bound to happen."

"But nothing was missing from the house," said the man named Levi. "The Marshal said so himself."

"They were scared off before they could get anything. They could have heard Mrs. Baysore, or Albert Dill coming, or even McClung himself. Robbers, I say."

As I said before, Mason fifty years ago might have been a small town, but it was far from a sleepy, idyllic little village; bad things happened in and around Mason, just like anywhere else. There were the usual arguments and fights you find anywhere. Around the time Hans got tied to the McClungs' front door, Albert Dill's sister-in-law got angry with some relation of John McClung's. He was walking along the road when he encountered Maggie Dill, who was helping her husband near their house, and he called out to her. He thought she was someone else, and called her by that name. Unfortunately, it was the name of a woman that Maggie despised, and she thought he was insulting her. She yelled at him; he yelled back, and then continued down the road. The more she thought about it, the angrier she got, and told everyone Joseph McClung had deliberately provoked her, and said she would bring charges against him. Finally, Joseph McClung got his lawyer and the marshal to accompany him to the Dill house to try to make peace over the matter. Maggie was waiting at the gate—with a revolver in her hand. The marshal took it away from her. Joseph McClung filed papers to have her committed for lunacy, and she was taken before a judge; but examination found her to be perfectly sane, and there was no more trouble from the incident.

Some problems did not end so well. Father was undertaker to several people who killed themselves out of true mental illness, or losing a job, or general despair. And of course, diseases of all kinds claimed the lives of people from infancy to old age, and there were countless accidents involving farm equipment, horses, trains, and weapons.

There was murder in Mason, too, and Rebecca's was not the first murder of a McClung. Back in 1887, Whitmore McClung, the 30-year-old son of John McClung's cousin, was shot in a Mason saloon trying to protect his father who had become part of a drunken fight over the death of a vicious dog. After some beer glasses flew through the air, one of the men whipped out a revolver. Whitmore jumped in front of his father to protect him and took the bullet that killed him.

And then there were robberies. Early in the town's history, there were so many horse thieves in the area that the Horse Rangers were formed in Mason and in nearby Lebanon to track them down. Later robberies were more alarming, some including assault and even murder. In the year before Rebecca McClung was murdered, there was a string of vicious, unsolved robberies in the area just north of Mason.

Just four months before Rebecca's murder, exactly one week before Christmas 1900, Michael Fryman, a reclusive bachelor, was asleep in bed just after midnight when four masked men burst through the door. Before he could register what was happening, they had seized him and wrestled him to the floor. Two held him down while the other two first stuffed a cloth in his mouth, tying it behind, and then tied together his hands and feet. They left him lying there, tossing about, as they stormed through the house, looking for money. Then they returned to Fryman, and pulled out the gag in his mouth.

"Where is it?" they yelled in his face. "We know your father just sent you three thousand dollars. Now where is the money?"

"I—I—don't have any money here," Fryman managed to get out.

One of the men punched him in the stomach. "You lie! Tell us where it is!"

"I don't have any money!"

One of the men swung at Fryman with a wooden club, hitting him on the head. Fryman's body went limp.

When he regained consciousness, the man with the club demanded again to know where the money was.

"I—don't—have money here," he sobbed. One of the robbers burned him with a hot poker taken from the fireplace. And then the club came down again, and Fryman was knocked senseless.

He barely escaped freezing to death when a passerby found him in the morning, unconscious outside his open front door.

Three days later, John Thompson and his wife were eating supper at their house two miles west of Lebanon, just north of Mason. Mr. Thompson had owned a grocery store in that town for fifty years, and the family was well known and respected by all. Their adult children were all married with homes of their own, and their son who had been visiting had left a few days earlier for Colorado. So now the couple was eating alone when four masked men burst through the front door. One of them shoved a revolver in Mr. Thompson's face while another tied up his arms and legs. As the other two men began to manhandle Mrs. Thompson the same way, she drew her hands apart in defense and one of the men slapped her hard across the face and hissed, "We've got you, lady, and if you don't keep still, we'll kill you."

The robbers demanded to know where the valuables were kept, and one of them tossed an iron shovel into the fire and said he'd burn the two of them with it if they didn't tell them what they wanted to know. But even before the Thompsons could answer, the ransacking began, with the couple on the floor bound hand and foot. Drawers and cabinets were yanked open, books and papers tossed on the floor, clothing scattered. "Ain't got as much money as when I used to be around here," Mr. Thompson overheard one of the robbers say. By the time they were done, they had pocketed over a hundred dollars in cash; they also took silverware and Mr. Thompson's gold watch, given him by his mother when he was young. But they weren't through with the Thompsons.

While two of the men kept guard outside, the other two stuffed handkerchiefs into the victims' mouths, tying them tightly in place with rope. They dragged them into a bedroom, flung them across the bed and then tied them to the bed posts in such a way they could not see each other. Just to be sure the Thompsons couldn't communicate in any way, they threw coats over their heads. The robbers then threatened they would return to kill the couple if they tried to get loose. "Good night," they said, turning off the lights and closing the door.

For four hours John Thompson picked at the ropes binding his hands with his fingers, finally working them loose enough to reach the knife he kept in his pocket. Together they were able to get the knife open. When Mr. Thompson had finally released both himself and his wife, their tongues were swollen and their mouths bleeding, and they could barely speak. They stumbled to a neighbor's house where they were cared for until morning.

The financial loss to the Thompsons was relatively small, but the brutal treatment they suffered outraged everyone in the area. A thousand-dollar reward was posted for the capture of the four men, and the Lebanon Horse Rangers said they would never give up until each of the men was either dangling from a tree or safe in the penitentiary.

A few days later, George Carey—not only the county coroner, but also a judge—issued warrants for four suspects; three of them were arrested on Christmas day, and the fourth soon after. But before most area residents learned of the arrests to breathe a sigh of relief, the suspects were dismissed; conclusive evidence was presented that all of them were on a train near their homes in Middletown at the time of the robbery.

Rumors popped up about other potential suspects, but there were no further arrests for the Thompson robbery; nor was anyone ever charged with the attempted robbery three days earlier of Michael Fryman.

The assault of Michael Fryman had shocked those who heard of it, but the reclusive bachelor was little known in the area and the story claimed only a couple of paragraphs in the local newspapers. The Thompson robbery, however, drew much interest and news coverage. While Fryman's house was almost fifteen miles northwest of downtown Mason, the Thompson house outside of Lebanon was only a couple of miles from one of the McClung farms. The proximity and the brutality of the robbery was enough for even the stubborn and usually unswayable John McClung to change his mind about moving to the countryside—and decide to stay in the relative safety of the village of Mason.

But he would still build a new house, and John McClung chose George Tetrick to build it. On the evening of April 11, 1901, Mr. Tetrick was discussing plans for the new design with both John and Rebecca at their house on Main Street. Just hours after he left, Rebecca McClung was found murdered in her bed, and George Tetrick's son Paul, about to board a train to Cincinnati as he did most days to attend medical school, was invited to observe her autopsy.

The Accused

April 15, 1901

We're going to the Opera House, they tell me. Too many gawkers showed up at the mayor's office, so they've got to move the show someplace else. They're walking me slow, Gallaher the sheriff and Williamson, who used to be Mayor; he's been staying at the house with me, acting as Deputy Marshal. Think I can't walk myself. Runyan, the lawyer Frank got me, is here too, cooing some words to me that I expect are to keep me quiet and moving. He needn't bother. I ain't weak, and I ain't stupid. Just a mite slower these days. My sister Sarah's close behind. She's a sturdy woman, one of only two of my sisters not already in the grave. I guess she's done well for herself, even after being a widow. I barely recognized her when she came to the house Friday. Hadn't talked, hardly, for twenty years, but now she's here, wearing a well-made dress, too.

Ain't never been upstairs in Sprinkle's building, in the Opera House. But I remember that day they brung the vault for the new bank. A whole team of horses it took, it was so heavy, and the gawkers were there then, too, watching as a team of men equal to the number of horses lugged that vault into the bank. Make it heavy enough, they figgered, and your money's got to be safe in there. I didn't buy that line of reasoning for a minute and still don't. You give your money to someone else and no matter how fancy the box they got to put it in, you might never see it again.

There's a crowd of people here around the bank and shop below the Opera House. Another deputy—can't remember his name—is telling 'em there's no more room inside, and they've got to make way. Make way for me, I see. He shoos them away from the entrance that's beside the bank, and they stare at me as Williamson grips tighter on my arm and pulls me through. Somebody I don't know opens the double doors, both of 'em, and we start up the stairs. Williamson sticks with me, holding my arm, and Sheriff and

Runyan follow. Then Sarah. Steps, so many steps. Sturdy, though, and no squeaks; Tetrick built this whole building, and he builds solid.

These steps never end. Lift one foot, lift the other, over and over. We make it to the top, and I can hardly breathe. So much parading around and the day's not half done. It's big and open up here, but filled to the gills with people. The only seats that's empty are up front, on one side of a wooden table, except for a big soft armchair just left of the table. Runyan points to it, and Williamson drops me in it. I ain't sure I ever sat in anything so comfortable. But I never cared about visiting this place, and sure wish I weren't here now. This is where they give them shows; squawking music out of horns, play-acting and such. Folks laying down good money to dance around like fools. Well, now they've got another show: see the old man whose wife got butchered.

It's hard for me to look them over, being up front and them behind. But I can turn my head a bit and see some of them on the side away from me. That woman, near the front—it's my other sister Elizabeth. She might have been at the funeral; not sure. Haven't seen her since she got married, must be more than ten years ago. Forty-nine, she was—got married when no one thought she would, to our cousin Robert McClung. That's him, sitting beside her. Elizabeth nods her head to me. She's fine looking, even if she's got gray in her hair. Marriage suits her, I suppose. It took all this commotion to get her out to see me. Course, I never did bother to see her, neither. She's got her life, I got mine. Relations are mostly just trouble, when it comes down to it. I look away.

Over there I see Carey, the coroner who spent all the time looking at Becca after—after everything turned crazy. He asked me a lot of questions, too, and wrote down what I said. Kept asking me if I knew anything about what happened, and how I was feeling. Asked me if I had an axe and hatchet, too—but told me it was a wooden club that did her in. Right now Carey's talking with Mayor Lowe, and Judge Runyan, my lawyer, is over there with them.

Runyan's the best there is; that's why I agreed to him. He's here in a plain brown suit, but it's a good one, cut and fit just as fine as the matching mustache and beard on his face. His old law partner is here, too—I forget his name; D-something, I think—but he's now the prosecutor, Runyan tells me.

108

I guess it's me he's prosecutin'. Back years ago, when he was with Runyan, he'd have been on my side; now he's the one accusin' me. Think of that.

I probably know most of the people here, but for the life of me can't remember most of their names. Some I ain't sure if I seen before or not. That man a few rows back, for one. He looks familiar—oh, I remember. The farm hand I had awhile back, the one who bought up the apples from one of my trees the year that was bad for apple trees in general, but mine did right well. He had a good eye for trees—paid me two dollars and ended up with a good twelve dollars' worth. Should have charged him more. I saw him not so long ago, last year maybe, and tried to sell him a bushel of walnuts. Said he didn't want 'em. He should buy them anyway, I told him, after getting a bargain on them apples. But the rascal wouldn't lay out the money. What's he doing here now?

Most of the town is here, seems like. I can hear them whispering to each other, behind my back. I sink deep in the chair and close my eyes. They can look at me all they want, but thank God I don't have to look at them.

Mayor Lowe stands up and asks for order; says court is in session. I open my eyes when Runyan comes over and sits in a straight chair at the end of the table next to me. He leans in. "Just relax, John. You won't have to say anything. We're here just so everyone can hear the truth about what happened Friday."

So I try to relax. Close my eyes if I feel like it. But I'll listen to every word. God knows I want to know the truth about what happened Friday, too.

Everyone gets quiet while Mayor Lowe goes on a few minutes, saying what day it is and where we are, like we don't know. He asks the two parties to say who they are. The prosecutor says he's here for the state of Ohio— Dechant, his name is, and he's got a fellow named Thompson with him too. Then Runyan says he's here for the defense, and Lowe asks if the defendant has been informed of the charge against him, and Runyan says yes, Your Honor.

And now Lowe reads it in front of everyone. I don't follow all the fancy wording, but some of it comes through: "Twelfth of April 1901 . . . one John McClung upon one Rebecca McClung did maliciously assault and with some blunt instrument strike her . . . deliberate malice with intent to kill . . . and did kill her the said Rebecca McClung."

Malicious. Intent to kill. Did kill. They're saying I'm a murderer. They think I killed Becca! I shake all over; cover my face. It cannot be true. The whole room is quiet; they already knew. I told Carey I couldn't have done it. Does everyone think I killed my wife? Dear God.

Mayor Lowe asks how the defendant pleads.

I ain't pleading with anyone. I tell the truth, I do what needs done, I live an honest life. Never begged from no one; I make my own way. But I watch while Mr. Runyan stands up and says bright and clear, "The defendant pleads not guilty, Your Honor." *Lowe says something, and Runyan sits.*

Mayor Lowe says the prosecution may call the first witness, and Thompson gets up with some papers in his hand and calls for Sallie Baysore. She puts a hand on the Bible and the other in the air and swears she'll tell the truth. Lowe tells her she can sit down, and she takes the empty chair off to the left of the mayor, facing Runyan and the gawkers.

"Mrs. Baysore," *says Thompson,* "Please state your full name and your age."

She smooths her dress and clasps her hands. "Sarah Burch Baysore," *she says, sounding a bit shaky.* "I'm forty-seven."

"You live in the same house as the deceased and Mr. McClung?"

"Yes, sir."

"How long have you lived there?"

"Six weeks. Mr. Dill and I bought the house from the McClungs and they now rent their rooms." *Not for much longer, though. Tetrick's starting in right soon on the new house, and we'll be moving before you know it.*

"Was anyone else living in the house with you besides Mr. and Mrs. McClung?"

"No. I've been a widow since my husband died in '97, and I live alone."

"Where are your rooms in relation to those the McClungs rent from you?"

"I use two front rooms on the first floor; the McClungs use the kitchen and sitting room in the back of the house and all the

110

rooms above it. There's a back door into their kitchen, and steps that go up to their rooms."

"What were the habits of Mr. and Mrs. McClung with their neighbors?"

"I can't say as to that."

"Were they of a cheerful disposition, and what were their habits at home?"

"I do not know, I never saw in their house; they did not keep either shutters or doors open and I always attend to my own business."

She'd better. Sallie sounds indignant. I would be, too. What right do these lawyers have asking about other people's personal business?

"Mrs. Baysore, please tell us when you got up on the morning of the twelfth of April, and what you heard."

"Well, I woke up at four-thirty, and ten minutes later I heard the first scream."

"And did you hear another?"

"I heard the first scream and then the second, and I thought to myself, Sallie, there is something serious the matter, and you had better hurry and dress; and I rushed out fastening my wrapper, with only my slippers on."

"Describe the screams, please. Was it as if someone was in great pain and anguish?"

"Yes, sir, it sounded like someone getting killed."

And then Sallie wails to demonstrate. "Oooohh, oooohh." Ghastly, and my heart jumps.

"Did you hear the McClungs previous to this time?"

"I heard someone stir up the fire."

"Are you sure about the fire being stirred, and did you hear Mr. McClung before that time?"

"All I know is that he stepped into the room and stirred up the fire when my alarm was going off at four-thirty o'clock. I am a truthful woman."

"Do you remember whether you heard Mr. McClung coming downstairs that morning?"

"I heard someone at two different times."

"The second time, was that when you heard the screams, or after?"

"After. I had already run around the house twice and back again when I heard someone come down."

"Where were you when they came down?"

"In the house."

"In what manner did Mr. McClung come down the stairs, with great speed?" *How does he know it was me?*

"In no special hurry."

"Will you swear that it was Mr. McClung who came downstairs?

"The steps were similar."

"Mrs. Baysore, when you heard those screams did you hurry to see what was the matter?"

"I immediately pulled on my wrapper and called to Mr. Morrison, who was passing on the street, and said something serious is going on in the other part of the house. He said that's too bad, and kept going. Then I saw Mr. John Gramlich coming up the street, and I said for pity sake, hurry, there is something in the McClungs' side of the house; someone is being killed. Then I rushed ahead, like a woman will, and not knowing just where the stairway was from the kitchen, I called, 'Mrs. McClung, are you sick?'"

"Did you get an answer?"

"No, only that sound like the death rattle."

Death rattle. My Becca's last sound. Why was I not there to ease her passing? I drop my head. Will Sallie never stop talking?

"What did you do then, Mrs. Baysore?"

"I thought to myself, Sallie, you had better get out of here and tend to your own business."

That's the matter with people these days. They don't tend to their own business. All the trouble we could avoid if people would only tend to their own business.

"After those steps came downstairs, did you not look to see who came out of the house?"

"No, sir. I could have seen someone coming out if I had been outside, but I wouldn't be able to see from inside in the house."

"Can you tell how long after you went in the house was it before you heard those steps come down?

"No, sir."

"Five or ten minutes or more?"

"I could not tell."

"Do you always get up so early?"

So early? I'm up every morning at four o'clock, earlier than Sallie. I'm a good farmer. Folks here in town, they like to take their ease, getting up at half past five and even later.

"I get up every morning at four-thirty o'clock. I'm not a lazy woman and attend to my own business; planning my work when I'll not be disturbed."

Thompson pauses, walks about the room a bit. I'm not looking at him, but I hear the steps.

"Mrs. Baysore," *he finally says, the steps stopping,* "did you ever know of the McClungs to have any trouble in their home, such as quarreling, harsh words or the like?"

"I never heard them have any trouble. I heard him speak a little loud at times, just like any man speaks to his wife once in a while, but no quarreling."

"You told the coroner that you had heard them wrangling, did you not?"

"Oh, yes, I heard loud talking, but that was none of my business; they did not bother me."

"Did that occur often?"

"I got used to it and went to sleep; I did not pay any attention to it."

All these gawkers here, everyone in town and beyond, and these lawyers see fit to ask about what goes on in my house. A man's business is his business.

Footsteps and chairs scraping, and I open my eyes. Thompson's sitting back down now, at the other end of the table, and Runyan gets up from next to me. It's his turn with Sallie.

"Mrs. Baysore, you have resided in Mason practically all of your life, have you not?"

"Yes, sir."

"And you purchased the McClung property with Albert Dill and moved in to your rooms there about six weeks ago?"

"Yes, sir."

"You occupied the two rooms, Mrs. Baysore, on the west side of the house, and Mr. McClung retained the rest of the house, did he not?"

"Yes, sir."

"Were there any doors between your rooms and their part of the house?"

"Yes, sir, there are three doors, one between my bedroom and their sitting room and two in my front room; one opening into their sitting room and the other opening into the hallway."

"Could anyone have gotten through those doors into the McClung side of the house?"

"Well, I should say not. I had my wardrobe against the door between my bedroom and their sitting room and I had my dresser in front of the other two doors."

"Well, would that prevent anyone from passing through your part of the house?"

"Certainly it would, as I had them tied with ropes."

Ropes! Does Sallie Baysore think I'm going to come stalking her in the night? Why would I want to see her or her rooms?

"Had you ever been in the bedroom occupied by Mrs. McClung?"

"No, sir."

"In order to get to their part of the house, you were compelled to go out your front door on the north side of the house, along the west side to the southwest corner, then along the south side of the house till you reached the kitchen door, through the kitchen and sitting room before you reached the stairs?"

"Yes, sir."

"Which room did you occupy as a bedroom?"

"The back room."

114

"You heard no conversation or talking after you retired the evening before?"

"I heard Mr. Tetrick talking now and then as his voice was loud. He seemed to be explaining something about the new house to the McClungs."

"Did you note any bad feelings that evening?"

"No, sir."

"Mrs. Baysore, is it not a fact that they were in a most excellent humor?"

"They appeared so, and I heard Mr. Tetrick laugh."

"Did you hear Mr. McClung laugh?"

"No, sir, I never heard him laugh in my life."

I reckon not. There's some whispering in the room, and Lowe bangs his gavel so Runyan can continue.

"Did you hear anything during the night?"

"No, sir. That is the first night since I have been in the house that I slept all night."

"You are sure the alarm went off at precisely four-thirty o'clock?"

"That is what I said and I speak the truth."

"You heard no commotion about the house until the alarm went off?"

"No, just as the alarm went off someone came into the next room."

"The next room was the dining room, was it not, and the room next to that was the kitchen?"

"Yes, sir."

"Was there any carpet on the hall that morning?"

"Yes, sir."

"Was there carpet on the steps?"

"There was none on the steps."

"Did you get up immediately after your alarm went off that morning?"

"I suppose it was in about four or five minutes and I immediately went to the window and opened the shutters."

"What did you do then?"

115

"I first went into the front room and stirred my fire. Then I blew out the light on the mantel that I leave on all night, and I was just bathing myself when I heard the first scream."

"Mrs. Baysore, had you heard any noise previous to this on the McClung side of the house?"

"I heard him stir the fire."

"Well now, could you tell whether it was someone stirring or building a fire?"

"It sounded like stirring; someone came into the room and stirred the fire."

"Had you heard anyone come down the stairs?"

"Yes, sir."

"Who did you take this person to be?"

"I supposed it was Mr. McClung. Someone coughed, and I took it to be him."

"Well, then it was after this that you heard the cries of distress?"

"Yes, sir."

"How many of these cries did you hear?"

"Just four cries, and they were terrible."

"How frequently did these screams occur?"

"Just as often as they could come."

"Was the screaming before the fire was stirred?"

"After."

"Well, could you hear anyone going up and down stairs before the fire was stirred?"

"I heard someone go upstairs after the fire was stirred."

"I believe you told the coroner you did not hear any blow?"

"No, sir."

"So you just heard a sound indicating someone to be in distress?"

"Yes, sir, just like a woman in distress."

"When did you hear the first scream?"

"Between four-thirty o'clock and twenty minutes of five o'clock."

"Immediately after hearing the screams you went out of your front door and you called to Mr. Morrison, but he did not stop?"

"No, sir."

"And you then called to someone else?"

"No, sir. First I ran around the house, and on my way back I saw Mr. Gramlich. I told him something was wrong with Mrs. McClung."

"Was the door to the McClungs' open?"

"No, it was closed."

"Did you and Mr. Gramlich go in to the McClungs' then?"

"Yes, we went in there. I went on ahead like a woman will—she's always getting herself in trouble, you know. I went into the kitchen and on to the hall."

"Was the door open between the kitchen and the hall?"

"It was closed."

"Did you go in?"

"No, it was dark in there."

"Then you called to Mrs. McClung?"

"Yes, but I got no answer. I could only hear a sound as though someone was moaning."

"Mrs. Baysore, did you notice if there was a fire in the grate?"

"Yes, sir. There was a good fire in the grate and a pair of shoes was in front of it."

"Were they shoes belonging to a man or to a woman?"

"I do not know."

"Could you not tell whether they were a man's shoe or not?"

"I cannot."

"Where was Mr. Gramlich?"

"He was in the kitchen, standing in the door, when I went back there. I wanted him to go up and check."

"And did Mr. Gramlich go upstairs?"

"No. He said he wasn't going to go up to old John McClung's room at that time of the morning unless Mr. McClung asked him to. So he left."

At least Gramlich had some sense. If Sallie Baysore keeps bringing folk into my house, she'll answer for it.

117

"What did you do then?"

"I went in my own room and commenced to put my shoes on. I had been running around all this time in thin slippers and I knew that would not do."

"But before you put your shoes on you heard someone come downstairs?"

"Yes, sir."

"Could you tell how long after you called to Mrs. McClung was it before you heard someone come downstairs?"

"I cannot say just how long it was—it could not have been very long."

"Was Mr. Dill there yet?"

"Not yet; he came after I had my shoes on."

"And did you tell Mr. Dill what you had heard that morning?"

"I told him that I had heard screams and about hearing someone going up and down stairs but he only laughed at me and told me I imagined all that and was frightened about nothing at all."

"He then took up the ashes from your fireplace and emptied them, and in order to do this he had to go out the front door?"

"Yes, sir, he took the ashes out and he certainly went out the front door as there was no other way for him to get out."

"Did Mr. Dill tell you that he saw Mr. McClung when he was out?"

"I do not know. He may have."

"Did you see Mr. McClung that morning?"

"No, sir."

"How long after Mr. Dill emptied the ashes was it before Mr. McClung came to your door?"

"It was shortly after; I do not know the exact time."

"When Mr. McClung knocked at your door from outside, did you open it?"

"Well, I reckon I did. He asked if Albert was in. I did not answer his question at all, but simply asked him what was the matter with Mrs. McClung, and he clasped his hands and said, 'My God, she is dead!'"

Dead. The word falls like an axe on wood, just as it did that morning when I pushed it out of my mouth. Tears well in my eyes, and everything gets blurry. I drop my head, close my eyes. My God, my Becca's dead.

"Then what happened?"

"Mr. McClung asked Albert to run for Dr. Van Dyke."

And what did you and Albert do?"

"Well, he ran. I went back in the house."

"What then? Did you go upstairs?"

"Well, I guess I did! I went up two steps at a time."

"Where was Mr. McClung at this time, and did he go upstairs two at a time?"

A few chuckles at that, picturing an old man like me taking the steps that way.

"He was right after me."

Runyan strokes his short beard. "I know this is difficult, Mrs. Baysore. But will you please tell us what you saw when you entered the room?"

"I could see someone was lying on the bed, but it was dark."

"Could you tell that it was Mrs. McClung?"

"Not at first; it wasn't light enough. But then when Mr. McClung picked up the lamp, I could tell it was her."

"What did you do then?"

"Well, the chimney on the lamp was so black and the light so poor that I ran across the room and I threw open the shutter."

"How did Mrs. McClung appear when you saw her lying on the bed?"

"She seemed to be lying with her arm over her head. Her body was covered with a blanket, but her feet hung off the edge of the bed."

"Did you see any blood?"

"No, sir. Not at that time. We came right back downstairs."

"What did you do after you came downstairs?"

"Well, I started after the doctor too."

"But Albert had gone after the doctor, had he not?"

"Yes, sir, but I thought I could go faster."

"Did you get to the doctor's before Albert?"

"No, sir. I met the doctor and Albert right at the front door."

"Well, then, Albert had been fleeter than you had given him credit for?"

"Yes, sir."

"So did you, Albert, the doctor, and Mr. McClung all then go upstairs?"

"Yes, sir."

"Did you see any blood at this time?"

"Well, I should say so. There was blood, blood, plenty of it."

Here it is, happening again. Becca sleeping, on her stomach, lying there, peaceful. But she's across the bed, red all around her. The doctor putting his hands on her, touching my Becca, his hands on her shoulders, on her back, pulling. Her head, coming around, turning her face toward me—her head, oh God! Her head broken, her head bashed in.

She was always so beautiful. So beautiful when she was young, I had to watch out and keep her away from scallywags. Her hair is gray now, but she is still beautiful. Still beautiful, in my mind. But not lying there on the bed.

"What did you tell the doctor?"

"I told him that I guessed Mrs. McClung had had a hemorrhage, and he stepped over to the bed and turning her head over with his hand, he exclaimed, 'This is murder, Mrs. Baysore; this is no hemorrhage. This is a case for the coroner.'"

"Did you remain in the room?"

"After the doctor had taken in the situation, he asked me to take Mr. McClung downstairs. I did so and helped him to a chair."

"Did he seem to be overcome with what he had seen?"

"Well, the poor old fellow was trembling so and making a low moaning sound and I was afraid he would collapse."

They are talking about me like I'm not here. And I don't remember Sallie taking me downstairs and sitting me in a chair, or moaning, or any of that. What I do remember is blood everywhere, staining the bedclothes, dripping onto the floor. Her blood, my beautiful dead Becca's blood.

"Mrs. Baysore, I believe you told us that Mr. McClung was a quiet man and you believed Mrs. McClung to be a quiet, peaceful woman?"

"As far as I know. They never bothered me nor I them."

"She was not a woman who mixed in society a great deal, was she?"

"Not that I know of."

"You had never heard Mr. McClung quarrel with his wife?"

"I told you a while ago that he talked loud sometimes, just like all you men talk to your wives at times."

Stifled chuckling in the room. Mostly from the women, by the sound of it.

"Yes, I understand," *Runyan says, his tone light.* "Nothing of a serious nature; only those things that make married life healthy?"

"I suppose so."

"Is it not true that these people were about the house all hours of the night?"

"I got used to that; they did not bother me."

"You knew they were old people, not well and perhaps being restless, were not able to sleep and you did not think anything about their being up at night?"

"That was not any of my business."

Runyan says he's through with Sallie, and she goes back to sit with the others. Runyan sits next to me again, gives me a nod and a quick smile. I don't see nothing to smile about.

Now here comes Albert, and he gets sworn in just like Sallie was. Thompson, Dechant's man, is up again, standing proud as a peacock in his fancy suit, and filled to bursting with more questions.

"Mr. Dill, please state your full name and age."

"Albert Dill. I'm forty-five."

"Your occupation?"

"I'm a stock dealer, and buy up crops, too."

The best in the county; the state, maybe. Always gave me a fair price. Other folk, too, can attest to that. But Albert would be better off if he learned a thing or two about money. Slips through his hands, it does, because he's mushy. Always letting folk take advantage of him. He could stand to be shrewder in his dealings. He's always trying to look out for other folk instead of his own rightful interest. If a man don't look out for himself, then who will?

"How long have you known Mr. John McClung and his wife?"

"I never knew her, but knew him many years."

"Were you ever in their house?"

"I have been in there a good deal."

"Mr. Dill, when was Mrs. McClung found dead?"

"It was Friday morning, April twelfth, 1901."

"Mr. Dill, please tell us where you were and what you witnessed of the happenings that morning at the McClung house."

Albert shifts around in his chair a bit to get situated before he starts. His voice sounds a bit tired, or maybe sad.

"I went over there somewhere about five o'clock to help Sallie with breakfast, and she told me about hearing the noise in the other part of the house. We talked awhile, and she cleaned out the ashes from the fireplace while I was sitting there. I took the bucket of ashes outside and emptied them over the fence in the back of the yard, like I always do."

"Did you see Mr. McClung when you went out?"

"Yes, as I turned to come back to the house, he was coming up from the barn with a bucket in his hand."

"At what time was that?"

"I should judge about ten minutes after five o'clock."

"What did he say and what did you say?"

"I spoke to him, but he didn't seem to hear me. I went around to the front and into the house."

"Do you know when Mr. McClung went in the house?"

"I don't know exactly, but right after I got inside I heard someone going up the stairs."

"How long after you heard someone going up the stairs was it before Mr. McClung came to the door?"

"It was a very few minutes until I heard someone coming down again, and he came right around to the front door, and Mrs. Baysore asked him if Mrs. McClung was sick."

"What reply did he make?"

Albert takes a deep breath and sighs. "Well, he just clasped his hands together and said, 'My God, she is dead!'"

They're saying it again. My words, my awful words, again. Will this never stop?

"What did he do or say then?"

"He asked me to go for the doctor, so I went."

"Did you go upstairs with the doctor?"

"Yes, sir."

"Did you see the bark found in the bed?"

"Yes, sir."

"What did it look like?"

"A piece of ash."

"Did you see any ash wood about the place?"

"There was plenty of it in the kitchen and woodhouse."

"Would you know the piece of bark found in the bed?"

"I think I would."

Thompson comes back to the table and pulls two pieces of tree bark out of the crate, and walks over to show them to Albert.

"Which of these two pieces did you see?"

Albert looks them over, and takes hold of one of them. "I am not positive, but this piece is more the shape of it."

"You say you saw ash wood in the kitchen?"

"Yes, sir. There's wood stacked next to the stove, and much of it looks to be ash."

Thompson says he has no more questions and sits down. Mr. Runyan gets up now, and walks over to Albert. Albert looks at him, and so his face is turned toward me, too. It's an honest face, the most honest face in the county.

"Mr. Dill, when you saw Mr. McClung coming up from the stable, what was he carrying?"

"He had a bucket in his hand."

"He carried a pail. Well, was it empty or full?"

"I don't know, but it certainly didn't have very much in it."

"When you spoke to him he was not disturbed and did not indicate that he had committed a foul murder, did he?"

"No, sir."

"Did you have occasion to go down and see about the stable later that morning?"

"Yes, sir; about an hour later."

I didn't know about this. What's Albert doing in my barn?

"What did you find in the vessels for the chickens?"

"They were filled with milk."

"And the indications were that they had just been filled, had they not?"

"I suppose they had; the milk was spilled over the sides onto the ground."

"You did not notice anything out of the ordinary?"

"No, sir."

"Was the horse curried?"

"I do not know."

"Was the cow stable cleaned?"

"I did not notice."

"Well, Mr. Dill, if Mr. McClung had done all his usual chores in the barn, about how long would this have taken him?"

"I'd say at least a half hour, probably more like forty minutes."

"And what time was it when you saw Mr. McClung returning from the barn with the bucket in his hand?"

"Ten minutes past five o'clock."

"So it is likely Mr. McClung was in the barn from about four-thirty until after five o'clock?"

"Yes, I would say that's likely."

Mr. Runyan takes a few steps across the room, stops for a moment and strokes his trim beard, and then walks back and faces Albert.

"You say that you have known Mr. McClung for a number of years and that he always had more or less money about him; in fact, he was known to be a man of wealth?"

"Yes, sir."

"And that he did not do any banking business, and it was the general belief that he kept large sums of money about the house?"

"Yes, sir."

"Is it not also true that you paid him forty-eight hundred dollars for the property, paying him one thousand dollars down and giving your note for the balance, thirty-eight hundred dollars?"

"Yes, sir."

"And later you paid him thirteen hundred dollars on the note?"

"Yes, sir, on the first of April."

"Did you tell anyone that you had paid him thirteen hundred dollars the first of this month?"

"No, I don't think I mentioned it at all."

"Had you told anyone, or if anyone knew you did that, it would indicate that since he does no banking business, that this money, at least twenty-three hundred dollars, was in his possession at the time of the murder. And he was getting rent money every day from his tenants?"

"I do not know that anyone knew of it."

"Do you know whether anyone within the past few weeks or months tried to break into his house?"

"No, sir, I do not know."

"Did not John McClung tell you that someone came to his back door one night a short time ago, after midnight, and wanted in and when he did not open his door, they tried to pry his shutters open?"

I remember; it was in the fall, just after I sold the property to Albert and Sallie. Someone woke me up, banging on the kitchen door. I told 'em to leave or I'd shoot 'em. They didn't get in, but jimmied the shutters pretty bad in the attempt. After my money, I reckon. They're after my money, all of 'em. Don't recall if I told Albert about it or not.

"I did not hear of it."

"Thank you, Mr. Dill."

Albert sits down.

Mayor Lowe bangs his gavel and says we're going to adjourn for lunch, and to be back in an hour.

Mr. Runyan walks back over and sits next to me, leans in, puts his hand on my arm.

"How are you doing, John?"

I consider. Becca is dead. Somebody bashed in her head, and instead of looking for the rascal everyone is up here in this Opera House talking about it.

"All right," *I tell him.*

CHAPTER ELEVEN

My father waited until after we children had gone to bed to tell Mother about the hearing in the Opera House. He had come home for lunch after the morning session, and I'm sure he told Mother the details of that portion, but I was at school then and the young ones were taking a nap. Of course Mother wanted to know the rest of it when Father got home just after I did, but he said that it could wait; and all he would say when I asked him at supper was that he had gotten a seat in the back, and how there were so many people they couldn't all fit, and that next would come a court trial in Lebanon. But he refused to say anything about the murder itself.

So I had to be resourceful. I waited until Mildred had fallen asleep, and then slipped out of bed and perched at the top of the back stairs. Mother and Father must have been sitting at the kitchen table, drinking tea or something; I could hear a cup being set on the table every so often. I had learned long ago that you could hear what was going on in the kitchen from the top of those stairs, and if you were quiet no one knew you were there.

"Did they question the marshal?" Mother was asking.

"Yes, the prosecutor Dechant did. Marshal Reed mostly talked about how he and his deputies searched inside and out and didn't find any bloody piece of wood that could have been the murder weapon. He said everything was in order in the stable, too; the animals had been cared for that morning. He also said they found footprints around the house and even near the fence where someone would have jumped over if they were trying to escape, but they couldn't tell who made them, or when."

"So it could have been robbers," Mother said.

"Or it could have been Sallie or Albert or McClung himself."

"But they never found the stick used to kill her?"

"No; they searched everywhere. The coroner figured it had been thrown in the fire and gone up in smoke."

"So what else did you find out?"

"There was a lot of discussion about the wounds on the body. Dr. Hall was the one in charge of the autopsy."

I knew who he was, because his daughter Marie was in my class. He wasn't our doctor, though; we saw Dr. Van Dyke when one of us was sick.

"Hall startled everyone by bringing her brain to court."

Mother gasped. "Her *brain*! Dear God!"

"You can imagine the shock in the room. A few of the ladies left, but most people just leaned closer to get a better view."

"I can't blame the ones who left." There was a pause. "But, of course, your curiosity would get the better of you."

I think Father chuckled, or maybe he was choking a bit on his drink. "When things calmed down, Dechant got Doc Hall to tell all about the injuries; he said they broke almost every bone in her face. Of course, I knew that—I had to put it back together for the viewing. The doc was very outspoken; he even talked about the brain oozing out."

Mother groans and murmurs something I can't hear. I feel something strange in my stomach.

"When Hall was done, Coroner Carey got up on the stand, and he said the bark they found in the bed had blood on it and it looked like it came from two different pieces of wood, one bigger than the other. He claimed he could tell that from the curvature of the bark. Carey had John's coat with him, too, the one he always wore and had on Friday morning. It had stains on it, and Carey said they looked like fresh blood."

"Oh, Charles. He must have killed her."

"Well, Doc Van Dyke doesn't seem to think so. Runyan cross-examined him, for the defense. Van Dyke said the stains might be blood, and they might not; they'd have to be tested. If it was blood, it could be from John himself. He said John has some kind of skin disease that makes his hands bleed at the slightest provocation. He's often seen the cuts on his hands, and seen John wipe them on the sleeves of his coat. Carey admitted John had sores on his wrist and his hands, and I guess John told Runyan he hurt his hand when he was out on one of his farms, and the lady who was the tenant there tied it up for him. One of the stains was on the back of the coat, though, and that would be harder to explain."

"Well, who knows how long that blood could have been there. You know how John's clothes never seem to find soap and water, especially that old coat of his."

"Doc Van Dyke also explained another way he thought there could be blood on John's coat, if indeed it was blood. I wish you had been there to hear it, Etta. You would have found it touching."

"What did he say?"

"Well, the attorneys kept asking if there was blood on the stairs, or on the railing, or if Van Dyke noticed blood on John's clothes. I think Doc was a little put out about it. He finally laid it out there plain." (Here, Father dropped his voice to a lower register to sound more like the doctor.) "'Suppose any of you gentlemen would get up in the morning, slipping quietly out of bed so as not to disturb your sleeping wife, go about doing your morning chores, build your fires so that the house would warm up; finally you are through with your regular routine and coming into the house from your barn, you go to your sleeping apartments which you have left less than an hour ago; go to awake that wife whom you left sleeping—and find her murdered. What would you do? Would you not get down over that woman and would you not take that woman up in your arms and would it be any wonder if you got blood on you?' The room was so quiet you could hear a pin drop. Then Van Dyke said, 'There, gentlemen, is the reason I did not look for blood. I would not give *that*' (Father snapped his fingers) 'for a blood stain of any kind.'"

"Good for him!" Mother said. "I don't know if John is guilty or not, but he's an old man who just lost his wife, and you've got to bring some humanity into this whole mess."

"Yes, Van Dyke said he felt sorry for him, and talked with him a bit while they were waiting for the coroner to get there. He asked John if he wanted him to get his attorney, and John said he didn't have one. The doc was also the one who asked John who he wanted for an undertaker, and John told him me."

"You know, Charles, I just can't picture that doddering old man being strong enough to smash up someone's head with a stick. He has trouble just walking around."

"Yes, I think others have wondered about that, too. Attorney Runyan asked Dr. Van Dyke about John's health the last few months. He said John looked like he had been a sick man all winter, and was failing rapidly. But when Runyan pressed him on whether he would have been able to produce such deathly blows, Van Dyke said it was possible."

I pictured it in my head, sitting there in the dark on the top stair. A white-bearded old man, wielding a club of firewood, sneering as he was about to strike. I could not help but picture Mr. McClung as he bent over Hans, tied to his front door, with a knife in his hand. But that picture was not quite what it seemed, was it?

"You know, Etta," Father was saying. "I was wondering about Mrs. McClung's position on the bed when I first saw her, before I moved her for the autopsy. She was on her back because Dr. Van Dyke had turned her over. But he said he found her lying crosswise on the bed like that, with her right hand hanging over the foot of the bed. It's certainly not a position she would have been sleeping in. Both doctors Hall and Van Dyke say they think she was sitting on the edge of the bed when the first blow came, and either that or the second one knocked her back."

"So she wasn't asleep," Mother said. "She must have seen her attacker."

"Yes, but not live to tell us who it was. Both doctors also said it was strange that even though all her bones were crushed in her face, there were no abrasions. They believe that was because the bedclothes were put over her head before she was struck."

"An act of mercy?"

"Perhaps; but I wonder if someone used the bedclothes as a restraint, pinning her to the bed, as a trapper might do with an animal and a net. They say that the first blow was probably not enough to kill her, or perhaps even render her unconscious; but there were no defensive marks on her arms or hands. If she were able, you would expect she would throw her arms up to fend off the blows."

"And the bedclothes kept her from doing that."

There was a moment or two of silence, and I heard Father set down his cup.

"Charles, do you think old John McClung has gone insane?"

Father must have pondered this, because there was a pause and he set down the cup again before answering.

"Runyan asked Carey about John's demeanor during the Coroner's inquest on Friday. Mr. Carey said he tried to be gentle, treating John as he would his father or uncle. He said John only answered the questions he was asked, without offering further information. Carey admitted John answered intelligently, even though he sometimes broke down with emotion."

"Did the coroner ask John straight out if he killed his wife?"

"He said John denied knowing anything at all about the murder; that he came in from doing his chores, and found his wife dead. Then Carey asked him if he may have done it in absence of mind. John said, "If so, I did not know it.""

"Oh, Charles. That's peculiar."

"I thought so, too. But Carey said John repeatedly claimed he did not kill her."

"What's next, Charles?"

"Well, the lawyers and Mayor Lowe talked for quite a while about what to do with McClung. Runyan was concerned about John's age and health; said he'd never survive being put in jail. In the end, the mayor said he was willing to change the charge to manslaughter rather than murder. That way, he could set bail and John could stay in his house."

"Doesn't someone have to sign a bond? Did anyone come forward?"

"Oh, yes. Lowe set bail at five thousand dollars, and there must have been ten people who rushed to the bench to go in on the bond. I was surprised, I have to say. In the end, the Court accepted John's brother Frank, his sister Sarah, and Frank Hughes, the fellow over in Liberty Township who handles many of John's business affairs."

I heard a chair scrape back and dishes being gathered, so I returned to bed. Needless to say, I had trouble falling asleep that night.

CHAPTER TWELVE

Butler County Democrat

Mason, April 13, 1901 - Mr. McClung is said to have wanted to build a small house, while his wife desired a large one. They quarreled, it is averred, on this point. But the old man gave in to his wife, and on the evening previous to the murder made a contract with George Tetrick for the erection of a fourteen-room dwelling. If built, it would have been the largest residence here. It is thought that he may have brooded over this contract, and revenged himself on the woman while temporarily deranged.

"You know, I've been thinking. I'm surprised they didn't have George Tetrick up there testifying yesterday," Mother said at breakfast. "Since he must have been the last person besides John to see Rebecca alive."

George Tetrick was the man John McClung had chosen to build his new house. He was probably the best contractor in Mason, and he designed and built many of the structures in the village, including the Opera House. Contributions he made during his lifetime included schoolhouses, bridges, sidewalks, and road improvements, and some of these are still being enjoyed by residents today. Highly respected by Mason residents, he served many years on town council and the school board. When George Tetrick talked, people listened, and so his views on the McClung murder became general knowledge. Mr. McClung might have been stingy in many ways, but he had high standards for whatever he spent his money on, including equipment, farm workers, lawyers and contractors.

Father finished chewing his toast, dipped in the yolk of his sunny-side-up egg, before responding. "I imagine it's because the hearing was meant to present evidence that would show charges should be brought against McClung. I don't think Runyan had any say in what witnesses would be called. If he had, he certainly would have had George up there. George has been clear from the beginning he thinks McClung is innocent, and the murder was done by robbers. He doesn't think McClung is insane, either. To hear Tetrick talk, he spent a pleasant evening with the McClungs, talking about building plans, the night before she was killed."

"Yes, he tells folks that the McClungs led a happy married life." I could tell by the smirk on her face that Mother couldn't imagine having a happy married life with John McClung. "I'm not sure how many believe that, but I guess happiness is a personal thing."

Father nodded and took a bite of egg. "I also heard Tetrick say that maybe they arrested John to throw off suspicion while they hunt for the real murderers."

Everyone in town and probably far beyond was talking about the murder and whether or not John McClung was guilty. Other stories about the strange old man also found their way into discussions, sometimes as supporting evidence that John McClung would do anything for money—perhaps even kill, if he was riled up enough.

Everyone knew he had more money than most anyone else in the county, and they even agreed he had earned it honestly. His success seemed to be due to a relentless ambition to achieve little else than land and money, and that overpowering drive was responsible for most of the couple's peculiar habits. The McClungs had the wealth of kings, but they lived like paupers.

In their younger days, people said, the couple drove to Hamilton once a month for their groceries, traveling the ten extra miles because there they could get seventeen pounds of sugar for a dollar, while in Mason they could get only sixteen. They spent their money only on absolute necessities, and never traveled farther from home than they did on those monthly trips to Hamilton.

They fed their farm hands well, but when John slaughtered a pig, he sold all the finest parts and they ate the scraps and offal. McClung's apple trees produced the best fruit around, and they sold at the highest prices, but they carefully converted the rotten and bruised ones into applesauce or some other edible condition for themselves.

The estrangement from both their families also was due to money. Rebecca's brothers had launched a lawsuit against John over their father's estate, and later John had filed one over settlement of his stepmother's estate, and the bad feelings generated had lasted ever since. Because all this was common knowledge in a small town like Mason, it was no wonder that some people believed that John McClung, having but few years left to live and knowing that all his wealth would go to his wife when he died, killed her to keep his money from going to her relatives.

This extreme would not be necessary, said others, if John followed through on what they had heard him say more than once: before he and his wife died, he would like to convert all their land and possessions into paper money and burn it, so it would not go to either of their families.

He may have gotten a start on this plan, since the first thing he did after the murder was to tell George Tetrick he didn't want the house built. The next thing he did was have placards printed advertising the sale of his household goods.

After the hearing at the Opera House when three people who cared about John signed his bail bond, he moved out of the house where his wife was killed and reluctantly moved in with his sister Sarah Jordan. She had a fine house just west of Mason in the village of Bethany, where she had lived alone since her husband died a few years earlier. She, too, owned valuable farmland, though not as much as her brother John. But sharing quarters with a widowed sister who fussed over him and liked having friends visit was contrary to John's reclusive personality, and he had other ideas.

A couple of weeks after the murder, Ethel Rebold was bursting with news. "Guess who I just talked with," she said in the hallway, just before school started. She didn't wait for me to answer. "Elsie McClung!"

Elsie was the daughter of Robert McClung, John McClung's cousin. He and his wife, John's sister Elizabeth, lived in town just a couple of houses down from Mr. Rebold's store. Elsie, the daughter of Robert's first wife who had died, lived with Robert and Elizabeth. We liked Elsie, because she often went out of her way to ask us girls how school was and if we had any boyfriends. She didn't really expect us to say yes, but she knew it would make us giggle and feel like we were more grown-up than we were.

"There was a wagon parked outside their house, filled with furniture," Ethel explained, "and Elsie was outside telling the men where to take it. So, I asked her if she was getting new furniture for her bedroom. She wasn't. But guess who she said it was for?"

"Not her parents, I guess," I said, realizing this would hardly seem exciting to Ethel. Then I had an idea. "Is Elsie getting married, and her husband is moving in, whoever he is?"

Ethel laughed. "Don't you think if Elizabeth was getting married and they had already bought furniture we would have known something about it before now?"

That was certainly true. Not much got past Ethel Rebold, and if she had news about someone we knew getting married, I would have been the next person to know.

Again, Ethel didn't wait for me to respond. "It's for Mr. McClung! Mr. *John* McClung! The one whose wife got murdered."

"I know who John McClung is, Ethel." She could hardly wait for me to show how impressed I was with her news. "Is he moving in with them?"

"Elsie said he's renting a room in their house, and he bought the furniture for it himself."

"Is he there yet?"

"No, she didn't know when he would move in. When I find out I'll tell you!"

There was no doubt about that. But days went by, and then a week, and then two, and there was no sign of John McClung at his cousin's house.

When I told Mother about it, she said probably John wanted to be in Mason where everything was familiar rather than in Bethany. It was hard enough, she said, to adjust to losing a spouse, without moving to a different town on top of it, especially for an old man. But Mr. McClung was not in good health, she said, and Sarah Jordan was more able to care for him in her home. She probably had put her foot down and said John was staying right where he was, so she could keep an eye on him.

So we didn't see John McClung those weeks following the murder. Not that that was anything new. But we couldn't help but think about him and the murder every time we passed his house, with the shutters open now and no one at the upstairs window.

Anticipation was great for the upcoming trial, and public opinion shifted back and forth about Mr. McClung's guilt or innocence. Those who believed he was the murderer said the blood on his clothes was certain proof, or they pointed out the disappearance of the ash wood club that killed Mrs. McClung. Would a robber have carried the bloody stick away with him? John, however, could easily have added it to the fire in the kitchen stove. (But, I thought, couldn't a robber do that too?)

The murder was not the only cause of excitement in town, however, at least among the children of school age. *The Mason Appeal*, our village newspaper, announced that it was teaming up with *The Western Star*, Lebanon's paper, to sponsor a marbles competition in June, just after school let out. The best marbles players from both towns, under age fourteen, would compete for real prize money, as well as the title of Warren County Marble Champion. Several of the boys my age thought they had a real chance in the competition, and started playing after school several days a week in preparation. Leavitte Pease was most vocal about his chances, bragging that he'd knock out those Lebanon boys one by one just as easily as knocking marbles out of a ring. But most of us saw that his real competition was Hans, and I secretly imagined my new friend not only winning the five dollars in prize money, but also the respect and admiration of kids throughout the county and, more importantly, of our own classmates.

With real money on the line and a healthy sense of competition in the air, the after-school marble games began to attract a small audience—younger kids, mostly, who wanted to learn from the pros and dream of when they might be a marbles champ; but also older kids who liked to root for their favorite player. I stayed for a game or two myself.

Hans didn't often stay after school for these games. I heard the other boys say he must think he was too good for them, or he was so cocky he thought he didn't need the practice. I didn't believe that was true. I never heard him brag, and he spoke very little about what he did outside of school, except that he helped his father and older brother work on the Wikoff farm just west of town. He said little about his mother, except that she was sickly and didn't go out much. Like Mrs. McClung, he said, except she would have been glad to get out of the house if she could.

This particular Wednesday, Farly Dwire was excited to play with some new marbles he had just been given by a visiting relative. When the other boys told him they had just the right number for a game and there was no room for him, I stuck around to console him. Farly was often left out, and I felt sorry for him. But he dashed off and caught up with Hans, already out by the street on his way home, and I followed.

"Hans!" Farly called out. "Let's play some marbles. I've got new ones I want to show you."

"Sorry, Farly, but I haff to go home."

"Please, Hans! No one else will play with me. You could teach me some things so I don't lose all my new marbles."

"I don't even *haff* my marbles."

"You can borrow some of mine. I'll even let you win some from me if you want."

Hans hesitated. He was a sucker for a pleading face like Farly's. "Vell, okay. But I can't stay long."

I smiled at Hans as he and Farly ran past me back to the schoolyard, and I continued on to the post office.

Hans wasn't at school the next day. I worried some, especially when I remembered what had happened the last time he had missed school. Sure enough, when he came on Friday, he was trying to hide a limp, and his lip was swollen and cut. I kept sneaking glances at him all during class, but he didn't look at me. Miss Dill was eying him, too, and at lunch she asked him to see her before he went outside. I don't know what they talked about, but I could guess.

When it came time to walk home after school, Hans hurried out ahead of me without a word. He was not getting away that easily.

"Hans!" I chided him breathlessly, after I had run to catch up with him. "Why didn't you wait for me?"

He kept his head down, studying the sidewalk. "Sorry."

I took his arm, and he winced. I think it was the arm he had hurt weeks before. I reached for his hand instead.

"Listen, Hans. You don't have to talk to me if you don't want. But I know someone is hurting you, and I want you to know I'm sorry, and I wish I could do something. It makes me really angry."

He continued to study the sidewalk and limp in silence as we passed Forest Street. "It was my own vault," he finally said, quietly. "I did not go right home like I vas supposed to."

"You mean on Wednesday, when you stayed to play marbles with Farly?"

He nodded slightly.

"Hans, did your father hurt you because you were late?"

He said nothing. His silence answered for him.

"Hans, did you tell Miss Dill? He really hurt you! That's not right!"

"I told Miz Dill a horse kicked me."

The anger welled inside me, and I clenched my history book tight enough to dent the cover. "*I'll* tell her then!"

Hans stopped dead and looked at me. "You. Vill. Not."

I studied his narrowed eyes, and his split and swollen lip. I read determination, and resignation. This was how things were, and he would live with it.

"If you tell anyone, it vill only be vorse."

I wanted to walk all the rest of the way to Hans's house, stride up to his father, and tell him just what I thought of him and what he had done to Hans. But I was old enough to understand that would only make the man more angry, and Hans would be the one to suffer. When we reached my driveway, I reluctantly told him I'd see him Monday.

That weekend I struggled with what, if anything, I should do about what I knew. Hans would feel betrayed if I told someone, and even be punished for it if his father found out. But how could I let my quiet, kind friend suffer another beating? At church on Sunday morning, I prayed fervently for Hans.

It was Father I finally approached on Sunday evening, as he played with baby Frankie in the parlor before Mother put him to bed.

"When you were a boy," I asked him, "did your father ever hit you?"

Father looked at me, surprised. "That's kind of an odd question. But yes, I was spanked when I was young, if I did something wrong."

I shook my head. "I don't mean a spanking. I mean really hurting you, like on your face, or so you couldn't walk right for a while."

Mother came into the room, and Father gave Frankie a kiss and handed him over to her. He waited until they had gone upstairs.

"Isabel, do you know someone that happened to?"

I hesitated. "Maybe."

I think Father understood my hesitation to say too much, and accepted it. "Beating a child, the way you describe, is not right. It happens. Some parents think it is the best way to teach a child a lesson. I think what a child learns from being really injured by a parent is something else entirely. But as hard as it is, there is nothing you can do about it. A parent has a right to do what he feels is best with his own child."

"So what do you do when you see someone getting hurt like that?"

Father thought a moment. "Well, if it continues, I think a relative should step in and try to talk some sense into the parent. But if it's not your family, Isabel, you have to let it go. And pray. Pray for your friend, and for the parent."

I continued to pray every night for Hans. And I prayed for his father, too—and I think now that what I prayed for him was not at all what Father had in mind.

The Western Star
Lebanon, Ohio.

April 18, 1901 – Franklin was the scene of another prize fight last Thursday night, the bout being held in the dining hall at the fairgrounds, where the Chautauqua has been held for several years past.

About nine o'clock that evening Warren County Sheriff Gallaher received a telephone call from Franklin stating that a prize fight was about to be pulled off there and that the Law and Order League had determined that it must be stopped. Accordingly, Sheriff Gallaher summoned Deputy Sheriff Bob Smart and together they drove from Lebanon to Franklin at a fearful rate, making the distance of ten miles in a little more than one hour.

Arriving at Franklin they were met by representatives of the Law and Order League and by Constable John B. Miller. The latter was somewhat excited and not a little out of humor. The promoters of the fight, being mostly Hamilton, Middletown and Dayton sports, had so carefully guarded their intent that people of Franklin who oppose such contests were entirely ignorant of any such proceedings until the "sports" seemed to fairly swoop down from the places above mentioned, coming in by the trolley load. Barney Walsh, of Franklin, and Patsey Moore, of Cleveland, were the "knockers."

No sooner had the Law and Order League become cognizant of the intended fight than it was determined to put a stop to it. Constable John B. Miller was sent for and awakened from a night's repose into which he had just entered. Miller soon reported for duty at the League chamber and learning of the task required of him started for the scene of action, accompanied by a Mr. Gamble and a Dayton newspaper man. The Constable was not received in an especially cordial spirit by the crowd assembled in and about the dining hall. When men pay a dollar to see a fight, as these men had paid, they are not quick to flee at the approach of a single officer, before seeing the sport. The crowd began to fling jeers and epithets at the officer from all sides and when he attempted to arrest the principals he was jostled and pushed from side to side by the crowd. Shouts of "put him out" came from all sides and Miller saw that he was powerless and discreetly returned to town.

About the time Miller had finished his report to the League, the Sheriffs and their deputies arrived. Someone on a bicycle had given the crowd a tip, and as the Sheriffs entered the grounds the crowd was pouring out in all directions, and running as if for dear life. While Sheriff Gallaher and his Franklin deputies guarded the doors, Deputy Smart rushed in and finding Moore placed him under arrest. Moore had just been knocked out in the fifth round and was at the time of his arrest in the charge of his second, Johnny Holweger, a sporty Irishman, of Franklin. Johnny resented the arrest and drew a hatchet blade from his pocket to attack Deputy Smart. With one hand holding his prisoner, the Cleveland pugilist, Smart with the other hand sent the Irishman sprawling across the room. Regaining his feet he again made for Smart, but Sheriff Gallaher was by him and covered him with his revolver while Johnny obediently put up his hands. The other deputies took charge of Moore while Gallaher and Smart searched Johnny, who with some plain advice was then told to "go," which he did at once. It was found that the friends of Walsh, the winning pugilist, had succeeded in getting him out and into a buggy before the Sheriff got to the grounds.

Moore was put in a buggy to be taken to town when he commenced to cry like a baby. All the sand had been knocked out of him and to Sheriff Gallaher's reprimand for thus boo-hooing like a baby he replied: "If you had come down here from Cleveland where you had no friends and was pounded to pieces by a man forty pounds heavier and who made off with all the receipts, you'd blubber too." This ferocious Forest City "pug" was taken before Squire Corwin, and pleading not guilty to the charge of participating in a prize fight, was bound over to the grand jury in the sum of $2000.

A warrant for Walsh was also sworn out but he has not yet been apprehended.

CHAPTER THIRTEEN

May 7, 1901

"I'm sorry we are late," groaned Aunt Inez, plopping herself into the softest chair in our parlor. "It's my fault, I'm afraid."

"Nonsense," said Grandma Miller. "It's not your fault the court made you stay past hours." She turned to Father. "Do excuse our tardiness, son. Inez had a very busy day at work."

"We're in no hurry!" said Mother, emerging from the kitchen and wiping her hands on a towel. "You're here now, and that's all that matters. The food is ready, so let's sit at the table. You can tell us about your day while we eat, Inez."

Although Mother had said nothing about the murder case when she invited my grandparents and aunt to dinner, it certainly was no coincidence that it was scheduled for the day that John McClung's case came up before the Grand Jury, or that Aunt Inez just happened to be a stenographer at the county courthouse. And although my siblings couldn't wait to be excused from the table, I wanted to hear every word of the adult conversation.

"I have never seen so many people or such a collection of characters in the courthouse," said Inez, now recovered somewhat with nourishment from Mother's table from her hectic day. "Pugilists and promoters, saloon keepers and saloon frequenters, all mingling with a couple of dozen of our neighbors from Mason. They filled the halls, talking and arguing and asking over and over how much longer before it was their turn to testify."

"I read about the prizefight in the paper," said Father. "The Law and Order League got involved."

"Yes, and some of them were at the courthouse today too, scowling at the sports fellows and making sure the grand jury knew what a serious offense this was. I recorded testimony from at least a dozen of the fight people before I got a break. And then I ran into Mason folks I knew—Sam Sprinkle, Jim Dwire, Mr. and Mrs. Crotty; I'm not sure why they were called. George Tetrick was there, of course. There were some McClung relatives I really don't know—his two sisters, and his brother Frank, and a couple of others, I think. A good two dozen people for the McClung case, and they were there all day, waiting while the clerks and guards were trying to herd all the prizefight people and get the right ones in the courtroom to give their testimony. The judge didn't get to the McClung case until 3:00, so only a few of the witnesses got to testify. They'll get to the rest tomorrow."

"Think of it," said Grandma. "You get a subpoena for court and don't have any choice but to go where and when they tell you, and when you get there you waste a whole day just standing around and waiting."

"Some of them got impatient," said Inez. "But most didn't seem to mind. They were talking to each other, giving their opinions about who killed Mrs. McClung."

"Did you hear what they were saying?" asked Mother eagerly.

"Some of it. Some of them thought John was guilty, mostly because he is so strange and they haven't found evidence of anyone else being there. Someone—I'm not sure who—said he heard John was seen beating his horse several times when he was out on his farm."

I scowled with indignation. Remember, I had recently read *Beautiful Joe*, the story of the dog that was abused.

"You can't tell a hearsay story like that in court," said Father. "And even if it were true, you don't convict a man for murder because he was rough with his horse."

"What else did people say?" prompted Mother, returning to the topic of her interest.

Aunt Inez shook her head. "I didn't really hear that much. I was very busy, and I just got bits and pieces."

"Did you hear anything more about robbers?" Mother asked, unwilling to leave any information untapped.

"Oh, yes. People talked about that couple in Lebanon—"

"John Thompson and his wife," said Grandma.

"Yes, and a couple of them who have property near there said most people know who must have done it but they don't have proof enough to bring them to justice."

"They arrested some men and let them go, I remember," said Father.

"Yes," agreed Grandpa. "Inez wasn't at court the day they brought them in—I think it was a Saturday—but the paper said they let them go because there was proof they were seen riding a train near Middletown, I think, on the day of the robbery."

Grandma shook her head. "I don't know why our sheriff and his people can't find any of these robbers and murderers. Why are they bumbling around arresting the wrong people when there are barbarians out there who run around doing what they please?"

Father looked at her and shrugged. "There's a lot of depravity out there, Mother." I wasn't sure then what depravity was, but it certainly had to be evil.

"But I know how you feel," Father continued. "I understand they've never found who committed the horrible murder last year in Butler County,"

"Stites," said Grandpa. "His name was Stites. An old hermit."

"Yes, that was it."

"I remember something else I heard," said Inez.

"Do tell, child," said Mother. I wondered if she'd still call *me* "child" when I was twenty-two.

"Gypsies. Someone said it could have been gypsies."

My grandparents and aunt left soon after that, so Inez could get some rest before she returned to court for the next day of testimony.

Young people today are not familiar with gypsies, except in stories, maybe. But when I was a girl you might see a gypsy caravan or even a parade of them passing through town on their way north in the spring or south in the fall. A caravan was a house on wheels, built on a wagon base but with a hard roof and a door and even windows with curtains. One camped on the railroad grounds on our side of town for a couple of days in a late winter snowfall when I was nine. High from the turret window I could see a curl of smoke sweeping from the smokestack on the caravan's snow-covered roof, and I pictured the family inside staying warm next to their pot-belly stove while their horse shivered outside. But the following spring, a year before the murder, I actually got to see the inside of a gypsy caravan.

Father had allowed me to ride with him on a Saturday to pick up a body at a lonely farmhouse more than two hours north of Mason. The deceased had been a relative of Mr. Weber, one of Father's friends in town, and the widow was left waiting for her grown children to arrive from places far away. As a favor Father was to bring back the body for embalming so the burial could wait several days for the family's arrival. Rather than the hearse, we took our wagon, for it was better suited for a longer trip and could seat three. Mr. Weber rode with us to assist with loading the body and comforting the widow.

The widow had been distraught and dreaded being left alone, so we remained at the house longer than we had planned. Father was much more patient than I, deeply anchored in his funeral persona of calm understanding. After cups of coffee and thick slices of bread and cheese, Father asked me to help the widow clean up in the kitchen while he and Mr. Weber loaded the body.

I knew well enough that I should keep the widow occupied so she wouldn't see her late husband's body pass through the door. When the men were finished, Mr. Weber joined us in the kitchen as Father watered Apollo and Ajax and hooked them to the wagon. He talked softly with the widow, assuring her that my father would devote the best care to her departed loved one, and promised that he would see her at the funeral. After the poor woman had finished shedding her tears, Mr. Weber squeezed the widow's hands in his and assured her of his prayers for her comfort and peace. Finally, she accompanied us to the door, tearfully thanked Father for coming all this way to transport her husband, and bid us goodbye.

It would be almost dark before we arrived, even if we made good time. But when we were just halfway home, and I had dozed off with my head on Father's shoulder, I was jolted awake as the wagon jerked to a stop.

Ajax had stumbled into a rut on the side of the road, much deeper than it had first appeared because it was still filled with water from the last rain. Ajax struggled to regain his balance, lurching his head at the stuck front foot, shaking the wagon and us along with it. Apollo nudged his teammate in helpless sympathy with his beautiful big white head while straining against the pull. Father hopped off the wagon and tried to calm Ajax, cooing "Whoa, boy" while pulling on the horse's bridle. When Ajax at last gained his footing, he shook his head with a powerful snort, and Apollo gave him a nod of congratulations. Father climbed back on the wagon and had to slap the reins to get the horses moving again. We hadn't gone far before he realized something was wrong, and brought the horses to a stop. Mr. Weber hopped off the wagon after Father and they both inspected Ajax's foot.

While trying to get out of the mud, Ajax had lost a shoe.

"I'm loathe to continue all the way to Mason with a three-shoed horse," Father told Mr. Weber. Ajax was a fine, strong horse, but he and Apollo had a full load to pull with a wagon, three live people and a dead one. Father would never risk injury to his best horse, but he had no tools with him to reattach the shoe, and he couldn't be sure that there wasn't already some injury to the leg.

The only lucky thing about this situation was that we had already reached the main road and even this late in the day there was apt to be traffic happening by from one direction or the other. So Father unhooked the horses and led them to some new green grass just off the road, and we waited.

It wasn't long before we heard a lazy clop of hooves from around a bend ahead, and two bright gypsy caravans appeared and moved toward us, one behind the other. They were boxy, like rail cars, each with a wooden curved roof and a little chimney poking out on one side. The body of the first caravan was painted a rich red and decorated all over with gold stripes on the sides and fancy curlicues on the front. The roof was decorated with dark green scalloped edging all the way around. The draft horses pulling it were tall, one sable and one black, both with big white feet. The dark one tossed its mane when he spotted us.

As the wagons drew closer I could see the people aboard— the driver of the front caravan a lanky man wearing a white shirt, dark coat and no hat, his wife on the other end of the seat in a print dress, and a girl who looked to be about my age sitting between them. My father waved as they approached, and the driver pulled his horses to a stop with a drawn-out "Whoooah."

"Trouble, mister?" the man asked. When my father explained what had happened, the man hopped off the seat to look at Ajax's foot.

The second wagon stopped behind the first, and the driver, a boy older than me with a red cap atop a shock of thick black hair and pimples on his nose, handed the reins to the old man seated beside him and hurried to join Father and Mr. Weber.

The gypsy man stroked Ajax's dark mane and crooned to him in the way only a true horse-lover can do. "Be calm, my strong boy. We'll just have a peek. There's a good boy. You'll be home soon."

While the three men talked together over the horse, the girl and her mother climbed from the wagon to greet me. Both wore colorful dresses with puffy sleeves, and strings of wooden beads hanging about their necks. The woman was plump and wore a yellow handkerchief on her head, with two dark braids hanging beneath.

"I'm Mrs. Stanley," said the woman, stretching out her hand to shake mine. Her smile was broad and genuine, lighting up her dark eyes and tawny skin. "And this is my daughter Anna."

Anna looked much like her mother, but lankier, with a prominent nose and chin. Her thick black hair fluffed loose about her face and hung just below her shoulders. I was pleased to see her eyes lined up with mine, another girl tall for her age.

After I introduced myself, Anna excitedly turned to her mother. "Can I take Isabel in the vardo, Ma, and show her my things?"

I knew "vardo" was what the gypsies called their house-caravans, and there was nothing I wanted to do more in that moment than see what is inside a gypsy caravan.

"Can I go inside with Anna?" I called out to Father, who was following Mr. Stanley toward the rear of the caravan while Mr. Weber stayed with the horses.

"I don't see why not. Mr. Stanley has tools and has kindly offered to reshoe Ajax," Father answered. Already the boy was pulling a large wooden case from under the rear of the caravan.

"We have a ladder for when the horses are unhitched," explained Anna, as she clambered up the footboard and onto the seat. "But we can't get it out now." I followed her onto the seat and then through the open Dutch doors into the wagon.

It was lighter inside than I expected, for there were two windows on each side of the wagon to welcome the late afternoon sun. They were real glass windows that could open but were closed now to keep out the road dust, framed with pretty pink-and-cream patterned curtains.

Under the windows on each side was a bed, one for Anna and one for her parents, draped with colorful linens. (Her brother, she explained, slept in the second caravan with their grandfather.) In the middle there was a small table and wooden chairs, and a stand with a washbasin in one corner. Pots and utensils hung from hooks on the walls set between the windows. It was a miniature house, neat and tidy with clean wooden floors.

"Do you always live in the wagon?" I asked, amazed at how all the necessities of home fit in such a small space.

"We don't *live* in it," she said, pulling a metal bin out from under her bed. "We mostly just sleep in it. We live wherever we are, in the woods or by a stream or in a golden field. What kind of living would it be if you were always in one place?"

I wondered about that. My house was much, much larger than her wagon. But was the place she lived in bigger than mine?

She looked over the row of books in the bin, neatly arranged with their spines facing up. "Do you like to read?" She chose a book and sat on one of the chairs, and I sat on another. "This is my favorite book. Have you read it?" She held it up for me to see. The book was a pale greenish-gray, and centered on the cover was a large drawing of a girl in a red-and-white dress, frowning and holding up one arm to ward off the onslaught of dozens of playing cards flying at her. Around her feet a rabbit and several other animals were darting away from them as well. The fanciful black script above and below the picture read *Alice's Adventures in Wonderland*.

"I've never read it," I said. "But I love to read."

Anna smiled and pulled her chair closer to mine so we could both see the book. It was all about a girl named Alice, she told me, who follows a white rabbit with a pocket watch down his hole, and she drinks something that makes her shrink and then eats something that makes her huge, and she swims in a pool of her tears with a mouse who she thinks speaks French but really speaks English. There's a cat with a grin who disappears but his grin doesn't, flamingos used as croquet mallets, and talking playing cards that are painting the white roses red because the nasty queen who wants to chop off Alice's head prefers that color. There were pictures, too, of Alice interacting with all the fantastic creatures of Wonderland.

I was enthralled. This was unlike any book I had ever read. Certainly nothing at school compared with it, and neither did the books I occasionally received as gifts from my parents and grandparents. This was a story that was the stuff of dreams and beyond, unexpected characters in a nonsensical world that was made to be very real. I wanted to know Alice; more than that, I wanted to *be* Alice, and visit Wonderland myself.

Anna read aloud to me some of her favorite parts of the book, including the story of the tea party with the March Hare and the Mad Hatter and the dormouse, who was sleeping. She stopped after reading the riddle presented by the Hatter: "Why is a raven like a writing desk?", and asked if I could solve it. I loved riddles, and thought for quite a while before giving up and asking the answer.

"There isn't one," said Anna, laughing. "None of them know the answer."

Too soon Father called out that it was time to go, and I reluctantly climbed down from Anna's little house on wheels. The sun was almost ready to set, but Ajax was hooked back up to the wagon wearing all four shoes, and Father was smiling and pumping Mr. Stanley's hand, thanking him for being so generous with his time and help.

"Let me tell your fortune before we part," said Mrs. Stanley.

Father tried to hide his shock. "No, thank you, Ma'am."

"But one dime is all it costs."

Father considered a moment. Only God knows the future, and divination is a sin. But I know now that Father realized paying for a fortune-telling was a way of paying the Stanleys for their help with shoeing Ajax.

"Perhaps my daughter would like to know her fortune," he said, pulling a coin out of his pocket.

Mrs. Stanley smiled and took the dime Father offered. She lifted her plump body with a bit of an effort onto the fork of her wagon and motioned for me to join her.

I sat down, shyly. Inside I was excited—my fortune! What would happen to me, who I would become. How could this woman possibly know? But her tawny skin and dark, shining eyes, her beads and bracelets and bright colors, made her somewhat other-worldly, and surely meant she could see things that we, in our plainer world, could not. I gave her my hand when she asked, and she studied it for several minutes without saying a word, turning it over, tracing the lines in my palm with a crooked finger.

"I see for you a long life," she said, looking up from my hand into my eyes. "It will be filled with love, and with loss, in equal amounts."

I smiled. Would I marry? Have children? I wondered. But she did not say, and I was too timid to ask.

"You will stay close to home, but travel to far places," she continued. "You will see things you can't learn, and learn things you can't see."

That was all. A bit puzzled, I thanked her nonetheless, and walked back to our wagon where Mr. Weber and Father were waiting.

"Here, take this," Anna said, just before I climbed back on to the wagon seat. She held out the Wonderland book.

"Oh no, I can't possibly—"

She pressed it into my hands. "I *want* you to have it. I'll soon have the second book about Alice going through a looking-glass—Pa has promised getting it for me after we visit my great-uncle Levi in Dayton."

I never saw Anna again, but eight years and one day after Rebecca McClung was murdered, I read in the newspaper about a funeral in Dayton for Levi Stanley, known as the last "King of the Gypsies." He had died in December of the previous year in Missouri, and his body, according to gypsy custom, had been kept in a vault until springtime, waiting for the ground to thaw and for gypsies from all over the country to make their way to the funeral. A well-known preacher and a choir from the United Brethren Church led the ceremony, and the 96-year-old man was buried in the large communal plot according to gypsy custom. I'm sure Anna and her family must have attended.

By that time I had passed *Alice's Adventures in Wonderland* on to my sister Milly, along with another favorite book that I had bought with my own money when I was thirteen. It was all about a girl named Dorothy who blew away in a tornado and traveled on yellow brick road with her dog, a scarecrow, a lion, and a tin man to see a wonderful wizard. I wished I could have given the book to Anna instead of to my sister. But then, I imagine Anna had read it before I did.

CHAPTER FOURTEEN

The Western Star

May 16, 1901 – John McClung, of Mason, whose wife was found murdered in bed one morning a few weeks ago, was by the grand jury indicted in this connection for murder in the second degree. He was brought to Lebanon Saturday and taken before Judge Clark who fixed his bond at $7,000. This was signed by F. H. McClung and Mrs. Sarah Jordan, brother and sister of the accused, John Swearingen and F. M. Hughes, the two latter of Butler County. The examination of these bonds-men by Judge Clark under oath developed that they were wealthy, Mr. Hughes himself owning six hundred and seventy-five acres of valuable land unencumbered. Judge Runyan, of the firm of Runyan & Stanley, which will defend McClung, stated that the aggregate wealth of the four was something like $300,000.

The trial of McClung was set for hearing June 24.

During the five weeks between the day John McClung appeared in court to be charged with second-degree murder and the trial to be held in Lebanon, life went on, of course. John himself, out on bail, went back to his sister's house in Bethany to await his fate. A few days after the indictment, Ethel Rebold had news of her own.

After school that day, she made me keep walking with her past the post office a little farther down Main Street, where she ran into an empty lot, flung down her books, spread her arms, and cried out, "Welcome to my new house!"

There was nothing there but weeds and a couple of trees, but Ethel explained that her great-aunt Ada Flenner had just sold the lot to her mother, one of several lots that Mrs. Flenner owned in town. The house her parents would have built there was going to be twice the size of the rented house they now lived in, and three stories high, like our house.

"I'll have a room of my own, and there will be two parlors, and two toilets!" she exclaimed. The Rebolds were moving up in the world. Although the house wasn't completed until the following spring, we saw lumber delivered and work progressing all that year. When it was finished, it was the largest house in that part of town.

The spring weather in southern Ohio is capricious—frosty or windy or warm, rainy or cloudy or occasionally sunny, and maybe all within one week. A tulip that cautiously opens its face to greet afternoon sunshine may be drooping without hope in frost the next morning. Farmers in those days alternately worshiped and cursed the rain, depending on when and how much it came down. They were not happy that year on the twenty-fourth of May, and they weren't the only ones affected. In one of the worst storms that people living around Mason had ever seen, rain pounded down until fields were flooded; a waterspout even sucked up part of Muddy Creek and Turtle Creek and dumped it on the ground, too. Hail pummeled our roof and the baby crops. Thunder boomed and lightning pierced the sky, striking several barns and setting them aflame, as well as one of the gunpowder mills in nearby Kings Mills. Fortunately no one was in the mill at the time, but the building exploded into a million pieces.

That evening Mason schools held its annual commencement in the Opera House, graduating seven students with pomp and circumstance and elaborate programs filled with names, accomplishments, honors and memories, all tied up in bright magenta ribbons. The festive atmosphere was dampened, however, by the news that the School Picnic for our neighboring district of South Lebanon was tragically caught in the storm. After hurrying through a picnic dinner as dark clouds rolled in, many attendees sought shelter in the host family's barn. A fierce flash of lightning struck near the barn door, stunning many of the students inside and throwing three men just inside the open door to the ground. Two of them eventually recovered, but the third, a young physician, died an hour later. As we do in such times, we all realized that the victims of the storm could just as well have been ourselves.

A week later, rather than holding a school picnic for all the Mason students as we had enjoyed in past years, each school held its own small celebration. Whether the change was occasioned by the tragedy in South Lebanon, or by an earlier decision, I don't know. But when the lemonade and cookies were gone and that last day of school was almost over, our teacher Miss Dill had a happy announcement—she was to be married in the fall to George Kohl, who worked as a blacksmith at his uncle's carriage shop in the eastern part of town. We were happy for her, as she was a wonderful teacher, and we (well, the girls, anyway) hoped to be invited to the wedding planned for the fall. She assured us she planned to continue teaching.

Before rushing out the door to freedom, we said goodbye to our farm friends, whom we would see but little during the summer months. It had been a rather rainy day, but a few sprinkles weren't about to ruin our vision of days on end of games and wading in the creek and visiting friends and family, without homework and waking up when we pleased.

Since that last day of May was a Friday, Hans walked home with me. I wondered if and when I would see him during the summer, but was too shy to ask him about it, so instead I brought up the subject of the upcoming event that many of the boys were excited about.

"Hans, I think I'll be able to go to Lebanon for the fair and marble tournament!"

"Zat's good, Izzy."

"Mother said if I could go with a friend's family it was all right with her, and Gracie Riker said she would ask her parents. They're going, because her father is going to be part of some kind of Civil War remembrance they're having as part of the fair."

"I hope you haff fun."

I was a bit disappointed with his reaction. Didn't he care that I'd be watching him play? "Are you excited about the marble tournament? Have you been practicing?"

"I'm not goink."

"What do you mean, you're not going?" From a going-on-sixth-grade perspective, Hans Schmitt not competing in the marble tournament would be equivalent to Percy Coleman, our local baseball player, turning down a chance to be on the Cincinnati Reds.

"My fadzer von't let me."

This was an outrage. "Did you tell him if you win, you'll get money? Does he know you're the best marble player in Mason?"

"He does not care about zat."

"Then I'll—I'll get someone to talk to him! An adult. Someone he'll listen to."

"No, Izzy. Zat is not a good idea."

"Well, then you'll just have to go anyway. You can tell him you're doing something else, and you can go with me and the Rikers. I think we're taking the train."

"Even if I go, I cannot play."

"Why not?"

"I haff no marbles."

"How can you have no marbles? You must have won lots from the other boys, and you've got all those you brought from Germany."

"My fadzer took zem."

"Well, you'll just have to find where he hid them."

"Izzy. He did not hide zem. He dropped zem down zee vell."

I pictured Hans's beautiful glass German marbles lying at the bottom of a deep well, their colorful swirls hidden forever from the sun. And then I thought how Hans, a gentle boy who could not have done anything to deserve such a fate, must have felt when he saw them disappear.

Can you hate someone you have never met? Of course, you can. I hated the man who first owned Beautiful Joe, the man who chopped off his ears and kicked him when he was just a puppy, and I only knew him from a book. How much more I hated the father of the friend walking beside me.

I did meet Hans's father, a little more than a week later, the morning after Mrs. Schmitt passed away. He appeared at our front door, dressed neatly in a suit with his mustache trimmed and hair combed neatly, looking sad and humble as he fingered the hat he held in his hand. You could tell he had been crying and probably had not slept well, if at all, and his quiet voice reflected both sadness and humility. He looked small next to my father, who escorted him to the parlor, and spoke with him quietly about funeral arrangements. This was not at all how I had pictured him.

Father was to do only the transportation and embalming of Mrs. Schmitt's body, generously paid for by their landlords, the Wikoffs. The viewing would be in the Wikoff house, and the funeral service at the German church in Foster that the Schmitts attended. Because Hans was a special friend of mine, Mother had a pot of pea soup and a batch of corn muffins baked early that morning for Mr. Schmitt to take home with him.

Mother and I attended the viewing at the Wikoff farm, a very meager gathering compared to the one that had assembled when Mr. Peter Wikoff, that family's patriarch, had passed away. The Schmitts nearest relatives were back somewhere on the east coast, and they had not lived in Mason long enough or been out enough to meet many people aside from those in their church. Hans and his older brother Wilhelm stood stiffly beside their mother's casket in their best clothes, their shoes polished and their faces grave. Mother and I shook the hands of all three and said how sorry we were. As Mother expressed her condolences to Mr. Schmitt, I pulled Hans aside.

"Hans, I know this isn't a good time, but I have to tell you something. The boys at school want to give you marbles so you can compete. Farly says you can have all you want of his, and even Robert and Leavitte have some set aside for you. You can come on the train with me and the Rikers, and you'll be able to compete at the tournament."

Hans looked surprised when I mentioned the other boys, but underneath a deep sorrow dulled his eyes and face. His hair showed no sparkling gold in the subdued light of the parlor.

"Tell zem I say zank you, Izzy. But I vill not go."

159

I nodded gravely and squeezed his hand just before Mother ushered us out of the parlor and toward home.

The Lebanon fair was held a week later; I didn't go. A boy from Lebanon took home the title of Marble Champ along with the prize money and the glory that should have belonged to Hans.

CHAPTER FIFTEEN

Dayton Daily News

Lebanon, June 25, 1901 – The jury to which John McClung of Mason, the alleged wife murderer, will be tried, was impaneled and the trial begun. It will be a most sensational one, it is believed. The sight of a man 75 years of age on trial for his liberty on a charge of taking the life of the partner with whom he has traversed the path of domestic happiness, is discomforting and sad and arouses the curiosity of the masses which wonder what his fate will be. The courtroom was filled with the greedy, curious people when the old man came in. He does not look perturbed, but is quiet and calm. The air of melancholia is peculiar to him and has suspended over him all his life like a dismal fog over a turbulent stream.

The coroner has pronounced the man guilty of killing his wife with an ash club while mentally deranged, or as the verdict expresses it, while in a spell of mental aberration.

The summer of 1901 was hot, sweltering hot. May and early June were pleasant, but by the last week of June, when the trial of John McClung began, it was so hot that tempers were short and nights were filled with tossing and turning. I asked twice if I could sleep in the ice house; the answer was no both times. We didn't play in the turret because, even with the many windows, it was far too hot. Father had to work extra quickly with the two bodies he had to prepare during that time so they would not become "unpleasant." As the calendar turned from June to July, the Cincinnati newspapers were printing two lists on the front page each day: one for deaths and one for "prostrations" from the heat. The papers also printed advice for preventing sunstroke and heat prostration; listed among things to avoid was "wearing heavy clothing, especially woolens," and "sitting in a draft to cool off when perspiring freely." Perhaps the most sensible thing on the list of what to avoid was "continually talking about the weather and asking everybody you meet if it is hot enough for them."

The heat alone might have explained Sallie Baysore's behavior and effect on the trial of John McClung, I suppose; but if so, she suffered more acutely than anyone else present. Mrs. Baysore was considered the primary witness for the prosecution, since she was the only other person in the house when Rebecca McClung was killed. Although three dozen others were subpoenaed as witnesses for the state, Sallie Baysore's testimony was needed to prove beyond a reasonable doubt that John McClung killed his wife.

Despite the weather, I was set upon my self-assigned project for the summer: find out who killed Rebecca McClung. From what I had heard about the failure of our local law enforcers in their search and prosecution of robbers in the area, I did not completely trust that the trial alone would determine if John McClung was guilty, and if not, who was the real killer. I used the resources available to me: any newspapers I could find, including those that I asked Ethel Rebold to salvage for me from her father's store; talk on the street and among the families of my friends; and pumping Aunt Inez for information from the court any time I could find her at home. I also was fortunate that Father found time to attend the trial two of the days, and he was remarkably cooperative in answering my demands; I believe he found it an educational exercise for me and a bit amusing for himself.

As I carefully recorded all I learned, on stenographer's pads thoughtfully provided by Inez, I fancied myself following in her footsteps, recording the words of witnesses to help determine the details of the crime and to record them for history. I still have those notes, and although my eyes can no longer see them, I read and re-read them so many times I remember most all of it.

The trial began on Monday, June 24. I went about the tasks Mother had assigned me, but my mind was elsewhere, anticipating what secrets might be revealed in court. I had planned to do all my chores so quickly that after supper Mother couldn't say no to my calling on Aunt Inez at my grandparents' house. But my network of informants acted even more quickly.

Not long before Mother was expecting me to help her prepare supper, Ethel Rebold was pounding on our front door. I found her on the step, out of breath, telling me I needed to hurry and come with her at once. The jurors—the very people responsible for deciding if Mr. McClung was guilty—were on Main Street at the scene of the crime!

Barely waiting for my mother's reluctant permission, I charged out the door. The day was not as hot as what was to come later in the week, and the sun was low in the sky, so we were able to keep up a brisk pace of alternately walking and running until we reached the McClung house. There was more traffic than usual coming down Main Street from Lebanon; people coming back from the courthouse, Ethel told me.

Although a small group was standing around outside the house, none of them looked like jurors. Leavitte Pease's mother was one of them, and we rushed to her, breathless.

"Oh, hello, Isabel, Ethel," she said, smiling. She lived at her mother's house, with Leavitte and his older sister Lucille. Leavitte didn't seem to have a father; I don't recall why, and it certainly wasn't polite to ask about things like that. But Mrs. Pease was what you might call approachable; she seemed to love people. I wonder if she was aware that her son was a bit of a bully back then.

"The jurors are in the house with Sheriff Gallaher and the lawyers," she told us, pointing to an upstairs window, where we could see heads moving as they walked around the room. "Seeing what the house is like and where the crime happened will help them better understand all its details."

It was only a couple of minutes later that the first two jurors emerged from the front door, their inside tour apparently complete. They waited on the sidewalk, whispering to each other, until the rest of the group assembled. Last of all was Sheriff

Gallaher, whom I knew by his uniform; he pulled keys out of his pocket and locked the door behind him.

Several of the jurors looked over at the small crowd of observers that had gathered, and a young farmhand I didn't know called out to them, "Quite a nice house for a dirty murder, ain't it?"

The sheriff spoke up immediately. "I'm sorry, but the jurors may not converse with anyone about their work on the case."

So we watched with a bit of awe and respect as the group walked around the back of the house and down to the barn. We were on the other side of the fence, and not close enough to hear what was being said, but we watched as the lawyers (Mrs. Pease told us who they were) pointed to a couple of places and some of them nodded or asked questions. Sheriff Gallaher mostly followed behind, saying nothing; he let the lawyers do the talking and guiding.

When they were through, the group broke up and reclaimed the carriages and buggies that had brought them to Mason from the courthouse, and I ran back home to Mother who complained about how behind things were for supper because baby Frankie was fussy and she had no one to help her.

I learned later that it had taken all morning for the lawyers and judge to appoint the dozen jurors plus two alternates, and the only real testimony that day came from Dr. Van Dyke, the first witness. Here is what I wrote on my steno pad for that day:

June 24, Day One of the Trial.
The jurors were picked and had to swear they would do all the things jurors are supposed to do.
Everyone had lunch.
When they came back, the prosecutor, Mr. Dechant, called Dr. Van Dyke to testify.
Dr. Van Dyke told how Mr. Dill came for him after Rebecca McClung was found dead. (From here on, I'll call her The Deceased, like they do in court.) When he got to the house he went upstairs with Mr. Dill and Mrs. Baysore

164

and The Defendant (that is Mr. McClung). He told everyone how she was lying on the bed on her face, and he turned her over and saw where her head was bashed in. There was blood all over the bed and the floor. He found a piece of bark on the bed and said The Deceased had been clubbed to death with a piece of wood.

Dr. V found blood on The Defendant's coat and said it probably got there when The Defendant lifted The Deceased up to see if she was dead or not. Or maybe it came from cuts on his hands, because Dr. V. said he had seen The Defendant before with blood on his hands and he wiped them on his coat.

**Dr. V said he was alone with The Deceased after Mr. Dill and Mrs. Baysore left to get the marshal, and he heard FOOTSTEPS coming down the stairs, and they sounded like the person wasn't used to being on those stairs. **Important Clue?

When court was over the county sheriff brought the jurors to Mason so they could see the Scene of the Crime. The lawyers came too. I saw all of them. Sheriff Gallaher said they weren't allowed to talk to anyone. That's OK, because I don't know any of the jurors or the lawyers anyway.

Tuesday it was really getting hot. In the afternoon I rode my bike to Ethel's house and we both then rode to the creek. There were lots of boys there splashing and dunking each other and causing general havoc, but Ethel and I managed to find a quieter spot upstream to cool off. I could have stayed there all day, except we both eventually got hungry and thirsty. We rode back to Ethel's house with soggy skirts, and Ethel's mother treated us to some lemonade and oatmeal cookies.

After supper I rode my bicycle to my grandparents' house so I could get the day's court happenings from Aunt Inez, being careful to leave before it got dark and the fire bell rang for curfew. That day was the first that Sallie Baysore had taken center stage in Lebanon. After Dr. Van Dyke finished his testimony that had begun on Monday, Inez told me, Dr. Hall took the stand and reported on the autopsy.

"He explained the wounds with a lot of medical language," she said, "and he used a model of a skull to illustrate them. Not her real brain this time—thank God!"

Mrs. Baysore was next on the stand. She told the story of events that I had already heard, several times over: The night before, George Tetrick had been with the McClungs in their downstairs sitting room to talk about the house to be built. He left around nine o'clock. The meeting sounded quite pleasant. After that, Mrs. Baysore went to bed and slept soundly all night.

When she first awakened at four-thirty the next morning, she heard four screams and then moaning from the bedroom upstairs. She also heard traffic on the stairs. A fire was burning in the kitchen, but no one was there. She dressed hurriedly and at the front door sought help from one passerby who didn't stop, and then from Mr. Gramlich, who came inside with her but they did not go upstairs. When Albert Dill came over for breakfast, she told him what she had heard, but he thought probably Mrs. Baysore was just imagining the whole thing. After Albert emptied the ashes from Sallie's stove, John McClung came to the door of her apartments and when asked if Mrs. McClung were ill, he exclaimed, "My God, she's dead!" The three of them went upstairs and saw the bloodied body lying on the bed, and Albert ran to get Dr. Van Dyke.

"Then Squire Runyan came forward to cross-examine Mrs. Baysore," said Inez. "And that's when she got pale as death. He asked her about some things she said at Mayor Lowe's hearing in the Opera House, details of when she heard footsteps, and what they sounded like. Mr. Runyan seemed to think some of what she said today didn't quite square with what she said then."

"Interesting," I said, in my best detective manner. My mind started thinking of all the possibilities.

"And then she fainted," said Inez. "She just keeled over to the side and would have fallen out of the chair if Mr. Runyan hadn't caught her."

"Did she come to? Did she finish the testimony?"

"No. Dr. Hall rushed up and carried her out and took her to the jurors' room. A couple of her friends followed. She never came back to the courtroom."

"What made her faint?"

"Well, it was ungodly hot in there, with the weather and all those people. She probably was nervous, too."

"Did anything else happen after they took her out?"

"Judge Clark called a fifteen-minute recess, and then the prosecutors called up John Gramlich."

I knew Mr. Gramlich; he was a grocery clerk in Mr. Rebold's store. He had a cute little girl who was about three in 1901. Mrs. Gramlich would stop in the store occasionally, and I saw little Reba running around once when I was there, with her mother continually calling out, "No! Don't touch that!"

John Gramlich was the first person to arrive at the McClung house after the murder, as he was by chance passing by the house a few minutes after Sallie Baysore heard the screams. He lived near my Miller grandparents, and was right in front of their house when Mrs. Baysore called out to him from the front yard of the McClung house. He must have gone with her reluctantly, because although he walked with her outside to the back of the house and up the steps to the kitchen door, he did not go any farther inside, not up to the bedroom or even to the bottom of the inside stairs. Sallie, however, did call up the stairs, and when there was no answer, Mr. Gramlich said he figured the couple must be asleep. Or something. And he left to go about his business.

Sallie Baysore was called up to the witness stand again the next day for cross-examination, and it happened again—she fainted dead away and had to be carried out. This time she was taken home to recover. Some said she had a heart problem; others said it was just the heat, or nervousness. Father, who attended the trial that day, said her corset was too tight. Mother said corsets must have been invented by a man and the world would be a much better place without them.

CHAPTER SIXTEEN

The Cincinnati Enquirer

Lebanon, June 27, 1901 – Interest in the McClung murder trial is still on the increase, and the courtroom was packed to almost suffocation today. Nearly the entire day was taken up in the examination of Albert Dill, owner of the property in which the McClungs reside, and who arrived at the scene of the murder soon after it was committed.

William H. Williamson, who was appointed as Deputy Marshal in charge of McClung until after the preliminary hearing, which was held April 12, testified to a conversation he had with McClung in regard to his habits. In the mornings he said he left his wife in bed at 4 o'clock and slipped out easy, so as not to awaken her, and built the fires and went to the barn and fed his stock, then returned, awakened his wife, and she would get breakfast while he took the cow to the pasture. That morning he went upstairs and saw the condition of affairs, and then went for help. He said, "To think the people think I murdered my wife."

Finally, on the last day of that week, the topic everyone wanted to know about was to be addressed: the blood on John McClung's coat. Was it the blood of the murdered woman, thrown in the air as he beat her with a stick of wood? The coroner had said the spots on the coat's lapels looked like they had been spattered there, similar in pattern to the larger splatters on the headboard of the bed. Or had they gotten there when John tried to rouse his poor wife when he first discovered the attack? Perhaps it was blood from John himself, wiped on his coat numerous times from sores on his hands, some of which were evident the day of the murder.

Or perhaps the spots were not even blood. Mr. McClung, after all, was often seen in that coat, and it was always dirty and stained. Those spots could be from most anything. So when word got out that the expert chemist from Cincinnati who had examined the coat and tested it for blood was subpoenaed to testify that day, the courtroom was full and people were hoping at last to hear a definitive answer that would shed new light on the murder case.

The day wore on, however, with testimony from Rebecca McClung's brothers, Nicholas and Servetus Dawson. Many people had said that John's animosity toward his brothers-in-law was strong enough to be a motive for his wife's murder, and it was all bred by what would happen to his money when he died. Since he was fourteen years older than Rebecca, he feared he would die before her, and his estate would pass to his wife; then, upon her death, since they had no children, her brothers would inherit the vast amounts of cash and real estate. Can you imagine, Mother had commented, that anyone—even someone as "unusual" as John McClung—would actually kill his closest companion to prevent her relatives from getting something he no longer had use of anyway, since he would be dead?

Unthinkable to Mother, perhaps, but not to the prosecutor, because he brought the brothers to the stand—one and then the other—to talk about why they and John McClung had a "case of the outs," as they put it. It went back almost thirty years, they said, to the division of their father's modest assets after his death. John and Rebecca filed a lawsuit against her mother and brothers to order partition of the land held by the Dawsons, so he and Rebecca could lay claim to their share. The Dawson brothers, too, carried animosity over the proceedings, and said they had not spoken to McClung since. Another witness, Charles Condon, who had a room at the Mason House Hotel where Albert Dill also resided, testified he had heard the old man say that if he knew when he was going to die, he would convert all his property into greenbacks and then burn them, rather than have "certain persons" get it.

But all of this was nothing but stale old news to everyone in our town, and rather than causing shock in the courtroom it prompted only nods and eye-rolling. Where was the testimony about the blood? By early afternoon the heat rose beyond all tolerance, and the expert chemist from Cincinnati, who had sweated in the courtroom for hours, was never called. The prosecution rested its case, and court adjourned early.

The heat wave continued through the weekend, with folks mostly lolling about trying to cool off. Mother said it was too hot to cook, so on Saturday we had cold leftovers, and Sunday after church we ate ham sandwiches and cold bean salad and canned fruit under the shade of our big maple tree in the backyard, on a folding table and the chairs we used for funeral services. Father filled three wooden buckets along with water and ice he had chipped from one of the big blocks in the ice house, two for him and Mother to put their bare feet in while we ate and one for the children to do with as we wished. Mildred, Marshall and Everett chased each other around dropping ice chips down each other's backs, and I popped little chips in baby Frank's mouth and bigger ones in my own. When Everett knocked over the bucket, we stomped around in the melting ice on the wet grass in our bare feet. Cerbie threw himself into the cool oasis and Marshall gleefully joined him, rolling around like a puppy until Mother told him to stop or she'd feed him dog food the rest of his life.

The relentless heat did not bode well for Sallie Baysore's return to the witness stand on Monday, the first of July. She came to court with her doctor, and he sat in a chair next to her during Mr. Runyan's cross-examination. She had only answered a few questions before she passed out again—again!—into the doctor's arms, and he carried her out of the room. One of her friends followed them out, Aunt Inez told me, to lend any assistance the doctor might need, and the people in the courtroom shifted in their seats, cooling themselves with paper fans and whispering to each other for at least ten minutes before the doctor returned. He reported that Mrs. Baysore was suffering from nervous prostration and would not be able to stand the cross-examination, and the lawyers were all called to the bench to talk with the judge about what to do. Eventually they agreed that she wouldn't have to appear again, but the defense, which had not had the opportunity for full cross-examination, could present evidence to challenge her earlier testimony.

A parade of witnesses came forward to prove the good character of Mr. McClung, that in conversation he was often heard to say, "It's just as Becca says," and that he always treated her kindly and affectionately. Several said that his hands often bled from sores. His sister, Sarah Jordan, said John and Rebecca lived a happy married life. George Tetrick, the building contractor, said John had told him to build the new house in accordance with his wife's wishes. Some of the witnesses hinted that men working on the cemetery fill near the McClung house may have been the guilty ones.

On the Fourth of July, Leavitte Pease drove a buggy past our house with his sister, his mother, and his grandmother on board, headed to the Wikoff farm for a family picnic (Leavitte's mother and grandmother were Wikoffs). Mother and I were outside watching Everett and Marshall run around the yard in the heat, and when we waved hello, Leavitte pulled the horses to a stop.

"Etta!" called out Mrs. Pease. "Happy Independence Day!"

"Hello, Minnie," said Mother, waving. "The same to you!" She walked closer to chat with the ladies. Everett chased Marshall around to the back of the house, and I followed the boys. I had little interest in chatting with the ladies, and none at all in chatting with Leavitte, if Leavitte even knew how to chat.

When I herded the boys back inside, Mother was in the kitchen talking with Father.

"He'll be back up there again tomorrow," she was saying. "I understand several other ladies are going."

"Who will be back?" I asked.

Father set down his water glass. "Your mother wants to see old Mr. McClung in Lebanon tomorrow." He seemed to find it amusing.

Mother explained that Mrs. Pease and her daughter Lucille had traveled to Lebanon the day before to see the trial and have dinner with one of Mrs. Pease's friends there. Mr. McClung himself had taken the stand in his own defense, and he would face cross-examination the next day when court resumed following the holiday break.

Well. If Lucille could sit in court, so could I. "Will you take the train? Can I go with you?"

"I don't see how anyone is going to Lebanon tomorrow," Father said. "Your mother seems to forget that several small children live in this house. Ethan Thomas's mother just died, and I can't see myself changing diapers and embalming a body at the same time."

Mother was quiet for a moment. "I could ask your parents to keep Frank," she said. "But the whole bunch of them is too much. Grandma and Grandpa aren't as young as they used to be." She sighed. "I guess you're right; I'll stay home."

My disappointment didn't last long, for I had an idea.

"I can watch the others, Mother. I'm eleven now."

I don't think it took Mother long to figure out that I expected something in return for my generous offer: a full report on the day in court. It wouldn't be the same as being there in person, but far better than nothing at all. After both of my parents looked me over as though trying to determine if I had indeed matured enough to be given the responsibility of caring for three of my siblings, they reluctantly agreed. Frank would go to my grandparents; I would watch the other children; Father could go about his work, but would be right there in the house, just in case; and Mother would ride the train to Lebanon with several other women from town.

The day for me was a trying one. But after enduring custody battles over toys and trials of my patience, hearing grievances of young boys and testimony from my sister, the only witness, and sentencing Marshall to fifteen minutes in the corner and Everett to hard labor cleaning up the milk he spilled, I nevertheless was ready for a report on the happenings in the county court. Mother was tired, too, but after she changed into an old housedress and put the younger children to bed, she and Father and I sat in the parlor to discuss the wheels of justice. I felt very grown-up.

John McClung walked to the witness stand very slowly, assisted by the bailiff, Mother said. His sister Sarah Jordan sat in a chair next to him.

"When John was up there on Wednesday, Mr. Runyan was conducting testimony for the defense. So today was the cross-examination by Mr. Dechant." Mother was addressing her comments to Father.

"The prosecutor," I said. My parents looked at me with a bit of astonishment.

"Yes. One of the first questions he asked was about the story an earlier witness—he didn't say who—told about hearing that John beat a horse with a rail in one of his fields, and Rebecca begged him to stop. He supposedly told her if she didn't shut up he'd give her some of the same."

I cringed. "What did he say?"

"He said it never happened."

"That hearsay again!" said Father. "I'm surprised the court allowed it."

"Then the prosecutor asked him if he didn't commit the crime, who else did he think would have a motive for killing his wife."

"Robbers," I said. "They cared more about money than they did Mrs. McClung."

Father smiled at me. "I think it's common knowledge John McClung has lots of money."

"That was John's point," said Mother. "He said he often saw people from town across the street from his house on the hotel porch pointing out his home to visitors, saying that's where the wealthy miser lives who never keeps his money in the bank. He said once he heard them say he had three barrels of money in the house, and when he was gone, he made his wife sit on them."

"That's what all the kids at school say," I said.

"He also said he often loaned money to others, and had more requests for loans than he could accommodate. He said the money was as much hers as his."

"Do you think Mr. McClung loved Mrs. McClung?" I asked.

"That's a good question, Isabel," said Mother. "Mr. McClung said he and his wife lived a quiet and happy married life, and they never had any trouble."

"That's not the same as loving her," I observed.

"No. But Mrs. Pease told me that the day she was in court his lawyer asked if he loved his wife. She said he just nodded and then broke down and sobbed. He wept again today while he was talking about their life together. I felt so sorry for him."

"Did he say why she always stayed in the house? Do you think he made her stay there?"

"Isabel," Father said, "You should know that Mrs. McClung's body showed no signs of anyone hurting her." I knew Father was following my thoughts about the "friend" I had asked about just a couple of months earlier. "She only had one old scar, on her leg, the kind that anyone would get from a scrape or minor cut."

This was helpful news, and I felt a sense of relief.

Mother added, "John said he was devoted to pleasing her, and that he spent considerably more time at home these last many years because she preferred to stay there. Then he talked about always providing for her every need and desire, and he mentioned all the bolts of linen and cottons that you saw, Charles, when you were there, as well as all the food that was in the house."

"But if Mrs. McClung had all that new fabric, why didn't she get nice clothes made?" I asked. "Mrs. Baysore is a dressmaker, and she was living right there."

Mother shrugged. "I guess fine clothes just weren't important to her, Isabel. If she wasn't going anywhere, it didn't really matter how she dressed."

"Did anyone else testify today?" Father asked.

"Yes, several people from town. After the noontime break Mr. Runyan called them up one after the other to support John's testimony. Mrs. Shurts talked about the fabric and the canned foods, and she also said she found plenty of underclothes and ordinary clothing that was Rebecca's. Charles Failor testified he had always known John McClung to be an honorable man, always paying his bills and honest to a fault. Brooks Crone said his brother used to work for the McClungs and boarded with them, and always reported they set a good table. He was quite a hearty eater, too, according to Brooks."

"That must have been years ago," said Father.

"Yes, I guess it would have been. Another man I didn't know who had worked for him said the same. Mrs. Hageman and Jim Dwire got up there, too, to say John McClung was an honest man of good repute and they never knew him to hurt anyone. Flora Tetrick rode up on the train with us and said she had been subpoenaed, too, but they never called her."

"John McClung has been around Mason a good long time," said Father. "All his life, practically, and I'm sure lots of people could swear he was of good character."

"And maybe a few might say something different," said Mother.

"Now, Etta. You may not like the man much; many don't. But you can't tell me of certainty anything he's done that's dishonest or hurtful."

Mother only shrugged, and Father changed the subject.

"Was anything said about the blood on John's clothes?"

"Oh, Charles! I plumb forgot. Flora Tetrick told me on the train up to Lebanon this morning that the prosecution never called the chemist to testify, but yesterday morning Mr. Runyan presented his report. He could not say conclusively that there was any human blood on John's clothes."

I took a lamp into the kitchen and wrote up all that Mother had told us in my trial journal, and then went upstairs to bed. There had been thunderstorms that afternoon, pushing out the stale hot air, and now a cool breeze gently fluttered the curtains in the bedroom window. For the first time in more than a week, I fell asleep right away.

The cooler weather lasted only a couple of days, but it felt glorious. Monday afternoon Ethel and her little sister came over so Mildred and Alice could practice their jump-roping. This get-together had been pushed by our mothers a couple of weeks earlier, but such vigorous exercise was ruled out by the hot weather. Milly and Alice had not forgotten, however, and with the change in weather we were soon in the road near our house with the jump rope Ethel had brought.

Ethel and I started a slow back-and-forth swing for my sister, the youngest, and after she got the rhythm, Ethel and I chanted: "Down in the valley where the green grass grows, there sat Mildred sweet as a rose. Along came Johnny and kissed her on the cheek; how many kisses did she get this week?" Then we started a full swing while Milly counted: "One, two, three . . ." before she tripped on the rope.

Next it was Alice's turn. We started her right off with a full swing. "I like coffee, I like tea; I like the boys and the boys like ME!" chanted Alice. Then, "Izzy and Hans, sittin' in a tree, K-I-S-S-I-N-G . . ."

I stopped the rope. "Alice!"

She stuck her nose up at me. "I get to say what I want when it's my turn!"

"Where did you learn that?" I snarled.

She looked at Ethel, who squeezed her lips together to repress a smile. "She's right, you know," said Ethel. "Don't be so *sensitive*, Izzy. It's just a rhyme."

I huffed a little, and then we started it up again.

"Izzy and Hans, sittin' in a tree, K-I-S-S-I-N-G. First comes love, then comes marriage; then comes Izzy with a baby carriage!"

As soon as she hit the last word, I pumped the rope faster and Ethel followed. Not quite hot pepper, but enough to get Alice to miss—and to make my point.

"That's too fast!" she cried.

"When I'm turning, I get to do it how I want," I said, "That's the rules." It wasn't the rules, but Alice didn't know that.

I had only seen Hans twice since school had let out for the summer. The first time he was too far down the street to talk to, and I watched him take off his field hat and walk into the carriage shop. On an errand for his father, I expect. I was glad to see he was walking briskly, without a limp, since I had had several dreams of seeing Hans without an arm or a leg, his father standing over him with a sneer.

The second time I saw him was from the window when I was up in the turret; he was with his brother on a wagon coming from the Wikoff farm where they worked. I tore down both flights of stairs and ran to the front door, pausing to catch my breath so I could walk out casually, as though I just happened to be headed for the front yard as they passed by.

"Hi, Hans!" I called out. His brother pulled up the horses.

"Oh, hi, Izzy!"

His face was ruddier than when I had last seen him, from working in the fields. He looked more muscular, too, although that might have been my imagination. I wanted to say how good it was to see him and how much I missed him. "Where are you headed?" was what came out instead.

"Vilhelm and I are on our vay to pick up zum horse feed and zum people feed, too." He smiled, and his teeth shone white in his tan face.

"Just don't get them at the same store."

"No, vee von't. Please tell your muzzer zhe make zee best cornbread!"

"I will."

Wilhelm slapped the reins and clucked to the horses. "It vas nice to zee you, Izzy!" said Hans.

That encounter had been several weeks ago, but after Alice's jump rope rhyme I looked around nervously just in case Hans might have been within earshot. Who I saw instead was Albert Dill, on his way home from the train station.

"Hello, girls!" he called out, walking toward us.

"Hi, Mr. Dill," we said.

"Are you coming back from Lebanon?" I asked.

"I sure am, Izzy. A bit earlier today. They've finished up with all the witnesses. Now maybe I can get some business done again!"

The trial had dragged on so long I had begun to lose interest. It seemed like it would always be with us, like the heat. "Does that mean the jury gets to decide now?"

"Well, pretty soon. First the lawyers get to make their speeches. Six hours for each side, can you believe that?"

"Six hours! That means twelve for both!" (There was nothing lacking in my mathematics education.)

"Yes. Lawyers like to talk and show off their learning," said Mr. Dill. "The case should go to the jury on Thursday." He waved to us all. "Enjoy the weather, girls!"

We enjoyed it, but it didn't last. By Wednesday it was in the nineties again, and on Thursday, the thermometer in Lebanon read a hundred and one degrees at four o'clock when the jury announced its verdict.

The Western Star

July 18, 1901 – John McClung is once more a free man. The jury which for fourteen days listened patiently to the tedious details of the trial wherein the defendant was charged with the murder of his wife in a horribly brutal manner, after remaining out some six hours found the defendant not guilty. McClung received the verdict with evident delight, though without any especial outward manifestations of his joy. McClung has stood the trial well, but it was a sorry sight to see a gray-haired man on the brink of the grave tried for the murder of his lifelong companion.

As in all cases where a trial becomes so important that its duration is measured in weeks, public opinion as to the guilt or innocence of the accused was divided. Yet in nearly every case those who heard a goodly portion of the evidence were agreed that the defendant, even though he did commit the terrible crime for which he was on trial, was not proven guilty by the State. The testimony introduced by the State was not sufficient to convict in any event, while the defense shattered practically every theory advanced against the accused. A detective had been employed who acquainted himself with all the reports current in the case and ascertained the points upon which the State would base its prosecution. Evidence was introduced to rebut every allegation against the defendant as well as to show his good character and the absence for any reasonable motive on his part for committing such a deed. Messrs. Runyan and Stanley, attorneys for the defense, showed remarkable tact as well as ability from a knowledge of the law, in the conduct of this case. The illness of the State's principal witness, Mrs. Baysore, which prevented a cross-examination, was generally regarded as against the State.

The verdict of the jury as a matter of fact does not convince the enemies of McClung that he is not actually guilty although the decree of the jury forever acquits him in the eyes of the law. On the other hand, it is stated that McClung and his friends have suspicions as to the guilty ones and will spare no expense to bring about their arrest and conviction. As the case now stands another awful crime committed in our county, the third within a little more than a year, is unaccounted for and the guilty one, whoever he may be, is still unpunished.

John McClung lived the rest of his remaining days at the home of his sister Sarah, in legal freedom but forever under a cloud of suspicion. He died quietly of heart failure at the age of 78 in October 1904. The small, private service was held at Sarah's home, and he was buried in the Mason cemetery under the stately marker he had erected following the death of his oldest brother Joseph in 1881. John's remains rest near those of his parents, and alongside those of his wife Rebecca.

CHAPTER SEVENTEEN

Sixteen Years Later

Nineteen-seventeen was the worst year of my life. Of course, there was a war going on, and the United States reluctantly entered it that spring. We prayed each week in church for the men from our town who were now soldiers, including my old classmate Pearlee Spuhler, and of course the war was always a topic of conversation. The farmers around us worked harder than ever, knowing that whatever they could produce was needed and would find an easy market. Father's work continued as usual; people are always dying and in need of undertakers, no matter what is going on in the world. He was glad as he got older to have the help of my brothers.

I was still living at home, feeling rather restless as I saw my friends getting married, having children, or finding jobs. Even Mildred was married, living with her husband in Flint, Michigan, where he worked at an automobile factory. Father for several years appreciated my help with the family business, but as the boys got older, he began to train them as potential partners. So when the Peters Cartridge Company in Kings Mills expanded into a new building and advertised for more workers, I was excited to join the company in the fall of 1916.

Peters continued to grow quickly when the United States entered the war the next spring. At the peak of production there were three thousand of us working at the factory on the other side of the Little Miami River from the town of Kings Mills, and one third were women. Many arrived at work via the Rapid Railway, a traction rail line that connected Cincinnati and Lebanon and several towns in between. For those of us working at the cartridge company and the associated Kings Powder mills on the near side of the river, it was ideal transportation—cleaner, lighter, and running more frequently than the railroad trains. I boarded the dark green car just a couple of blocks from our house, and it traveled the same route I had ridden many times on my bicycle, up Main Street and along the road to Kings Mills, where it dropped us off on our side of the river before heading north to Lebanon. Those of us working at Peters would then walk down cement steps on the steep hill to the river and across the bridge to the buildings that stretched along the water on the other side. I worked in the shell factory, where we made the cartridge tubes from rolled paper, waterproofed and ironed them, and added paper wads into the bottom of the shells before they were sent to the loading mill. It was meticulous and tedious work, but we chatted with each other while we did it, and we could get a fresh-cooked dinner in the factory dining room during our midday break—at a reasonable price, of course.

But none of this was related to the devastation I felt by the end of 1917; for me, the first year our country was at war found me in a more personal trench. And ironically, it was Rebecca McClung's unsolved murder that pulled me out of it.

The last day of June that year was a typical warm, summer day, following two days of rain. It was good to see the sun again, especially on my day off. I had taken a walk up to the croquet field and back and was relaxing with the newspaper that afternoon when a sharp, insistent knock came at the front door, and I answered it with the paper still in my hands.

There stood Farly Dwire, tall and handsome now that he was grown, a husband and a father of three children. But today he was sopping wet, covered in mud, his hair pushed away from his face in tufts that thrust several directions. He wasted no time with pleasantries.

"Izzy." It was a voice struggling to sound calm. "It's Marshall. There's been a terrible accident."

"What? What's happened?"

Farly broke down in sobs. Unable to speak, he stepped aside from the door and pointed out toward our driveway. There stood the horses and wagon Marshall left with that morning, hired to do hauling for some folks just outside of town. Tied with a rope behind the wagon was a third horse, Farly's horse. From the porch steps I could see into the wagon—stretched out beside some equipment was a bedraggled body.

I threw down the newspaper and ran to the wagon, followed closely by Farly, and climbed up on the fork so I could get to Marshall. He was wearing only his underclothes and was soaking wet. His face was white, his mouth drooping open.

"I did everything I could." Farly had climbed up beside me and placed his arm around my shoulders. "He was already underwater when I got to him. The water was so high, and running fast. As soon as I pulled him out I tried and tried to revive him, but it was too late."

I pulled a soggy leaf out of Marshall's thick, dark hair and brushed it back from his handsome face. It was as cold as the melted ice under Father's embalming table.

"Oh my God, Farly—he's—he's—!"

"I found him in Muddy Creek, just under the bridge on the road to the cemetery."

That was Section Line road, just south of the McClung house. "But Marshall is a good swimmer," I wailed. "The *best* swimmer. How could he—how could he *drown*?" The word felt like poison on my lips.

"The creek is high after all the rain," Farly said. "There are some funny currents in there, and you can't see where it's going to drop off."

I must do something—I had to make it better. What could I do? My brother drowned. He was *dead*. I tried to grasp reality. "Dear God! I've got to get Father and Mother!"

"Go ahead," said Farly. "I'll stay here with him."

We learned later that Marshall had stopped by the bridge to water his horse at the trough that is maintained there for the purpose, and he decided to cool off in the creek on his way home. He left his horses in the charge of a young boy who was playing nearby, and it was this boy who yelled when Farly came

185

along the road on his horse. Marshall was swimming in the creek, the boy said, and suddenly he was gone. Farly leapt off his horse, putting the reins in the boy's hands, pulled off his shoes, and dove in. He had to dive several times before he found my brother, and he pulled him out of the water and laid him on the bank, doing all he could to revive him. When nothing would bring Marshall back to life, the boy called his older brother who helped Farly load him on the wagon to bring him home.

We never really understood why a good swimmer and strong young man like Marshall would drown in Muddy Creek. It was more dangerous than usual, of course, being swelled by the recent rain. But that hadn't stopped many other young people from cooling off through countless summers past. Mother said maybe he had just had his lunch and got a cramp. She was always telling him not to go swimming right after eating, she said; why hadn't he listened?

We held the viewing in our parlor, where so many other people from Mason had received their final goodbyes. Father, of course, did not do the preparations; he called on an undertaker friend from Lebanon to handle the preparation and burial arrangements. But Marshall was laid in one of our best caskets, and buried in Rose Hill Cemetery where sixteen years earlier Rebecca McClung had been laid to rest. Marshall had drowned less than two hundred yards from the bedroom where Mrs. McClung was murdered.

I called the cartridge company to say I wouldn't be coming in for a few days. But I knew after those few days I was still not capable of concentrating on the precise work needed to produce the best shells for our servicemen, so the days stretched to a couple of weeks. Besides, I needed to be at home. Unlike many less fortunate families, my parents had never lost a child until that day Farly Dwire faithfully brought Marshall home to his family. At the C. C. Miller Funeral Home, the business of death needed to go on, even while the experience of death was still raw. I helped Mother with household tasks, for my sake as well as for hers, and tried to pamper my father with hugs and fresh-baked cookies. Inside, we all were hurting.

I sent a letter to Hans Schmitt to tell him about Marshall's death. Hans was in Columbus at that time, and I had encouraged him to be there. How I would have loved to have him nearby to be a comfort after Marshall's passing. But he was in Columbus partly at my urging.

Hans had grown to be almost six feet tall by the end of high school, and even though I was still taller than the other girls, I had to look up to him. His father had died in 1906, I think, from infection following a horrific accident with a grain thresher. Following his death, Hans and his brother Wilhelm continued as tenant farmers on the Wikoff property until Hans graduated high school. Wilhelm had never attended school in Ohio, and had only a grade-school education. He wanted more for his brother, and insisted Hans continue in school, even though it made his own life more difficult on the farm. High school wasn't free in those days, but every year city council granted several scholarships to promising and needy students, and Father, serving then as councilman, made sure Hans was one of them.

Hans and I continued to be friendly through the years, although we did not often walk home together when we were older. On the evening of our graduation in the Opera House, Hans and I hugged and promised each other we would always be friends.

All through high school, Hans was smitten with beautiful Elsa Bergstrom. Her parents were Swedish, and she had the fine features and long, flaxen hair of her ancestry. We all assumed she and Hans would be married one day. But that last summer after graduation, Lucille's older brother came home from the college he attended back east, bringing a friend who was going to spend the summer on their farm, and by August the friend and Elsa were engaged. The town was shocked. Most of us suspected that Elsa's family probably encouraged the romance with the medical student who had a seemingly more promising future than Hans the farmer. In October Elsa and her parents boarded a train to

Boston for the wedding, and I never saw the woman in Mason again. It's probably a good thing; if she had shown up, I might have ripped her eyes out for what she did to Hans.

After high school, Hans and his brother moved to a small farm outside of Lebanon, where Wilhelm hoped to soon buy his own land and start a family. I didn't see Hans for several years after that, because Lebanon was closer than Mason and larger for buying supplies.

But then, one spring evening in 1917, we met again. A few years after the Rebolds moved in to their big, fancy house on Main Street, Ethel's father built himself a new store right next door to the old McClung house. The building's second floor became Rebold's Hall, a social hall that brought bands and entertainment and lots of young people from Mason and others who lived or worked along the Rapid Railway. One Saturday evening in April there was to be a dance, and I had arranged with Sharon, a new friend from work, to meet there.

Mr. Rebold greeted me warmly when we entered his store. We had to walk inside and then up the stairs to get to the social hall, so he was there to oversee the evening. I asked him about Ethel, and he said she was doing well and happy living in Cincinnati with her husband, but she missed her friends in Mason.

The band that evening included a couple of saxophone players, a trumpet, trombone, and drums. Sharon and I were enjoying the music, watching some of the dancers, when I felt a touch on my arm from behind. I whirled around, and there he was.

His face was ruddy and rougher-looking than when he was younger, weathered from farm work. But his smile was just as sweet as always.

"Izzy! I'm so glad to find you here."

And I, of course, was happy to see him. I introduced him to Sharon, and Hans asked her some polite questions, but Sharon understood the situation and was soon off chatting with another group and eventually found her way to the dance floor.

Hans and I danced, two-steps and fox trots, and in between we caught up with each other. I told him about my new job at the cartridge factory, and Hans said he had been thinking of going to work there as well. His brother wanted his help on the farm, but the pay was better at Peters.

We didn't go too deep into our work lives; this talk was too serious for a fun evening. We danced some more, and I was surprised to see that Hans was a natural. He had lost much of his German accent, too, having spent more of his life in America now than in his native country. We finished the evening dancing to "By the Light of the Silvery Moon," and I gave Hans our family telephone number. He promised to call soon, from a public telephone in Lebanon, probably, and we'd get together again.

Instead, he surprised me early one morning after I started walking up Main Street to board the trolley at the Rapid Railway station. Coming toward me was a one-horse buggy, with Hans driving.

"Izzy! Hop aboard!" he said, pulling the horse to a stop. "No rail car for you today. I'll drive you to work!"

I was delighted, of course, and climbed up next to him on the seat. Before we turned and started off, he handed me a little package wrapped in paper. I didn't even have to open it to know what was inside—the wonderful aroma gave it away.

"You bought me a donut!"

"I thought you might like a bite to eat on the way, so I stopped at the bakery." The waiting room for the Rapid Railway was inside the bakery, and on days when the weather was unpleasant, I would sit inside until the trolley came. But being frugal with my money, I only enjoyed the aromas instead of the tastes. So, Hans's offering was a treat.

"I have to admit I have a selfish reason for giving you a ride today," Hans said, as we turned right onto the Kings Mills road. "I need your opinion."

He told me about George, a friend whose father ran a butcher shop in Lebanon. One day when Hans was buying some

189

meat at the shop, George told him he would no longer be working for his father. He was on his way to Columbus, to train at an Army flight school housed at Ohio State University. Hans was enthralled. All of us, and perhaps the whole world, were excited when the newspapers trumpeted the news of Wilbur and Orville Wright's first flights in 1903, and we eagerly followed the development of air flight in the years following. Hans said that in early summer the Army had completed a training field outside of Dayton on land where the Wright brothers had tested their early fliers. George had been there, and watched one of the double-wing fliers land and roll to a stop, trailing a cloud of dust. But before a prospective pilot could train there, he must first complete ground training at the university, and that's where George was headed.

I'll always remember the next moment. The sun was just coming up, and when Hans turned toward me on that buggy seat, the rosy rays lit up his face, and his hair that had darkened some since fifth grade caught the sun, too, and lit it up in a hundred shades of gold. But it was his eyes that shone the brightest.

"I've been thinking, Izzy." I sensed what was coming, and he almost whispered it, a combination of reluctance and reverence. "Do you think I could learn to fly?"

I saw it all—the long voyage from Germany when he was so young, adjusting to a new country and learning a new language, losing the girl he hoped to marry, and especially all those years subject to his father's temper and control. What better way to break free than to soar into the sky?

I didn't say this to Hans, of course, but I did tell him I thought it was a wonderful idea, and of course he could learn to fly.

His expression dulled when he recited the reasons not to follow this dream that had dropped into his head and heart like a star from the sky. He had an obligation to his brother, who had encouraged him continuously during the school years to learn all he could, and who now counted on his help on the farm because he was to be married soon. And what about money? Certainly there would be some cost. Maybe the Army wouldn't even want him. As he explained all this, our buggy passed a couple of automobiles parked on the side of the road by the entrance to the King Powder Company, along the steep winding road toward the river. We were about to cross the bridge; in a minute or two we'd be at the cartridge factory where Hans would leave me.

"Go find out," I told him. "Do everything you can. Otherwise, you will never know, and you'll wish you had. Your brother can hire someone on the farm if he needs to. And promise me that when you do learn to fly, I'll be the first person you tell what it's like."

Hans continued working on his brother's farm, giving it all he had for as long as he was there, just in case. He telephoned me when he was accepted into the flight program in early June, and we planned a date to celebrate and say goodbye before he left for Columbus on June 16.

Hans arrived on the trolley, and from my family's house we walked down Main Street to Mr. LaMar's newly-opened restaurant and ate the best hamburgers I'd ever tasted. From there we continued down Main Street to the new Princess Theater, almost across the street from the McClung house where our friendship started, and watched a Charlie Chaplin movie called *By the Sea*. It was my very first movie, and the first time I ever saw moving ocean waves, never having traveled to the seashore to see them in person. Hans and I started laughing from the moment Chaplin carelessly dropped a banana peel on the pier and then stepped on it, his feet flying out from under him. I especially liked how when a pretty woman came along, he'd raise his eyebrows, and his hat would go up right along with them—how did he do that?

Hans walked me back home after the movie was over, and we promised to write to each other while he was in Columbus. He expected the ground training to take about eight weeks, and after that, if he did well enough, he would train at Wilbur Wright field near Dayton, where he would actually fly. He thanked me for encouraging him, and held both my hands as he kissed me on the forehead to say goodbye.

So Hans was in Columbus when Marshall drowned two weeks later, and all I could do was write him a letter. He wrote back right away, saying he wished he could be with me but he could not take any days off from the intensive ground training. He would pray for our family, he said; I felt his prayers, and they were some comfort.

I finally returned to the Peters factory. They had been hiring like crazy ever since our country entered the war in April, and during this time of peak production we were turning out one-and-a-half million cartridge shells a day. A division of Ohio Army soldiers guarded the gunpowder and cartridge-making factories to prevent any enemy attacks on these vital supplies. We loved seeing the soldiers, many my age and younger, patrolling the property in their uniforms and broad-brimmed hats. They were billeted in a barracks in the village of Kings Mills, and sometimes I'd see a couple of them walking sleepy-eyed down the road to the factory as I arrived at work. We had all been saddened in May when one of the newly-arrived recruits drowned while swimming in the Little Miami River that ran between the two factories, but I didn't know him personally. Perhaps it was a foreshadowing of what would happen to Marshall the next month.

The high points of that summer and fall were the letters from Hans. None were long, as he was not used to being so "paddocked," as he called it, spending long hours in stuffy classrooms and his small dormitory room studying. In the free time he had, he preferred walks outside to sitting and writing letters. But he made it clear he was anxious to get in an actual airplane rather than just talking and reading about it.

Hans and I had such a short time together between the dance at Rebold's Hall and his departure for Columbus that I was unsure how to view our relationship. He was a friend, as always, but was there anything more? Could there be, in time? I tried to push the thoughts away. He was chasing a dream we both hoped would come true, and that was enough for now.

He sent the news in September that he had passed his ground training and had moved in to the barracks at Wilbur Wright Field just east of Dayton. "Look up!" he wrote. "I may be in the sky when you read this!" He signed his letter "Hans Schmitt, Flight Cadet."

He probably was not in the air when I read that letter, because it was about a week later before he wrote, as promised, the letter that described his first flight.

He explained that the cadets flew in aircraft designed by Glenn Curtiss, the famous flight pioneer, and all of the airplanes were girls named Jenny. Hans sat in the front seat, under the top wing, and his instructor sat in the other seat behind him, under the open sky. The flying machine had two spoked front wheels like those on my bicycle, he said, and a small one under the tail; and the airplane tore across the field faster than he had ever gone in his life before rising from the ground, leaving the dust behind.

"You may think I felt like a bird," Hans wrote, "but the clattering of the engine and the buzz of the propeller were louder than any bird I know, and Jenny lumbered into the air like a dog plunging into the creek. It's smoother when she levels out in the air above, but still there are updrafts you can't see until you're in them, and the big wings catch them all.

"But the view—that's when I felt like a bird. All around me were struts and wires, but you can look beyond them to the horizon stretching as far as you can see, the big blue sky with its puffy clouds sitting atop the crazy quilt of earth. The fields of corn and tobacco and beans below are patches of brown and green, each patch the realm of a farmer tied to cycles of planting and harvesting. I saw brown stripes of road, and even a gray one, paved with macadam, I guess. On the stripes you see little squares that are wagons with toy horses pulling them, and the occasional automobiles that move a bit faster but are still crawling along like ants on a leisurely stroll.

"It is amazing to think that most of us live all our lives crawling like them on the earth, when above us is another whole world that stretches without end, all the way to the stars. To look down and see how small each of us is on the world is humbling, but it is more humbling yet to realize that infinitely higher than Jenny and I can fly there is God, who watches over it all. And I never felt closer to God than when I was flying in that airplane."

I read that letter over and over until I knew it by heart and I could close my eyes and imagine sitting with Hans in that airplane, freed of the bonds that hold us to earth.

Hans completed his primary flight training in December, and although he (and I) hoped he would have time to come home for Thanksgiving, the Army was anxious to get its new pilots trained as quickly as possible so they could join the war. So in mid-November Hans boarded a train in Dayton (I pictured how the train would look from the air, a caterpillar crawling along a line of track) that took him all the way to California for advanced training on the Army's Rockwell Field.

A couple of weeks later, I was excited to bring home a letter from the post office that had traveled all the way across the country, addressed to me. In perhaps the longest letter I had received, Hans wrote of the long train ride from Ohio, including some of the stops along the way, and then of his new home in southern California. The flight school was on a peninsula of land that the Army shared with the Navy, sticking into the Pacific Ocean with San Diego Bay on one side and the ocean on the other. It was warm there, even though Christmas was only a month away, and once he had walked barefoot along the skinny strip of land that tied North Island to the mainland, with water on both sides of him. It was hard to believe, Hans said, that he dipped his feet in the same ocean we had seen in the Charlie Chaplin movie less than half a year earlier. He wished I could be there with him to hear the crashing surf and the gulls calling in the salty air, and to see the sun glitter on the water like a million diamonds. I had to set the letter down to keep a tear from falling on it.

Hans ended his letter by saying he wrote such a long one because he was confined to quarters that day, laid up with a cold.

He expected to feel better in the morning, and although it was nice to have a day of rest, he couldn't wait to get back in the air.

Two weeks later, on a dreary day in early December, my supervisor at work called me away from my cartridge-stuffing work station. "There's a young man here to see you," he said, not looking happy about it. "He says it's urgent."

I felt a shiver of dread. It had not been long since one of my co-workers had been interrupted at work and learned her older brother had been killed in the war. No one in my family was fighting, but I assumed the young man must be one of my brothers, and immediately thought something must have happened to one of our parents.

I hurried to the office where my supervisor directed. There, with hat in hand and head bowed low, was Hans's brother Wilhelm.

"Hello, Izzy," said Wilhelm, his voice hollow and soft. "Hans would want you to see this."

He unfolded a letter and handed it to me. I took a deep breath, and searched Wilhelm's eyes, seeing nothing but defeat.

"Sir, I regret very much to inform you that your brother, Hans Schmitt, has died in the line of duty at Rockwell Field. After becoming ill he was under care in our infirmary but sadly succumbed to pneumonia . . ."

Wilhelm took me home; I don't remember the ride. But I do remember looking at him and seeing Hans in his blue eyes, and the desperation of wanting him to *be* Hans, my friend whom I would never see, never talk with again.

Still bewildered from Marshall's tragic death, I lost all sense of order and purpose with this new loss. The whole world had gone mad and taken me with it. Pneumonia? My dear flight cadet who had soared to the skies died in a lowly infirmary bed? It was not noble; it was not fair. It made no sense, and suddenly everything I thought I knew made no sense.

Father informed Peters Cartridge Factory I would not return to work. My family tip-toed around my feelings; even Milly tried to cheer me with smiles and crayoned pictures of dogs and rainbows. Mother tried to keep me busy with household chores, and my hands and feet dutifully performed them, but my heart refused to awaken.

Months later, it was Father who was able to first stir my interest in anything. "You need a project," he said. "A crusade; a quest; a challenge. Think back. What is something you always wanted to do—or to learn?"

He held my gaze, waiting for an answer. And so I thought back.

"Who killed Rebecca McClung," I heard myself say.

He didn't laugh; he didn't shake his head; he didn't even smile. "Then find out."

CHAPTER EIGHTEEN

Dayton Daily News

Lebanon, July 12, 1901 — The failure of the authorities to convict in this case only adds another murder mystery to the nomenclature in Warren county. The list of dark and unsolved tragedies now numbers 16. Several of these crimes can be safely numbered among the most foul and revolting murders of the age, but the murderers have cunningly hidden their trail and tangible clues have never been discovered.

I needed information, as much as I could get. First, I retrieved from the top shelf in my clothes closet the journal I had made during the trial in 1901. Despite my determination then to be meticulous and professional like my aunt the stenographer, I was dismayed to find that my notes, not surprisingly, looked like those of the child I still was. I mostly neglected to record the sources of my observations, tending to trust what adults told me and recording it as truth, without considering possible bias on the part of those who had known John McClung for years. Ironically, the most helpful insight I gleaned from my notes was not the information they contained but the answers they lacked. Many of the questions I scribbled then, that I hoped to answer in further research, were still relevant today, such as these:

Would a man hate his wife's brothers so much that he would kill that wife to hurt them?

Could a man as old and sickly as John McClung really be able to come downstairs, start two fires, pick up two pieces of firewood, carry them up the stairs, beat his wife to a pulp, come back downstairs with the same wood, throw it in the fire and wash his hands, and then go out and do his chores in the stable like nothing had happened?

These were questions that mere facts and information probably could not answer, and John McClung, the only one who could really speak to his motives and physical strength, was buried in the Mason cemetery.

My journal was not the only record I had from 1901, however; I also had saved every newspaper article about the murder I could lay my hands on, and stuffed them in a big brown envelope that I found on the shelf under the journal. The newspapers ranged from our hometown *Mason Appeal* to big city papers in Dayton and Cincinnati that I had gathered from friends and family and even bought myself from Mr. Rebold's store. Perhaps the most helpful newspaper was Lebanon's *Western Star*, because it came from the nearby seat of our county government, where the McClung trial was held. It was only a weekly paper, but I had clippings from every issue pertaining to the case, thanks to my Aunt Inez who had indulged my pleas to get them for me since she worked right there.

As I read through the yellowed articles, the horror, amazement, anger and craving for justice the whole town felt toward the crime came alive again and stirred in me the same feeling of *unfairness* I had felt as a child. Bad things happened to people who weren't careful or who stirred up trouble, not to quiet old women who stayed in their house. Even at age eleven I knew that life was not often fair, but that didn't mean you had to accept it. Now that I had seen so much more of both the evil and the good in the world, I read the articles more carefully. I began to see a thin thread of possibility woven through the evidence—references to other horrendous crimes around the same time as Rebecca McClung's murder. As the news of her demise spread quickly through Mason, the first thought of most was that would-be robbers were responsible. It was widely known that the McClungs did not use banks, and so they must hold their great wealth within their big shuttered-up house. The robbers, it was thought, entered the house as soon as they saw John make his customary early-morning trip to the barn, killed his wife so she could not identify them, and then were frightened away before they could find the money they came for. Sallie Baysore, after all, was a relatively new resident in the house, and her commotion after hearing Rebecca's screams may have surprised them.

The infamous day was not yet over, however, before people heard Coroner George Carey's verdict that the death was caused by "multiple blows upon her head and face inflicted by some blunt instrument in the hands of her husband John McClung." He also announced Mr. McClung had murdered her while under "mental aberration," although this was not part of the official verdict. Was it the coroner's job to declare who committed the crime, and why? John was arrested that day due to Carey's statement, and the horror of an old man beating his wife to death right in their village drew a great crowd to the preliminary hearing in the Opera House.

But alternative views continued to float like dark mists through the proceedings. John McClung himself said he had suspicions as to the guilty party, and some of his friends felt the same. George Tetrick, the contractor, said John was certainly not insane, and that possibly he was arrested to allay suspicion while the authorities were running down the robbers who were the real murderers.

The papers noted that the McClung case was dragging along slowly; one article said the defense seemed to be prolonging the trial as much as possible, but no one knew why. The defense team had employed a detective, the papers said, and hinted more than once that he would have something startling to tell. Finally, Judge Runyan, McClung's defense attorney, shed some light when he stated in his closing argument that the detective's work had led him to the conclusion that sometime in the near future a confession or a conviction would be made that would exonerate John McClung. Runyan referred to several other cases of robbery and murder, apparently carried out by a ruthless gang that attacked people known to have money, and thought the McClung case was another of these. But the detective's work could not be introduced as evidence.

Who were these gang members? Were they ever brought to justice? Could they have been responsible for Rebecca McClung's murder?

Judge Runyan mentioned three examples in his statement: the Stites murder, and the Thompson and McCammon robberies. These all happened shortly before Rebecca McClung's murder. The Thompson robbery I remembered; the elderly couple were gagged and tied to the bed while several robbers ransacked the house, and only escaped death by Mr. Thompson cleverly accessing a knife in his pocket to cut the cords. My parents had talked about the crime, and said it was the cause of the McClungs deciding to stay in Mason village rather than moving back out to the countryside. The Stites name sounded familiar; of McCammon I had no recollection.

For help, I turned again to my Aunt Inez. She had been married for eight or nine years now, and lived in Cincinnati with her husband Elmer, who worked in real estate. Inez had left her stenography job when she got married, but she and Elmer continued to live in my grandparents' house in Mason until first Grandma passed away in 1908 and then Grandpa in 1910. During that time Elmer worked as a pharmacist in Lebanon, so Inez, too, continued to visit the county seat where she had worked in the courthouse. If she had still lived nearby, I might have enlisted her as a partner in my murder investigation, for she had no children to keep her busy; instead, I had to make a long-distance telephone call to Cincinnati.

"Stites!" she exclaimed, as soon as I mentioned the crimes I wanted to investigate. "Of course I remember the case! I saw the full range of humanity in that courthouse, but I never saw such a parade of riff-raff in all my life as those brought in for the Stites murder. Illiterate, many of them, signing the court documents with their "X"; they came from both the tenements of Middletown and the hills near Oregonia. Both black and white, young and old; I never could figure how they all got connected in the affair, except that lowlifes seem to attract lowlifes, and none of them were to be trusted."

Inez told me that court records were stored in a stuffy room deep inside the courthouse, and I may be able to look at them. She also recommended visiting the offices of the *Western Star* newspaper, for she had heard they kept copies of every newspaper they ever printed. The Stites murder, she remembered, had received much press because of its brutality and a number of twists and turns in the case.

The next day I boarded the trolley to Lebanon armed with a notebook, two pencils, and my notes from the telephone call with Inez. The *Western Star* offices were on Mulberry Street, not far from the trolley station, housed in part of an imposing three-story brick building topped with a clock tower. I climbed the stairs to the second floor, and was greeted by a young receptionist who listened to my request with interest. After she consulted with someone farther down the hall, I was escorted to the archives room by a young man with smudges of ink on his white shirt and across his left cheek.

The room was small and stuffy, lined with steel shelves that reached to the ceiling. The young man seated me at a wooden table with two straight-back chairs, and ventured into the shelves to find the boxes holding newspapers from 1900 and 1901.

"There's at least one copy of each of the papers," he explained as he set the last of the boxes on the table. "Please be gentle with them, and refold them and place them back in the box in the proper order when you are finished. You can leave the boxes on the table when you are done."

I thanked the man, took a deep breath, and dug in.

Hezekiah Stites was seventy years old at the time of his murder, a giant of a man, six-and-a-half feet tall and sturdily built. A bachelor, he lived all his life in the same log house where he was born, just outside Oregonia, a village east of Lebanon and about fifteen miles from Mason. The house stood in a mostly secluded area on a hill overlooking earthworks of the ancient mound-building natives. He was known as an honest, upright, and worthy man who quietly tended strictly to his own affairs.

Entirely self-educated, Stites was a great reader, especially of scientific works, and his home was cluttered with books, newspapers, magazines, and memorabilia. For forty years he carefully observed the weather, recording temperature and rainfall every morning and evening at seven o'clock. Although a recluse, he was not miserly; he freely bought literature, flowers, and other simple comforts of life.

He was known to have money, and for this he lost his life in early February of 1900. The murder was discovered by a neighbor named Emmons who came to borrow a magazine, and getting no answer, looked in the window and saw him lying on the floor. After forcing entry and discovering Stites bloody and dead, Emmons immediately called for Coroner George Carey, who began an investigation.

Mr. Stites's pants had been removed and the pockets rifled; four or five pocket-books were found emptied and tossed into a bucket. The motive of the crime seemed to be robbery, and the amount taken was eventually estimated to be about $250.

Coroner Carey arranged for a post-mortem examination by another doctor, who found that Stites had been dead for about three days before the body was discovered. A partially written letter to a friend was found on the desk, along with Stites's meticulous weather records. The date and time of the last entry was helpful in determining when the murder occurred. The cause of death was blows to the head with a heavy blunt object, aggravated by strangulation.

Blood was pooled on the floor and spattered the walls and furnishings. Bloody bits of paper were found, apparently used by the murderers to wipe their hands after the deed was done. The apparent murder weapons were also found on the floor: two pieces of bloody wood, the same type as that stacked by the kitchen stove.

When I first read this in the newspaper archive, I drew in my breath so sharply the receptionist stepped in to see if I was all right. Two pieces of stove wood were used to pound Hezekiah Stites on the head until he was insensible. Two pieces of stove wood were used to beat Rebecca McClung on the head until she was dead. Two pieces of bloody wood.

Of course, I told myself, this was a full fourteen months before the McClung murder. If the robbers who killed Hezekiah Stites had been found, they must have been safely in jail by the time Rebecca was killed. I continued to search.

Immediately the *Western Star* reported that it seemed to be "well understood" that those people guilty of Mr. Stites's murder lived not far from the scene of the crime, and nearly everyone in the area felt assured of their identity, but people were afraid to make their suspicions public and there was no proof available. One week after the murder, the county commissioners offered a $1,000 reward for information that would lead to the arrest and conviction of the murderers.

From the beginning, several names appeared often in the newspaper articles detailing the arrests in the case. The first of these was Ralston. One month following Stites's murder, two Ralston brothers, Clarence, age twenty, and Leon, fourteen, of Oregonia, were arrested for theft of a revolver taken from the Stites home. The window had been broken and several other articles taken along with the revolver. The theft had occurred almost a year earlier, and the gun sold and resold before the murder, so it was astonishing that the crime should be pursued at this time. Clarence pled guilty to the charge, and Leon served as a witness and was later released. In their trial, testimony from fourteen witnesses established that the theft had not been made public at the time it happened because Stites feared retaliation from the burglars. Much of the testimony was startling because of its seeming relation to the murder case, but the defense was careful and would not allow Leon to testify for fear he would incriminate himself. The Ralston brothers were never charged in connection with the murder.

The next name that filled the papers, beginning three months after the murder, was Upton—Newton, age 40, and his nephew

Frank, 25, who lived in Morrow, a town not far from Lebanon. The events leading to their arrest began a sensational, convoluted story of greed, rejected love, collusion, ignorance, and perjury that must have been more suspenseful than a crime novel for readers of the *Western Star*.

It started with a visit of two strangers to a Lebanon restaurant. Following their meal, one of the men, when pulling money from his wallet to pay at the counter, dropped a page from a letter on the floor. Because of its startling contents, the paper was turned in to the sheriff's office, and a transcript printed in the newspaper. In scribbled phrases with many misspellings, in handwriting that looked like a woman's, the writer said she had been told by a woman named Hessie Berger that Newt Upton and a relative killed Hezekiah Stites and got cash. They had robbed him once before, the Berger woman said, and told Stites if he said anything about it, they would kill him. Hessie Berger told the writer that she was supposed to marry Newt Upton, but found out he was already married so she changed her mind.

This letter led to the arrest of Frank and Newton Upton, as well as a supposed accomplice named Harry Ring. They were brought before Justice Carey (the one who also served as coroner in the case), and charged with the murder of Hezekiah Stites. Miss Hessie Berger, age eighteen and illiterate, was arrested to serve as a witness.

In the preliminary hearing, it was discovered that Frank Upton had once worked for Stites on his farm, and the two were on bad terms. He was seen in the neighborhood shortly before the crime was committed. Two witnesses testified they had heard Newton Upton make threats to Stites. Newton Upton was held to appear before the grand jury. But due to a lack of firm evidence, his nephew Frank was released.

The next day Robert Harlan, of Middletown, was arrested to serve as a witness; he had succeeded Newton Upton as the lover of Miss Berger.

When Hessie Berger, considered the star witness, testified in the hearing, she said "Newt Upton told me that he had killed old

Stites. He said he and his nephew, Frank Upton, did it. They took sticks of wood from the woodpile, went in through a window and pounded the old man over the head."

Her testimony and that of other witnesses established that five months before the murder, Newton Upton had robbed Stites at night, and threatened his victim with death if he talked. Finding the old man so easy, Berger said, Upton returned in February, pried open the window, and robbed and killed Stites. In response to this damning testimony, the grand jury indicted Newton Upton on a charge of first-degree murder.

It seemed justice would finally be served. But the grand jury's charge against Upton came with the intent to reconsider his case a few weeks later when they hoped evidence more than hearsay would be found. Not finding any, and believing that Upton, who had been sitting in jail for two months, was entitled to either a trial or his freedom, they released him in July 1900.

The poisoning of a young woman under very odd circumstances at the end of August may or may not have been connected to the Stites murder. Abbie Mountjoy, a seventeen-year-old girl in a poor family living less than ten miles from the home of the murdered Hezekiah Stites, became deathly sick from drinking water containing Paris Green, a strong pesticide found in her family's woodshed for use on their potato vines. Suspicions pointed to Edward Lewis, who was married to her older sister, as compelling her to drink the poison. Abbie's eleven-year-old brother Robert saw her talking with Edward, and their older sister Susie met Edward coming from their house as she returned home. Abbie, however, said a tramp had come along and made her take the drink, saying he would kill her if she refused. Robert said he hadn't seen any tramp. Edward's wife Nancy Lewis, although not present at the Mountjoy home, said she believed her husband had forced her sister to take the poison. Abbie died two days later, and George Carey, the coroner, investigated and declared it was murder. There was talk among some folks that Abbie's death was connected to that of Stites. She may have had knowledge about the murder, and was poisoned to keep her out of the way. Abbie, however, had shown some symptoms of depression in the past, and her death was eventually ruled a suicide. Edward Lewis was not charged.

There was no more news about the Stites murder the rest of that year. But just a few months later, one week before Christmas, the reclusive bachelor Michael Fryman, who lived in a house near Middletown, was assaulted. He was the one who, after he was tortured and robbed, lay bound, gagged and unconscious outside his front door all night until he was found the next morning by a passerby. Several things struck me as I read the short article about this crime. First, those assaulting him were four masked men. Second, they knew he had recently received money. And third, he was pounded with a wooden club until he was unconscious. I found no record of any arrest in the case.

Three days later, on December 21, it was four men again who broke into the Thompsons' house while they were eating dinner, gagged them and tied them to the bed, and ransacked the house. Mr. Thompson heard one of them comment, "Ain't got as much money as when I used to be around here," indicating the robber lived in the area or at least had at one time, and knew they had money. Another similarity to the Fryman case was the threat of torture; Mr. Fryman was burned with a poker heated in the fireplace to elicit information, and the Thompsons were threatened with a hot fireplace shovel.

This time, however, the perpetrators had left a trail. A witness had seen four men with two rigs in the woods near her home; the men had hitched the horses there and were feeding them. The authorities brought in bloodhounds that caught the trail where the horses had been hitched and followed it to the Thompson home and back again to where they had left the rigs. They were unable, however, to follow the trail once the men were back in their buggies. The neighbor who had spotted the men and their rigs remembered that one man was very large, something Mr. Thompson also mentioned. She said one of the horses was white, and another a dark bay, and both buggies had red running-gears and rubber tires. Some people in the nearby Shaker community saw the men and buggies later that evening at a local saloon. The men were very drunk, witnesses said; the Thompsons had noticed a strong smell of liquor on the breath of the robbers.

Four days after the robbery, three men answering the description of those seen at the saloon following the time of the robbery were arrested. One had worked recently for the Thompsons; the others were familiar with the neighborhood. Just before the last day of 1900, however, the charges against the men were dropped when the prosecutors discovered they had been positively identified riding on a train near Middletown at the time of the robbery. This was remarkable! Either the ones arrested were not the same ones seen by witnesses at the saloon, or the supposed timing of the events was badly mistaken. Whatever the case, the actual culprits were still at large.

No other arrests were made and no one was being held in any of these cases—Stites, Fryman, and Thompson—in the first quarter of 1901. Any of the perpetrators theoretically would have been free, then, to murder Rebecca McClung on April 12.

CHAPTER NINETEEN

If all of these hours and days and weeks spent poking around in old newspapers for stories about murder and criminals seems gruesome, it actually was a kind of escape from all the news about the War. Battles and tactics, bombs and deaths, Germans, Turks, Brits and French filled the newspapers, and served only to depress me. In May came news of the first death of a soldier from Warren County, and the solemn reality of the Great War settled on our town like a heavy fog. In June, twenty-one-year-old Marine Luther O'Banion of Mason was killed in action in France. Later that year the son of our postmaster, an Army Private, was buried in French soil. So studying crimes long past seemed almost tame compared to the reality of an ongoing war.

Of course, there were lighter moments in my life, too. Especially memorable was a family outing to our town theater to see two Charlie Chaplin movies. Although at first I thought only of Hans and the Chaplin movie we had seen together, I soon was laughing right along with Mother, Father, and Frank. The next day I wrote a letter to Mildred in Michigan and told her all about the movies. My favorite was *The Adventurer*, in which Charlie played an escaped convict in a striped prison suit; he eluded the police chasing him just as easily as murderers closer to my home seemed to elude the county sheriff. Charlie, however, was of much better character than our local criminals; in the movie, he also rescued several people from drowning in the ocean. The funniest part was when Charlie and the policeman got in a kicking match, a woman came up from behind, and the policeman kicked her by mistake, right in her derriere. The movie ended with Charlie running again from the police; I had a good feeling he would never be caught. Maybe he ran all the way to Ohio.

After I finished my letter to Mildred I was off to Lebanon again, this time to the courthouse to search official records of the McClung case. An elderly woman with her hair in a tight gray bun and round spectacles perched on her nose was there to assist me. Staid as she may have first appeared, she broke into a smile that took twenty years off her face when I explained to her my mission. "I never see normal people back here," she said. "It's only lawyers' assistants and such. Not that they aren't normal, of course; but they just talk about precedents and jurisdictions and former indictments. Never the *people* involved. These are not just court cases, you know; they are the stories of people's lives at their most crucial and exciting points; their sins most despicable, their justice most sweet."

The dear, lonely woman was happy to help me. The court records, however, were mostly disappointing, lacking all sense of the excitement of people's lives she spoke about. First, I was given a heavy, oversized book of court proceedings, and the friendly attendant helped me find the beginning point for the McClung case. The handwritten record began with the names of the jury duly impaneled, continued with the indictment against John McClung accusing him of murder "contrary to the form and statute in such case made and provided, and against the peace and dignity of the state of Ohio." Next came a daily record of the court proceedings, each stating in identical words that the prosecutor and his assistant came to court, along with the defense attorneys and the witnesses; it was studded with words like "heretofore" and "aforesaid." What I wanted to see was not there: what did the witnesses say? Their names were not even given. Each daily entry ended with a statement that since the proceedings were not complete and the time of adjournment had come, the case was continued until the next day.

Of little more help was the records of expenses for the case. At least this included a list of the various witnesses, along with the amount of travel expenses paid to each. Most of the names I recognized; some I knew well; a few were unfamiliar.

None of this provided any information that would help me in my quest. But the diligent attendant kept digging, and at last presented me with what I was looking for: a handwritten transcript of George Carey's coroner inquest held at the McClung house on the day of the murder. I copied it all into my notebook, my hand cramping with the effort.

The notebook is here beside me now, the corners of the faded red cover peeling and the edges of the pages soft and fuzzy with age. I thumb through to about two-thirds back, just before the pages that feel newer, unused, and open it. With the desk lamp turned on and my magnifying glass in hand, I can still make out my handwriting, if I bend close, even with my failing eyesight. I turn back several pages and find the where the transcript begins, and I remember the excitement I felt over thirty years ago in the courthouse basement when I first read the actual words spoken by John McClung just hours after his wife was murdered.

One phrase from the many newspaper articles that appeared soon after the murder occurred had always stood out to me. The stories reported, over and over, that John McClung never denied killing his wife; the only answer he gave when asked was, "If I did it, I didn't know it." A variation of this comment was, "If I killed her, I must have done it in my sleep." What a peculiar comment! When I first read these articles, back in 1901, I thought this was not what an innocent man would say when asked if he killed his wife. There should have been shock and outrage at the suggestion, horror just at the thought of murdering his beloved partner.

The occasion of this comment was not usually stated in the papers, but at least one reported it was an answer given to George Carey during the coroner's inquest. And that day at the courthouse in 1918 was the first time I had ever seen a transcript of the inquest. I read it eagerly.

Mr. Carey interviewed John McClung, Sallie Baysore, and Albert Dill within hours following the murder, with a few neighbors present to record the questions and answers. He began with John McClung. After some initial questions about John's actions that morning, Carey asked him if he knew how his wife was murdered; John said no, he saw what had happened and immediately sent for the doctor.

At the end of the interview, Carey asked John, "You are quite sure you do not know how your wife came to her death?"

John: "I don't know."

Carey: "Did you in absence of mind do it?"

John: "I don't know. Not to my knowledge."

Here, at last, was the source of John's supposed comment, "If I did it, I didn't know it." Carey's question put John, an efficient, practical man, in a logical dilemma. If he was not mindful of something he did, how could he now say whether he did it or not? Carey himself understood this when he was testifying at the preliminary hearing in the Opera House. He explained: "In fact he denied knowing anything about it and said if he did it he didn't know it, and if there was an absence of mind, why of course I did not know I did it."

In the coroner's inquest transcript, John several times denied he killed his wife: "It must have happened while I was at the stable," "I had nothing to do with it," and finally, when Carey asked him again if he could have killed her without knowing it, John replied, "I couldn't have done it. I didn't do it."

I learned something else from the transcript that I felt was important. John told Carey that the previous fall, one or more men tried to get in the McClung house. When they ordered him to open the door, John told them to leave or he would shoot them. Later, he found a shutter had been damaged where someone had tried to pry it open. John said he did not recognize the intruder's voice, but he had a suspicion of who it was.

Here was some substantiation for the robbery theory. The attempted entry at the McClungs' house was right after he sold the property to Albert Dill and Sallie Baysore, a time when he would be known to have money in the house. Could this attempted robbery be connected at all with Rebecca McClung's murder? Could either event be connected with any of the other three crimes I had researched? And the ultimate question: was

John McClung wrongly accused of his wife's murder, and if so, who was in fact responsible?

Although the perpetrators of the other crimes I had investigated had not been caught by the time of the McClung murder, I realized the cases remained open and the culprits might have eventually been brought to justice. Finding news that one of them had confessed to murdering Rebecca McClung was too much to expect, I knew; that would have been headline news across the county and perhaps the state. The murder was still occasionally talked about in town, and people still thought John McClung was probably responsible. The best I could hope for was to discover details that might provide links between the cases.

First, I considered the Thompson robbery, for interest in this case was revived during the time of John McClung's trial. The front page of the *Western Star* on the last Thursday in May 1901 included separate articles about each case. There was a detective in town from the northern part of Ohio, the paper said; he was investigating a crime that had occurred there that was similar in many respects to the Thompson case. Three men had been arrested up north, and two of these were said to be said to be from Middletown. "It is said" —by who, the paper did not report—"that it can be proven beyond a doubt that the men held for the crime in northern Ohio were at Lebanon at the time the Thompson robbery was committed." Lebanon, of course, was where the Thompsons lived. And less than ten miles from Mason.

The Thompson robbery had a different feel to it than the Stites murder. First of all, those who broke into Mr. and Mrs. Thompson's house had a revolver; none of the other crimes involved a gun. Secondly, the robbers were dressed well, according to the Thompsons, and they had enough money to rent themselves two buggies with rubber tires, probably from Dayton. Men such as these would have stood out as city folk in the backwoods where Hezekiah Stites was murdered in his log house, and seemed to be looking for a richer haul than Stites would have provided. Could these four men have killed Rebecca McClung? It seemed unlikely. Neither Rebecca's killer nor the one or ones who attempted a break-in the previous fall had a gun. If the Thompson robbers had been at the McClung house, John and Rebecca probably would have received a treatment similar to that of the Thompsons, and the house would have been ransacked. If someone had tried to rob the McClungs on the day of the murder, they left without attaining their goal; the only explanation for this was that they were scared away before they could find what they wanted. And, of course, many people found the simpler explanation to be that the one man known to be on the premises at the time, John McClung, was the murderer. The question was always, "If he didn't do it, then who did?"

Perhaps the answer could be found in the rogues' gallery of suspects and informants in the Hezekiah Stites murder. By the time John McClung went to trial and was found not guilty, due primarily to a lack of evidence, at least half a dozen suspects had been arrested in connection with the Stites case and released for the same reason. No further arrests were made in the Stites murder for more than a year after the release of Frank and Newton Upton, Harry Ring, and Robert Harlan. Then, in January 1902, the county commissioners increased the reward for an arrest and conviction in the case by $300, making it total $1,300.

This incentive apparently bore fruit. The next day, two women and three men were charged at Lebanon with the murder of Hezekiah Stites. Warrants were issued for the five because of an affidavit signed by a Middletown woman who had been living with Robert Harlan, the man detained in 1900 as a witness in the charges against Newton Upton. She was informing the authorities of the terrible crime committed by these men because she had become angry with Harlan. Harlan, it was believed, had been with Newton Upton when in 1898 they had robbed Hezekiah Stites of $200. If he talked, they told him, they would kill him. Stites had told some relatives of the theft, and the robbers apparently heard of this, providing the motive for the killing. If all the allegations of people robbing Hezekiah Stites were true, he had been robbed at least three times before the final theft when he was murdered.

Arrested along with Upton and Harlan was Vernon Lewis, brother of Edward Lewis, the one suspected in the poisoning death of Abbie Mountjoy. In addition to the three men, two women were also arrested; one of them was Hessie Berger, the "star witness" for the earlier hearing for Newton Upton. The other woman, Nellie Heron, claimed that William Lewis, a relative of Vernon and Edward Lewis, had told her before the murder that Stites was to be killed that night.

Exactly two years following the murder, in February 1902, the five charged appeared before Justice Carey. According to the story that unfolded, the gathering at the home of Hezekiah Stites sounded like a murder party. Vernon Lewis picked up Nellie Heron in his buggy, saying they would visit a sick neighbor, and took her to the Stites house instead, where they found William Lewis outside, looking in through a window. They saw Stites on the floor, with Newton Upton clubbing him; Robert Harlan was trying to choke him. The old man was fighting back, so William went in to help finish him off. Hessie Berger removed Stites's pants and took a pocketbook from his underclothing. Nellie Heron said she watched all this through the window, and afterward Vernon Lewis took her to the home of his brother Edward, who was caring for his wife who was ill. Nellie Heron's story was substantiated by Vernon Lewis, who said he had lived in terror ever since the murder, because Harlan had put a knife to his throat and said he would kill him with it if he ever told about what he saw that night.

Vernon Lewis, Hessie Berger, and Newton Upton were all held without bail awaiting a grand jury. Nellie Heron had been summoned to appear as a witness, but was not called to the stand, and was not sent to jail. William Lewis had not been apprehended.

The grand jury specially called to hear this case convened less than a week later. Witnesses testified to earlier conduct and conversations that portrayed Upton and Vernon Lewis as violent men who went about threatening residents of the area. During the proceedings, the name Ralston again arose—this time it was a man known as "Colonel" Ralston, the father of Clarence and Leon who had been arrested for stealing Stites's revolver and other items. He had been called as a witness, but soon found himself arrested for perjury and placed in jail. He was released a week later after the grand jury heard all the testimony and entered indictments. The hearing of Nellie Heron, Hessie Berger, Vernon Lewis and Newton Upton was continued to the May court term.

There was a whole gang of them! Young and old, white and black, male and female, from two or three neighboring counties. About all they seemed to have in common was poverty, lack of education, and a moral compass gone awry. The connections among them were not clear, nor was an understanding of who did exactly what, but it looked like justice would soon be served for Hezekiah Stites—and perhaps others. The *Western Star* commented, "There is a general feeling that at least a part of these people are guilty of old man Stites' cruel murder and that the others at least know more about it than they should. There has been so much lawlessness in this county that it is time to put a stop to it."

But more surprises were to come. Before the grand jury convened again in May, Nellie Heron and Vernon Lewis began to weaken in their story, and the prosecutors feared they could not be relied upon when called up at the trial. Finally, both admitted that the story they had told was false, and they knew nothing at all about the murder. Nellie said the story had been fed her by Allie Logan, a "lewd woman" from Middletown. The Logan woman had promised her a share of the $1,300 in reward money if she would testify to the story she told her.

Since the testimony of Nellie Heron and Vernon Lewis were the basis for the murder charges, Newton Upton and Hessie Berger were released from jail. Robert Harlan remained, serving an earlier sentence for pickpocketing. William Lewis was never apprehended. Nellie Heron, Vernon Lewis, and Allie Logan were later indicted for perjury; Logan also was charged with subornation of perjury. Vernon Lewis was found guilty and sentenced to three years in the penitentiary. Nellie Heron, however, was found to be too feeble-minded to understand the nature of the oath she took in court to tell the truth. Because she was not found guilty of perjury, Allie Logan could not be tried for compelling the perjury, and both women were released.

"Again have the efforts to apprehend the murderers of Hezekiah Stites proven futile," reported the *Western Star*.

By the time I had sifted through all these newspapers covering a period of more than two years, I must admit I had begun to lose confidence in the judicial system. Dozens of witnesses had been heard; another dozen arrested. Certainly, there had been a gang of vicious people in the area near Mason. Couldn't anything be done to stop them?

The final chapter in this convoluted story came immediately after the perjury cases. On June 19, 1902, Richard "Colonel" Ralston and his son-in-law Carl Posey were arrested and charged with the murder of Hezekiah Stites. Posey was soon released, there being no evidence found against him, but Ralston was held.

Richard Ralston, for some reason known as "Colonel" despite his lack of military service, lived with his wife Melinda and several of the younger of his nine children in a small house on an acre of land not far from the home of Hezekiah Stites. He had worked as a farm laborer, and was 67 at the time of his arrest. The murder charge came as a result of testimony concerning an old English sovereign coin that Ralston had in his possession. Stites was known to have carried this coin in his pocketbook, and following his murder one of the empty pocketbooks was found to have a piece of paper with the imprint of the coin on it. Ralston's coin matched the impression perfectly. The "Colonel" had concocted a story that his son had found it in an alley, but while he was in jail waiting to testify the previous February, some other inmates overheard him telling his daughter to put the blame on the boys, because he was too old to be in jail.

Another conversation involving Stites was also telling. Mrs. Emmons, the wife of the man who found his neighbor Hezekiah's body, testified that on the day following Stites's burial, Ralston knocked on their door while Mr. Emmons was hitching up his horse in the barn, and asked if her husband was planning to go to Lebanon to get the reward offered. She evaded this question and then he asked her if there were any arrests to be made that day. When she was again silent, he said to her, "If you know anything about this case you had better keep still or your life won't be worth *that*," snapping his fingers. Other witnesses testified that Ralston had sold some fine pieces of cloth they recognized as coming from Stites' formal coat to a junk dealer.

The testimony from these reliable witnesses was enough for Ralston to be bound over to the grand jury under a charge of first-degree murder. But none of the evidence against him was conclusive of guilt, so bond was set at the low sum of $500, and Ralston returned home.

The case was never brought to trial. In January 1903, the $1,300 reward was rescinded, and no one was ever convicted of the murder of Hezekiah Stites.

CHAPTER TWENTY

Cincinnati Enquirer

Lebanon, July 7, 1901 — W. R. Kemper, civil engineer, examined the two pieces of bark found on the bed the morning of the murder, and gave as his opinion that one piece was off an inch and a half stick and the other a two-inch stick. The first stick would have weighed nine ounces to the foot and the latter twenty-five ounces to the foot. The physicians also testified that they believed that the two blows made on the top of the head were made with the small club, while those that crushed in the bones of the face were with the heavy one. It was also the opinion of these experts that someone had held the hands of the woman when murdered, as the wounds on the top of the head would not have rendered her unconscious, and her natural inclination would have been to have thrown her hands up to her head. There were no bruises found except on the head.

The failure to find the murderer of Hezekiah Stites left the citizens of Warren County disappointed and disgusted, not only for the justice denied a quiet old man killed in his own house, but for the frustration of seeing no end to the many vicious crimes that were plaguing the region. The case did, however, make public that what the *Western Star* called a "gang of ignorant and vicious people who reside in the river hills" of our own county and a similar gang in Middletown had been in collusion for many years. "To this fact," continued the *Star*, "may well be attributed some of the heinous crimes which have disgraced this county and almost terrorized certain communities."

Many people who read these words probably counted the murder of Rebecca McClung as one of those heinous crimes. Was there any evidence that connected her murder to that of Stites?

The McClungs were known both for their wealth and mistrust of banks, not only in Mason but in the surrounding area as well. They lived just over ten miles from Hezekiah Stites, and some of their farmland was closer to his home than that. John had feared a robbery similar to that of the Thompsons or Mr. Stites so much he changed his mind about building a new house in the countryside and planned to construct one in town instead. The McClung house was not secluded like that of Hezekiah Stites, but at four or four-thirty on an early spring morning, the sun would not yet have risen and few people would be seen on the streets. John, a creature of precision and habit, could be expected to exit that rear door of his house and spend half an hour or so in the stable every single morning, leaving the door unlocked. The house's proximity to the cemetery and the creek offered some natural hiding places where robbers could lie in wait for the house to be temporarily accessible.

If it was easy to picture how would-be robbers could get *in* to the house at that hour, it was a bit harder to imagine how they could get *out* without being seen. Sallie Baysore was awake when she heard the screams of Rebecca McClung, and was soon running back and forth between the front door she used and the rear doors accessed by the McClungs, calling out to people on the street and up the stairs to Mrs. McClung. She had only been living in the house for six weeks, not there when John McClung reported someone trying to get in at the window the previous fall; she may have unwittingly surprised anyone breaking in and put them in a frantic search for how to get out of the house undetected.

Footsteps seemed to be tramping all through Sallie Baysore's testimony, going both up and down the uncarpeted stairs that led to Rebecca McClung's bedroom, many times over. If John McClung had killed his wife, here is how the footsteps in Sallie's account described John's movements:

John awakens at four a.m., his usual getting-up time, and comes down the stairs. He stirs the fire in the dining room (next to Sallie's bedroom), and then goes to the kitchen and starts the fire in the woodstove. He picks up sticks of firewood there and climbs back up the stairs, beats his wife to death, comes down the stairs again with the bloody wood, and throws it in the kitchen stove. He washes his hands, proceeds out the kitchen door and across the yard to the barn, and takes care of the animals. A half hour later he returns to the house through the kitchen door, climbs the stairs again, finds his wife dead, comes back down the stairs, and goes out the kitchen door and around the house to the front door where he summons Sallie and Albert Dill.

From the beginning, there were inconsistencies surrounding Sallie's description of all those trips up and down the stairs. At the preliminary hearing, she said she awoke to the sound of someone stirring the fire. Not until the prosecutor asked her did she say she first heard him come downstairs, that he coughed, and she took it to be Mr. McClung. But in answer to a question from the defense attorney, she said it was the *second* time someone came down that she heard the cough.

The sound of the steps, too, was puzzling. When questioned by the coroner just hours after the murder, Sallie said the steps she heard coming down the stairs after she heard the screams sounded just like she'd heard on other mornings; she assumed it was John McClung. His shoes screaked, she said. But in court, she said the McClungs always took their shoes off before going upstairs, leaving them by the fireplace in the dining room. In fact, as she went to investigate the screams, she saw Mrs. McClung's shoes there by the fire as always; Mr. McClung was wearing his at that time, out feeding the animals. Later, during the trial, she admitted that the noise of the shoes was *not* what she normally heard when Mr. McClung came down the stairs. The prosecution pointed out this discrepancy during their closing remarks in court.

Sallie was not the only one who heard footsteps. Dr. Van Dyke testified both at the preliminary hearing and during the trial that after he first viewed the murdered woman, he sent the other witnesses out of the house, staying himself to secure the room until the marshal arrived. While examining the pieces of bark he found on the bed, he heard someone descending the stairs and "walking around as though they did not know where to go." He left the room to investigate, but didn't find who was downstairs.

With all the emotion of that morning, I could understand that the events may not be remembered exactly how they occurred; but the testimony of those who were at the scene certainly allows for the possibility of a stranger or strangers to enter the house, kill Mrs. McClung, and slip out unnoticed. If they didn't escape immediately after the murder, the layout of the house gave numerous hiding places for someone to wait for an opportunity. Upstairs, there were several rooms that were not used by the McClungs on a daily basis, and these would have been dark. Some rooms downstairs were unused, too; Sallie said when she entered the back of the house to call out to Mrs. McClung, she did not go into the hall, because "it was dark in there." The house provided multiple exits; there were four separate doors to the outside—one in the front, built for direct access to a room that was once used as a business office, was locked; the other front door accessed Sallie's sitting room. In the back, one door exited the kitchen; the other exited the McClungs' sitting room. Although this last door was probably locked at the time of the murder, someone already inside the house would have been able to exit there.

Having satisfied myself that robbers could indeed have accessed the house and left again undetected, I next considered the subject I had long avoided—the dead woman herself and how she was murdered.

Sallie Baysore and Albert Dill were the first to see the body after John McClung told them she was dead. They found Rebecca lying with her face down in a pool of blood, and without touching her, assumed she had suffered a hemorrhage of the lungs. It was Dr. Van Dyke, who arrived a few minutes later, who turned her over and exposed the fatal head wounds. He put his finger in the worst wound and said it was sufficient to cause death. The next one to examine the body was Coroner Carey. Dr. Van Dyke told the coroner the details of his actions and how he had found the body before the coroner's examination. The postmortem, led by Dr. Hall, added more information.

She was found lying across the bed, not in a sleeping position. The doctors and coroner agreed that it appeared she had been sitting on the edge of the bed when she was first struck, and these two wounds, on the top and side of her head, would not have caused death and may not even have knocked her unconscious. She probably fell back onto the bed and then received the fatal blows to her face. Perhaps she had begun to get dressed for the day; she was wearing only underclothing and some other clothes were lying near the foot of the bed. The doctors were surprised to find no defensive wounds to her hands and arms, as it would have been instinctive to throw up her arms to protect her head when she was struck. It also was remarkable that despite the powerful blows that crushed her bones, her facial skin was scarcely marked or broken. These clues suggested that someone had thrown the covers over her head before she was struck.

From the lack of rigor mortis and the temperature of the body, Dr. Van Dyke judged that death occurred at about twelve minutes before five o'clock, no more than a half hour before he arrived at the house. I looked back over the Opera House testimony of Sallie Baysore and Albert Dill. Sallie heard screams between 4:35 and 4:40 a.m., and someone coming down the stairs between 4:45 and 4:55. Albert saw Mr. McClung coming back from the barn between 5:00 and 5:10, after finishing chores that would have taken about a half hour. Either someone was mistaken in their testimony, or someone other than John McClung was in the house when his wife was murdered.

Throughout all my methodical consideration of the various aspects of the murder case, there was one thought that kept nagging at me, a simple question I had recorded in my journal when I was only eleven. The importance of it now shot like a bolt of lightning through all the other complicated details: Why would *one* man pick up *two* pieces of wood to use as a club?

223

It was well accepted by all the experts that two pieces of wood, consistent with what was found piled next to the kitchen stove, were the murder weapons. Two pieces of stovewood, one a bit fatter than the other, and both of them were used. Didn't that suggest two attackers? And someone had apparently thrown the bed covers over Rebecca's head and maybe held her arms. I simply could not picture one elderly man with only two hands restraining Rebecca and beating her with two different clubs.

There was something else remarkable about the murder weapons. Coroner Carey, when investigating the death of Hezekiah Stites, found near the body two pieces of kitchen stovewood covered with blood, and determined they were the murder weapons. Two pieces of bloody stovewood. The similarity may not have held up in court as evidence, but to me, it was the final element that convinced me that John McClung had not only been wrongly charged with the murder of his wife, but had also been wrongly convicted in the minds of many of our citizens. It was a stigma he bore the last few isolated years of his life and it has stained his reputation for all the years since.

I closed my investigation of Rebecca McClung's murder with a visit to her grave. It's easy to find in the town cemetery, because John McClung had an elegant, tall monument erected on the center of a family plot following the death of his older brother Joseph in 1881. Circling the family marker are smaller stones for each individual. John's parents, Samuel and Susanna, are there; so are his sisters Rebecca, Elizabeth, Mary, Rachel, and Charity, as well as markers at Charity's feet for two infants and a two-year-old.

I found Rebecca's stone easily; her name is inscribed in large capital letters. I stood before her marker in the shade of mature trees under a bright blue autumn sky. Golden leaves hung above me and sprinkled the trimmed green grass. I thought of the drawing Rebecca had made me, and consciously connected the smiling woman on the back of the bicycle with the name engraved in granite at my feet. I closed my eyes and prayed that she was at rest now, healed of the wounds she had endured. Then I laid a white rose in front of the stone.

Next I took a step to my left, to John's marker. I thought of him standing over Hans with a knife in his hand when I was only ten, a man who spoiled children's fun and fought about sidewalks. Then I thought of the lonely old man who lost his only companion, enduring weeks sitting in courtrooms, surrounded by people who believed he was a murderer. It struck me then that here lay a man who closely guarded his monetary treasure, no benefit to him now, at the expense of losing his only true treasure. I laid a second rose on his grave, and left the cemetery.

CHAPTER TWENTY-ONE

December 1951

I found something today in the closet. I was a bit clumsy with the skirt I wanted to wear and as I struggled getting it off the hanger, I heard something hit the wooden floor and bounce a couple of times. Although puzzled for a moment, I soon remembered that a few days ago, the last time I had worn this skirt, I had been tired after returning from a walk to the drug store and lay down on the bed for a bit of a nap. I pulled off my clip-on earrings to be more comfortable and stuffed them into the skirt pocket, and there they stayed until this morning when one of them escaped.

Because of my damaged eyes, my fingers often have to be my sight, so I got down on my hands and knees to search. I shook each of the shoes lined up on the floor; nothing. Then I systematically groped every inch of the floor, moving from the center to the left, the direction of the bounces I heard. Although not deep, the closet stretches far behind the wall on each side, so I was almost all the way inside before reaching the end. Against the side wall leaned what felt like a little table with short hinged legs, the kind of thing you might set across a sick person's lap so they could eat a meal sitting up in bed. I temporarily moved it aside so I could feel behind it.

Way back there my hand found the earring—and something else. As I slid my hands around it and felt its shape, the memory came back as fresh as it had been yesterday.

It was only a few weeks before the murder. Father had taken the train to Cincinnati to attend a meeting of undertakers; they would talk about the latest ideas and procedures, and perhaps see old friends from mortician school and past meetings.

Often Father would bring back something for the family from the city—a book, a piece of pottery from the Rookwood ceramists, chocolates, or—once—some interesting pebbles and shells he found along the Ohio River. This time he brought something special—bottles of a drink called Coca Cola, one for each of us children (except Frankie, of course, because he was just a baby).

I had tasted Coca Cola once before, at a drug store in Dayton. Before baby Frank was born, we left Mildred, Everett and Marshall with my Miller grandparents, and took Aunt Inez, who was twenty, with us on my first trip to the big city. Inez had recently started her new job as a court stenographer in Lebanon, and she wanted to shop for a couple of ready-made dresses now offered at the big Rike's store. Mother was excited to help her and to try on some new fashions for herself, and I was just excited to see what a big city looked like. Father would drop us off to enjoy the store while he picked up some undertaking equipment and looked at caskets at a supplier nearby.

Rike's was a beautiful white, two-floor store in downtown Dayton, modeled after the Exposition Building at the 1893 Chicago World's Fair. The building next door was many floors higher, the tallest building I had ever seen, but Rike's stood out on its street corner because it was filled with soaring windows and topped with a tower and cupola. Inside it was bright and airy and open, with the center ceiling rising two stories and the sides lined with galleries on each floor. A boy was assigned to us when we entered, to carry any merchandise we might choose and to take our purchases to the cashier. Aunt Inez tried on several dresses in a private room made for the purpose, and finally chose a beautiful jade-green dress and a more conservative tiny floral print with white cuffs and collar. Mother restrained herself and bought only a scarf, and she bought me a little manicure kit that snapped together like a change purse.

Father had parked the carriage along the street in front, and the boy carried our purchases out and loaded them on top of a crate of embalming bottles Father had just bought.

"And now," he announced, when we had all settled into our seats, "I think we all deserve a little treat." He slapped the reins and drove us just a few blocks away and stopped the carriage in front of a big drug store. After tying the horses, he led us inside. The store was bigger than the drug stores in Mason, and to our left was a long counter that stretched most of the way across that end of the store, with stools set before it. On the wall behind the counter was a large sign printed in curly script that read:

Soda Fountain.

One Dozen Flavors!

"Father!" I cried. "Can we try some soda?"

He just smiled and bowed, swooping his arm toward the counter like a butler ushering us forward. I climbed up on a stool near the center and motioned for Aunt Inez to sit next to me while Father helped Mother get seated.

A smiling young man emerged from a door behind the counter and walked up to the glossy white marble machine in front of me. "Good afternoon, folks!" he said. "What will you have today?"

"This is our first time in your establishment," said Father. "Perhaps you might suggest something."

"Well, as the sign says, we've got a dozen soda flavors! Popular ones are strawberry, orange, chocolate—raspberry and pineapple are good too—but if you're asking my opinion, I'd say try our newest soda—Coca Cola!"

I had seen advertisements for Coca Cola in the newspapers Father brought home from his trips to Cincinnati, but it was not available yet in Mason. The advertisements showed a fashionable young woman in a big hat sitting at a fancy tea table, sipping the drink through a straw. The ad promised the drink cured headaches and gave you renewed energy.

The choice for me was simple. "That's what I want, Father!"

Aunt Inez ordered a Coca Cola, too, but Father and Mother chose one of the fruit flavors.

I kneeled on my stool so I could see over the top of the soda fountain in front of me as the man made our drinks. Each flavor soda came from one of the many shiny brass spigots lined up across the machine. The man fixed my drink first, lifting the spigot with one hand while holding the glass under it with the other. The soda whooshed into the glass sending bubbles sparkling to the top of the dark brown liquid, then erupting in a foam that spilled over the edge into a catch pan at the base of the machine. Watching the bubbles and froth dance in the glasses was almost as much fun as drinking it after we were all served.

The fizz tingled in my mouth, and the sweet-tangy-spicy taste of the drink was something brand new. I took little sips, making it last as long as possible, watching as two teenage boys sat down at the end of the counter and ordered Coca Colas and sandwiches.

I used the little manicure kit I got on that trip to Dayton, but to me that visit to the soda fountain was more exciting and memorable than any merchandise from Rike's. I couldn't wait to tell Ethel about the Coca Cola, and tried without success to come up with words to describe its unique flavor. I would tell her father that he must get some for his store.

But Coca Cola, like the other fountain drinks, was not something you could drink in your home. You had to pay your nickel to the druggist who had the fountain machine, and then drink it from a glass sitting at the counter, or maybe just outside the door if the weather was fine.

That's what made the bottles of Coca Cola Father brought us that year from Cincinnati so special. For the first time, we could drink the famous soda right in our own home, whenever we wanted. Father put the bottles in the ice box so they would be cold to drink the next day. The plan was for us children to enjoy them as part of an after-school snack as soon as I got home.

It was a Friday, and Mildred was waiting for me outside the front door as I came up the street. She called out to me as I said goodbye to Hans. At the sound of her voice, Marshall pushed open the door to join her on the stoop.

"Izzy!" he said, flapping his arms. "Coca-coca now!"

Mother had a plate of oatmeal cookies waiting on the kitchen table and my brothers and sister took our seats around it, except for baby Frank who was taking his nap; of course, he was too young for Coca Cola anyway. I set out glasses for everyone while Mother got the corkscrew and the bottles from the ice box.

Mildred got the first bottle. Mother popped the cork and poured it slowly into her glass, and the little ones giggled at the bubbles that rose to the top. I watched Milly take the first sip, loudly slurping the foam, her eyes growing wide at the tingle of the fizz, and I smiled as a grin spread across her face. Everett imitated her when he got his glass, and then Mother opened Marshall's bottle. She passed me the corkscrew so I could open and pour my own.

Mother poured a small amount of soda in Marshall's glass and helped him take a sip. Surprised at the fizz, he opened his mouth and some dribbled out. He smacked his lips, screwed up his face, and shook his head as Mother wiped his mouth with a napkin.

Mother laughed. "You don't like it?" Marshall vigorously shook his head again. "Would you like Mother to finish it for you?" Marshall nodded and Mother enjoyed her first taste of Coca Cola.

"Izzy, aren't you going to open yours?" Mildred asked, reaching for a cookie.

I looked at Everett and Milly, delighting in watching the bubbles rise up in their glasses and then slurping them up to tingle in their mouths. Then I looked at my own bottle, the liquid dark and still, waiting for the joy to be released.

"I think I'll save mine till later."

The next day I rose early to catch Mr. Dill before he left his hotel, and asked him to give my bottle of Coca Cola to Mrs. McClung. I knew better than to entrust the task to Farly Dwire— the temptation would be too great.

I wondered if Mrs. McClung received the bottle or, if she did, whether she opened it or not; I never heard. The weather grew rainy for several days following, so I didn't ride the bicycle past her house again until a week or so before her death. I think she waved from her window that last day, but it was hard to be sure—it was so dark behind the mostly-closed shutter that all I could see was a flutter of shadows.

So today as I sat on the wooden floor outside the closet where I had searched for my earring—the same closet where Mrs. McClung had hung her clothes fifty years ago—and ran my hands over the smooth glass Coca Cola bottle, something stirred inside me. The bottle was one of the old straight-sided ones, made before the familiar curvy bottles of today, with a neck made for a cork rather than a bottle cap. I read the embossed lettering on the bottle with my fingers: "Property of Coca Cola Bottling Co.," the drink's name even back then written in the classic script.

The bottle was empty. It had been hidden far back in the corner of the closet, empty and untouched for fifty years.

Right now I am picturing Rebecca McClung sitting in her shuttered room with the door closed, sipping the Coca Cola I had given her, delighting at the bubbles rising from the bottom of the bottle and smiling as the spicy, sweet liquid tingles her mouth. I feel, with her, the joy of that moment, and tears run down my face.

A door opens and closes below me, and soon I hear tramping up the stairs. This will be Belle, my niece, coming to pick me up. Belle is my brother Frank's daughter; he is a master carpenter, and their family lives right across the street from the house where we grew up. She will have brought my early Christmas present, a new typewriter ribbon and a package of paper. She always lets me know when the words I'm typing become faded, and the ribbon needs to be changed. Today Belle and I are walking to the Dream Theater just down Main Street to see the new movie—an animated version of *Alice in Wonderland*, made by the great cartoon creator, Walt Disney. I won't see much of the picture, of course; but I'll be able to hear Alice and the White Rabbit, and the Mad Hatter ask his riddle that has no answer, and Belle will whisper to me what's happening on the screen. My niece's real name is Isabel, the same as mine; I go by Izzy and she goes by Belle, and together we make a great team.

The Historical Characters

Sarah (Sallie) Baysore was the daughter of William Burch, proprietor of the Burch House Hotel in Mason. Sallie's husband George Baysore, a contractor and carpenter, bought the Mason House Hotel in 1886; following his death 1897, Albert Dill bought the hotel. Sallie worked as a dressmaker and had no children. Sometime after her brief residence in the McClung house, Sallie Baysore purchased a house in Dayton and rented rooms to boarders. She died in Franklin, Ohio, in 1922.

George Carey, described in an 1890 article as a "hustling insurance agent" and one of the best-known faces in Lebanon, Ohio, became a county coroner and later a judge. He served in both capacities for several years, and his name appears frequently in county crime reports of the time. He also served many years as the Secretary of the Ohio State Fair, and in 1903 he ran unsuccessfully for State Senate. Judge Carey died in 1914.

Nicholas Dawson, middle brother of Rebecca McClung, was born in 1847. He never married, and lived with one or both of his brothers most of his life. He was a wagon maker and later in life a day laborer. He served on city council, and died in 1911.

Nimrod Pingree ("Pen") Dawson, youngest brother of Rebecca McClung, was born in 1849 and worked in his own shoemaking shop on Main Street in Mason. He never married and spent his whole life in the village, dying in 1925. He served for a time on the village council.

Servetus ("Vete") Dawson, oldest of Rebecca's brothers, was born in 1843. He served in the Civil War, and afterward received regular pension payments listing him as an "invalid." However, he worked as a wagon and plow maker, like his father, and sat on the Mason village council. He married Hulda Hulse and had one son; Hulda died at age 30, and Servetus lived as a widower the rest of his life, but usually with one or both of his brothers in his household. He died in 1925.

Albert Dill lived in Mason and the surrounding area all his life and never married. A dealer in cattle, hogs and grain, he was known for his honesty, fairness, and generosity, and served as a village trustee. Although he owned much land outside of town as well as several buildings, including the Mason House Hotel where he lived in his later years, his wealth was gone by the time of his death. He died in his hotel room in 1906.

Maude Dill, a school teacher and Mason's first elected female council member, married George Kohl, a carriage maker, in October, 1901. They had one daughter. In 1927, when her infant grandson died suddenly, Maude became despondent over the loss and never fully recovered. She died at age 49 while apparently cleaning a car in the closed garage with the engine running.

James McFarlane Dwire, known as Farlane, was born in 1891 in Mason, the oldest of four children in the only Catholic family in the town. His brothers had unusual nicknames, too; "Tiny" (Donald), who ran a popular tavern in Mason; and "Toad" (Joseph). After serving two years as a fireman in the U.S. Navy, Farlane struggled to support a wife and four children with manual labor jobs; three of the children were housed for a short time at the Catholic orphanage in Cincinnati. By 1940 he was working as a bartender in a lodge, and his wife Waneta as a seamstress in a shirt factory. It was Farlane who recovered Marshall Miller's body in 1917 after he drowned in Muddy Creek, according to Miller's obituary. Farlane died in 1952 and is buried with his wife and children in Cincinnati.

Alonzo "Lon" Miller, father of Charles C. Miller, was first a contractor and then a reaper expert for a farm equipment company. He served as a First Lieutenant in the Civil War. He and his wife **Louisa** had five children.

Charles C. Miller and **Etta Irwin Miller** moved their undertaking business to a large new house at the west end of Main Street in Mason in 1897, where the business continued for almost forty years. It was one of the first in the area that provided space for funerals and visitations. Charles served multiple terms as a member of the Mason city council. The couple had six children, and died within six months of each other in 1935.

Charles Marshall Miller, born in 1898, was known by his middle name. He worked both as a traveling salesman and at odd jobs before his tragic drowning death in the Muddy Creek near his home at age nineteen.

Everett Miller, born in 1897, left school after eighth grade to work as an undertaker in his father's business. He married, but his wife died young. After the death of his parents, he worked as a decorator in a painting business.

Frank Miller, born 1900, played on the Mason High School basketball team. He married Margaret Bergen and the couple had two daughters and a son. Frank worked as a laborer in a machine shop while single and living in his parents' home; later he became a carpenter and lived with his family across the street from his childhood home. He died in 1982.

Ineze Miller, youngest daughter of Alonzo and Louise Miller, was born in 1879. She worked as a stenographer before marrying Elmer Evans in 1906. The couple lived with her parents until their deaths, with Elmer working as a real estate salesman and later as a pharmacist. They moved later to Cincinnati where Elmer worked again in real estate. The couple had no children.

Mildred Miller, born in 1895, married James Marshall, acquiring the last name of her brother who had drowned. They moved to Michigan where James worked as a machine operator for an automobile company. They had at least two sons. Mildred died in 1970 and is buried with her husband in Mason.

Leavitte Pease was born in Mason in 1889. His parents were **Minnie Wikoff** and Charles Pease, who later divorced. His mother and sister **Lucille** really did attend the McClung trial on July 10, 1901. Leavitte became an accountant for an automobile parts company and died in Florida in 1912.

Ethel Rebold, born in 1889, had just one sibling—her younger sister Alice. When she was 24, Ethel married John Miller, a Cincinnati laborer who was eleven years her senior. The couple divorced sometime before 1940, when Ethel was back in Mason living with her mother. She had no children, and died in 1989.

John ("Jack") Rebold started working for $12 a month in a general store in Mason when he was 14, and owned a general store of his own by the time he was in his twenties. He was successful in the mercantile business all his life, and built two major business buildings and an elaborate home in Mason. Each of the business buildings had a social hall on the upper floor; the second hall had a freight elevator and its own entrance so patrons wouldn't have to go through the store to get to the dance floor. All three buildings still stand today. John Rebold died in 1939 at the age of 78.

James Runyan, John McClung's defense lawyer, was also a judge on the Warren County Common Pleas Court and tried many important cases in the area. He lived in Lebanon, Ohio.

Pearlee Spuhler, born in Mason in 1890, was the oldest of eleven children. His parents for many years were proprietors of a lunchroom and later a candy store. After serving as a private in World War I, Pearlee returned to his parents' home in Mason and worked at Peters Cartridge Factory in Kings Mills. He later married and moved to his wife's hometown of Dayton where he worked as a machinist at the National Cash Register Company. He had a son and daughter and died in Dayton in 1960.

George Tetrick lived in Mason all his life and served many years on the village council and school board, and even a stint as street commissioner. His career, however, was as an architect and builder, and his projects included installing blackboards at a school, moving the jail, laying cement sidewalks, building a footbridge to the cemetery, and building the Opera House, a school, and other buildings in town. He was married fifty years to **Flora Wikoff**; their son **Paul** became a physician after attending medical school in Cincinnati; he was present at Rebecca McClung's autopsy. George Tetrick died in 1924.

Robert Tucker, born in 1890, was third eldest of eight children. Robert first worked as a carpenter with his father, then as a packer at Peters Cartridge Factory; he returned later to carpentry. He married and had seven children; he lived in Mason all his life and died in 1968.

Dr. John Van Dyke, physician to the McClungs, was born in Mason and worked as a doctor there for many years. He also served on the school board and was the first chief of the Mason Fire Department. In 1905 Van Dyke was elected mayor, a position he held until 1911. He died in 1915.

About the Author

Janet Slater is a writer and editor and a former writing instructor at the University of Cincinnati. In addition to *Murder in Mason*, she is the author of *Time Trail*, a novel based on local history near her home in southwest Ohio, and *A Home in the Storm*, a historical fiction book set during the Revolutionary War for children ages eight to twelve. She loves the outdoors, travel, reading and researching history, inline skating, and golfing with her husband.

Learn more about her books and contact her at www.facebook/janetslaterbooks. Books are available at Amazon.com.

Made in the USA
Las Vegas, NV
25 April 2021

22021695R00134